Sooo Not Looking For a Man

CJ MORROW

Tamarillas Press

Cover images: CJ Morrow,
Man image by Alexander Lesnitsky from Pixabay
Design: © CJ Morrow
Copyright © 2019 CJ Morrow

ISBN: 9781700448446

For my family.

The Beginning

I never used to believe in love at first sight.

Then I met Leeward. Well, not met, more glimpsed across a crowded, noisy bar on a Friday night when I was my friend's plus one at her after work end-of-financial-year celebration booze up.

And it was only a glimpse, yet though our eyes met for only the briefest of moments we just connected. It was as though a thousand words had been exchanged between us. He had dark eyes, deep eyes and I don't just mean deep set, although they were, I mean I felt I was seeing into his soul. A tortured soul. Don't ask me how I knew that, I just did.

Then he was gone, pulled away by an unseen force and I was back listening to my friend's inane, drunken rambling about auditors and virements and other nonsensical stuff. I did actually know what a virement was, because she'd told me three times in the taxi on the way to the bar and about twenty times since we'd been here – the transfer of a surplus from one account to cover a deficit in another.

I looked around me and saw everyone having a good time, there was plenty of drink sloshing around, anything you wanted from the free bar; I dread to think

1

how much money her company had spent on this evening – I wondered what the auditors would think of it. Not that I was availing myself of it, I had an early start the next day, one which hadn't been on the rota when I'd accepted this invitation. I thought I was the only person in the entire place, other than the staff, who wasn't completely off my face.

'Hey,' a voice said from behind me.

I turned, and there he was. Leeward. Not, of course, that I knew his name at that point.

'Hi.' I offered a shy smile. It was genuine too; I was just so knocked out by his presence.

'I feel as though we've already met.' He didn't smile. His face was serious, intense.

'Yeah.'

'Across the bar.' He nodded over to where he had been when our eyes first met.

'Yeah.'

'Would you like a drink?'

'Um, yeah, but not alcohol.' I didn't say I was on an early shift in the morning, in my head it sounded sort of lame.

'Not drinking?'

'No. I'd love a coke or something soft, though.' I didn't want him to think I was turning down his offer, even though we both knew the drinks were free.

'Cool. I'm having a coffee.'

'They do coffee? I didn't know that otherwise…' My voice trailed away, because he was smiling and it took my breath away. It wasn't a full on, teeth bared smile, just a little upturn to the corners of his lips, slightly crooked, and it had the most profound effect on me. I felt my knees start to buckle and I pulled myself upright. What was wrong with me? I wasn't even drunk.

'Would you like a coffee instead?'

'I would. Oh yes, I would.'

'Cappuccino?'

'Yes, please, err...'

'I'm Leeward.' He held out his hand. I was afraid to take it, afraid to touch him. What the hell did I think would happen? Sparks, fireworks, explosions, that's what. 'And you're Lauren.'

'Yeah. How did you...?' Over his shoulder I saw my friend grinning, holding up her thumbs, nodding in that stupid way drunk people do, especially in front of the stone cold sober. 'You asked my friend,' I said, answering my own question.

'I did. You sit there.' He nodded at an empty table for two. 'I won't be long.'

I flopped into the seat and watched him as he made his way to the bar. I don't know why I was so attracted to him; he wasn't my type at all. I went for tall, fair-haired men, I liked them on the lean side, not quite male model heroin chic, but getting that way. I was twenty-five and my two serious ex-boyfriends had been *exactly* my type. And neither had worked out well. I was only three weeks out of my latest relationship which had lasted seventeen months. I thought we had a future, it seems he didn't and he dumped me, rather unceremoniously at my brother Sam's engagement party. I was still smarting from the rejection and definitely not looking for another relationship.

Leeward was short, not tiny, just not much taller than me, and he was stocky, not fat, but definitely not lean. He had dark hair, cut short, but long enough for me to see a few licks of curl around his collar. Definitely not my type, but I still found him attractive.

I think it was his eyes, deep, dark pools of

unfathomable something – I just didn't know what.

'I gather you don't work with this lot,' he said, putting our coffees on the table and sitting opposite me. I was staring straight into those eyes. I read pain and sorrow and a troubled soul but not a loser, definitely not a loser; not someone who needed fixing.

'No. You?' Maybe I should have had a glass of wine, it might have helped my speaking abilities.

'No, I came with my brother over there.' He nodded in the direction of the bar but I couldn't tear my gaze away from his eyes to bother looking.

'Where do you work then?'

'In the hotel industry.' He smiled again. Oh God. Don't do that. 'Where do you work, Lauren?' I adored the way he said my name.

'Just started at a nursing home,' I said.

He nodded; his face impassive.

'I'm a nurse there.' I felt I needed to justify myself, I don't know why.

He smiled again and he let the smile stay on his lips as I babbled on about my few years in the NHS and how I loved working with old people and this was such a golden opportunity to do that *and* it was a promotion.

Over in the corner someone dropped a tray of drinks and as the glasses smashed to the floor a loud cheer went up, followed by a communal chant that everyone knew except us.

'I've got my car outside,' Leeward said, fixing me with those damn eyes. 'Would you like a lift?'

'Yes please.'

And I wasn't even drunk.

Sitting next to him in the car was driving my senses wild. I could smell him, of course he smelled of expensive aftershave, but there was something else

4

there: man. Being so close to him made my body tingle.

We pulled up outside my parents' house and he turned to me.

'Would you like to meet up again? We could go for dinner somewhere.'

It was hard to say no, but no is what I said. I was still smarting, I really didn't trust men, any men. In the end we exchanged phone numbers and left it at that. For a while…

One

Ten years later - late August

I so don't want to be a bridezilla.

'Brides usually lose weight but your weight loss is quite shocking.' The seamstress who has altered my wedding dress for the fourth time in as many months pulls up the zip and smooths the dress down, spanning her hands around my waist.

I can't remember the last time I was this thin. In fact, I don't think I have ever been this thin. Is it wrong to revel in it?

'It still feels a little loose,' I say, smiling.

'I really don't want to take it in any more. I think it will spoil the line of the dress.' She smiles at me, a smile that defies argument. 'Also, you're wearing flat shoes, heels are going to change your posture, that can affect the fit.' She frowns down at my cream, silk ballet pumps, the pearl-encrusted toes peeking out from beneath the dress. It's the first time she's seen them, but I've told her all along that I'll be wearing flats. 'I hope the dress is long enough,' she says, in a weary tone.

'Length is perfect,' I say, sounding just a little snappy. Then I smile, because no one wants to be a bridezilla, do they?

'The dress is perfect, Lauren,' Mum says, perched on a tiny stool in the corner. She's by the open window and wafts outside air into the room with her hands; it is so hot today, especially with three of us cramped into this tiny room. 'You want to be able to eat on your wedding day.' She laughs and stands up, waving her hand over her face. 'I'll wait for you in the car.' Mum totters out of the room, the smallest bedroom in the seamstress's home, down the stairs and lets herself out of the house.

'I think your mum's right.' The seamstress unzips me before I have a chance to comment and she's whipping the giant dress-bag off the hook in the corner and getting it ready to receive the dress.

'Okay.' I offer a smile and wiggle myself out of the dress. I'm so thrilled with it, with myself, with everything.

'I couldn't bear to be in there another minute,' Mum says as I approach the car; she's sitting on the open boot and swigging from a bottle of water. 'Sorry. It was just so hot and airless. I was starting to feel quite sick.'

'I know. It was. But we're done now.' I wiggle my bagged-up dress and smile at it.

Mum stops swigging and leaps off the boot so I can place the dress inside. I lay it down and can't resist another smile.

'I've never been this thin,' I say as we get back into the car.

'No. You haven't. Shall we drop the dress home and go and get some lunch or do you have plans?'

7

'No, no plans. Leeward is spending the day with his brothers doing man things.' I imagine Leeward, Kenton and Steve arranging a special treat, a surprise that Leeward will spring on me at the last moment. I wonder what it will be?

Either that, or they're getting their bits waxed in some kind of macho dare all arranged by Kenton. Much more likely. And why not, Leeward doesn't get many Saturdays off work, so he should just enjoy himself.

At Mum's I take the dress upstairs to my childhood bedroom and hang it on the hook behind the door. Mum has come up with me, but only so she can change her shoes; she says her feet have swollen in the heat of that tiny room.

'While we're up here, can I get a photo of *your* dress?' I ask Mum as she frowns.

'Why?'

'Not all of it, just a bit that shows the colour. Jayne is paranoid about you turning up in the same colour.' Jayne, Leeward's mum, has been bugging me for weeks about what Mum will be wearing to the wedding. She's convinced they're going to turn up looking like mismatched twins. Well, it wasn't my idea to insist that all the guests wear blue, it was Leeward's, and I suspect Jayne had a hand in that.

'Help yourself. I'm going to the loo.' She waves at her wardrobe and disappears.

'Ah, there you are,' Grimmy says as we burst into the kitchen together. 'I've been waiting for my lunch. It's past twelve you know.'

'Where's John?' Mum asks, meaning my dad.

'Hello, Grimmy.' I lean in and give my great-grandmother a quick kiss on the cheek. She flinches.

'Mmm. I don't know. In the garden.' She shakes her head. 'Shed. I don't know. I haven't seen him for hours.'

Mum's eyes widen, not in shock or concern, but in disbelief. You cannot trust Grimmy's estimate, or grasp, of time.

'He's supposed to be doing your lunch,' Mum says, glancing up at the clock. It is indeed past twelve; three minutes past.

'Well he hasn't. He let me in, made this cup of tea hours ago and disappeared off.' She makes a motion with her hand suggesting he vanished into thin air. She looks cross, but then, she always looks cross. The only time her super pearly whites make an appearance is when there is food on offer. She eats a lot for someone so small.

'We're going out for lunch, Grimmy. Why don't you join us?' I can't imagine she will, but it's polite to ask.

'No thank you. I want cheese and pickle and proper white bread with a decent cup of tea, not a toasted panny and a cup of froth. I went with your mum a few weeks back. Not nice, not nice at all.' It was actually six months ago and we'll never hear the end of it. There's no point in wasting a treat on Grimmy, she doesn't appreciate it.

Grim by name and grim by nature; my oldest brother, Mark, had given her the name Grimmy when he was about fourteen. It had stuck, we all called her Grimmy, except Dad. To be fair parts of her life have been grim, she lived in London during the war, had a daughter who ran away at sixteen and returned at seventeen about to give birth. Her name was Catherine and that's who my oldest sister is named after.

Catherine died in childbirth and Grimmy brought Dad up. She's also outlived three husbands. So maybe she has a right to be grim, but it can be wearing, especially as she lives in leafy Wiltshire now with my parents running around after her.

Mum goes off in search of Dad and I tell Grimmy about my dress. She appears to listen and her mouth curves up at the sides, suggesting she is smiling, but her eyes dart quickly towards the door when Mum and Dad make an appearance. It's all about the food.

'Where have you been?' Her tone is sharp. 'You left me alone for hours.'

Dad waves a loaf of bread at her, white sliced that only she will eat, gnawing on its viscous dough for what can seem like hours.

'I told you I had to pop out for fresh bread. I've been gone ten minutes.'

'Mmm.' She frowns at Mum and Dad before turning to me. 'What's happened to your hair, Lauren?'

'I had it done last night. Blonde slices and stuff. Ready for next weekend.' I let my voice go up at the end, as a verbal reminder without the words.

'What's happening next weekend?' I don't think she's joking.

'My wedding. Next Saturday. We sorted out what you are going to wear last week. Remember?'

'Of course I remember, I'm not senile. How is Gollum?'

'What?' Did I just hear her correctly?

'Well…' Mum butts in, 'Now you're sorted, Grimmy, we'll be off. John will make you a lovely sandwich, just the way you like it.' Mum pats Grimmy on the shoulder.

'Bye, Grimmy,' I add, grabbing my handbag and still

10

wondering if she said what I thought she did.

'Eat plenty,' Grimmy says. 'You're very thin.'

I smile as I turn away; I know I am and I love it.

'Bye Dad,' I call. 'Did Grimmy just call Leeward Gollum?' I ask Mum as we head out of the door.

'God knows. Best ignored.'

'Has she even seen Lord of the Rings?'

'I've no idea,' Mum answers, a bit too quickly.

'She has, you know, I remember. Last Christmas with the boys.' I definitely remember her sitting in the middle of my nephews watching TV, with Leeward sitting alongside and constantly telling them not to talk over it – it's his favourite film, if you don't count the other Lord of the Rings films, while us girls – well the adult ones anyway – drank wine and giggled over YouTube videos shown to us by my nieces.

'Where do you fancy for lunch?' Mum asks, changing the subject.

'Your favourite,' I say, laughing, because we both know that's where we'll be going even if I suggest somewhere else.

Twenty-minutes later we're sitting in Metcalf's ordering our lunch. Mum's having a panini stuffed full of God's knows what, because, unlike me, she can eat like a horse and never put on weight. I've ordered salad, with a half portion of tuna for the protein. I can't afford to put weight on before my big day because despite there being room in my wedding dress, there definitely isn't any room in the holiday clothes I've bought for my honeymoon. Leeward helped me choose, ensuring they were appropriate, but without telling me where we're going; it's a surprise. I think I'm more excited about the honeymoon than I am about the wedding, after all, we've been together for ten years, and only been on holiday three times and two of those were city minibreaks.

I give an involuntary little shudder when I think of how much the wedding is costing. Mum and Dad have chipped in, not that I wanted them to, Leeward's mum has contributed *what she can*, which has mostly been advice.

'Are you all right?' Mum frowns her concern.

'I'm fine, fine. Just a little hungry.' It's half lie, half true. I've been on a diet for six months now, and I'm permanently hungry.

It was Leeward's idea; we'd both go on a fitness regime. For him it meant sessions down the gym, for me it meant eating less. A lot less. Not that I was fat to start off with, just a normal, average, not-look-twice size. He wanted me to be a knockout, after all, every bride should be the star of her own wedding. He was determined no one would outshine me. And, with my twenty-two-inch waist, I doubt anyone will. Especially now I have the hair; sliced and coloured and all the rest of it, and with a dozen or more hair extensions glued in. It's a good job I'm not at work this week, or God knows how I would have coped with the hair. As it is, I can just let it hang down and enjoy it. That was Leeward's idea too; he loves a long blonde *do*.

If I'd realised I was going to go hungry for six months I might not have agreed to the diet, but he caught me with my guard down. We'd just booked the venue for the wedding; it wasn't quite what I had imagined - which was something small and intimate with just close family and a few friends. It turned out that Leeward wanted big and showy. God knows why we hadn't synchronised our expectations before we looked at the venue – a visit he had arranged. It was a stately home, lovely, massive, expensive and the minimum number of guests we could have were two-hundred. Two-hundred. I didn't think we even knew two-hundred people. But it was what Leeward wanted, and, as he reminded me, he always gets what he wants. After all, he'd chased after me for weeks all those years ago, before I gave in and went out with him, hadn't he?

So, here we are, a week before the biggest wedding I have ever been to – my own. And we're having everything, six bridesmaids, including my forty-year-old sister as matron of honour – not that she was too keen. The men are all wearing top hat and tails, with cravats. My dad, with what he calls his middle-aged comfort roll – read fat belly – looks like The Penguin out of the Batman film, the one where Danny DeVito plays the baddie. There's a live band, a six-course meal and champagne for the toast – not sparkling wine, which is normal at all the weddings I've been to. Personally, I think it's all a bit excessive, but, as Leeward says, he's paying for it and only the best will do for his bride. Me. Even if I would have been happy with something a lot less ostentatious.

What you up to? A message comes through on my phone; it's from Leeward.

Just having lunch with Mum xxx
Don't eat too much x
Lol xxx

He doesn't reply.

Another beep from my phone and this time it's Jayne telling me Mum's dress isn't the same shade as hers, so we're all fine and no one is going to have to go dress shopping again. Thank God for that. I don't tell Mum, because she would most certainly not be going dress shopping again, no matter what Jayne thinks.

Mum and Jayne don't really see eye to eye. My hen party is a good example. Jayne wanted to go to Barcelona. I didn't. At thirty-five I'm the last of my friends to get married, most of them are having babies or staggering under the weight of big mortgages so I just wanted something simple and cheap. We went for afternoon tea and prosecco at a little café in town, though not Mum's favourite café, because they don't open for private parties. I enjoyed it. Mum enjoyed it. My sister, Cat, enjoyed it because it didn't need too much organising and it didn't take her away from her family for too long, and the same applied to my friends, most of whom I hardly see now anyway. So, something low key fitted the bill and everyone was happy. Except Jayne.

You can't please everybody.

'This time next week,' Mum says, her voice breezy. 'You'll be the new Mrs Quinn.'

'As opposed to the old one,' I say with a smirk.

'Huh, has she ever been a Mrs? Is that even her name?'

'They're all Quinn, I've told you this before.'

Mum shakes her head. She's trying not to sound judgemental, not to be condescending. We all know that Leeward and his brothers have different fathers and that none of them were around during their childhoods. No one really knows where the name Quinn came from, except that all the boys have it as their surname and at some unspecified point in the past, Jayne changed her name by deed poll, adding a 'y' to her previously plain Jane and becoming Mrs Quinn.

'You'll be the genuine article,' Mum says, before wincing as she realises she's said it out loud.

'Stop it.' But I laugh. I can't help it. Sometimes it's fun to be bitchy.

After our long, leisurely lunch we stroll around the shops because I still need to buy a nice gift for my sister, jewellery, I think. After a lot of looking Mum helps me choose a silver brooch.

'That way she can pin it on her jacket and forget about it, and she'll always be wearing it when she wears the jacket.'

'If you think so,' I say, not convinced.

'She's got four kids and a busy life. She rarely wears jewellery, does she? She's too busy running around after everyone else and organising them.' Mum pulls her *I know what that's like* face, which is true, she does. There are four of us, me, my sister and my two brothers, though not in that order and it's not as though any of us are children anymore, far from it. I'm the youngest, next is Sam, he's thirty-six; my partner in crime, apparently, when we were kids. Then Mark who's thirty-eight, then Cat who's forty. When I was born Mum had four children under five, sounds insane. At least Cat has spread hers out.

I get the brooch gift wrapped; when I get home I'll add it to box containing the other bridesmaids' gifts. They're all children, the oldest is Cat's daughter Natalia, who's thirteen. The rest are my brothers' girls, ages ranging from a cute and uncontrollable two, to eleven. Neither of Leeward's brothers has any children yet.

'Has Kenton decided who he's bringing?' Mum asks, referring to Leeward's older brother.

'No, and Jayne's getting in a stress about it especially because Suzi keeps crying on her shoulder.' Jayne adores Suzi, she certainly prefers her to me. 'Whoever he brings, Jayne won't like her.'

'Do you think they'll get back together? Ken and Suzi.'

'I don't know.'

'Maybe he'll come alone.'

'I suspect not. He seems to have no problem attracting women.'

'I can see why.' Mum giggles. It's true, Kenton, or Ken as he prefers to be called and who can blame him – is tall, dark and handsome. In fact, he's the epitome of tall, dark and handsome. He's well over six feet tall, has dark brown eyes and dark olive skin; some say his father was Spanish or Italian, or even of Caribbean ancestry, but Jayne never lets on. Whatever the mix is, he's certainly benefitted in the looks department and he'll steal the show on the photographs too because he's incredibly photogenic.

'Good job I never had Suzi as a bridesmaid.' Jayne had pushed me, but I wouldn't. I like Suzi, but I know what Ken's like, he's had fifteen girlfriends in the ten years Leeward and I have been together. Few of them last a year, and like so many of her predecessors Suzi hasn't even made it past six months.

'Imagine how awkward that would have been.' Mum and I exchange grimaces. Fortunately, I don't have to imagine, or worry about it. I just hope Jayne doesn't egg Suzi on to come anyway; I wouldn't put it past her though.

In the car on the way home Mum and I chat about our plans, I've taken this week off work as holiday, followed by two more for my honeymoon. So we're arranging lunches and outings to pick up last minute things. We're also getting our nails done on Thursday. This is especially luxurious for me as my job prohibits me from painting my nails.

'How is work now,' Mum asks, when I say how much I'm looking forward to my three weeks off.

'Since I went part-time, you mean?'

'Yes.' Mum and Dad didn't really agree with me cutting my hours at the nursing home. Not that they've said anything, but I could tell from their faces when Leeward and I announced it over a big Sunday tea at their house, that they weren't particularly happy. I don't know why; you'd think they'd be pleased that I won't be exhausted all the time. Yes, I've had to take a bit of a demotion, but it's okay.

'Yeah, it's fine.'

'Big drop in money though.' Mum says this while driving and staring straight ahead. 'And status.'

'Yeah, but Leeward earns enough.' I ignore her status remark.

'Just seems a shame when you worked so hard to get there.'

'I'm a nurse, Mum. All nurses work hard. I still work hard.'

'Yes, but…' Mum's voice trails off.

Yes, I was *the* senior nurse in the home, the one with the most experience, the one with the final say but I still have the knowledge. Nothing can change that.

'Are you're definitely not going to go back to full-time?'

'No. Couldn't even if I wanted to, they've already replaced me.' I laugh. It's true it wasn't my idea to go part-time, it was Leeward's. We were running around in circles trying to get everything organised for the wedding, when he came up with the solution. If I went part-time I could sort everything out – his job in hotel sales means he works long hours and often has to travel – so it just seemed the obvious solution. And we'll probably be trying for a baby as soon as the knot is tied, so there's no point in stressing with a full-time job then, either.

'Oh well, on the bright side I'll see much more of you once the wedding is over and you're not spending all your time on it.' Mum pastes on a big bright smile and I find myself feeling more than a little irritated.

We pull up outside my house and Mum keeps the car running as I get out.

'You not coming in?' I ask, poking my head back through the car door. 'Come and keep me company 'til Leeward gets home.' His car isn't on the drive so I know he's not in.

'No, Grimmy will be needing her tea, you know what she's like.'

'Yeah.' I laugh. I do know what she's like. No one dare deviate from her meal timetable. It's ironic how she's never wrong on meal times yet loses track of days and weeks. Still, she's amazing really. She'll be ninety-four soon and she's definitely got most of her marbles, unlike some of the poor souls I see every day at the nursing home. She's a tough taskmaster and the irony is she doesn't even live with Mum and Dad; she lives across the road from them in sheltered housing.

'Shame you had to sell your car,' Mum says, musing as she stares at the empty drive.

'Yeah, well. All in a good cause.' It seemed the logical thing to do to pay for the wedding. I can walk to work easily enough but Leeward needs his car for his job. I'll get another car once we settle back down. And I'm sure some of it has gone towards my secret honeymoon surprise, so definitely money well spent.

And the wedding rings, I know exactly what they cost because I took a sneaky peek at Leeward's credit card bill which he'd left in his study. He insisted on choosing them, wanting them to be a surprise for me, and since I've never had an engagement ring, I am expecting something special; I've dropped enough hints about diamonds being a girl's best friend. Judging by the bill from that rather chichi jewellers he likes, there should be several diamonds. Each. I can't wait to see them.

Once indoors, I send Leeward a message asking what time he'll be back and if he's bringing his brothers with him. After about half an hour he replies that he'll be home in an hour and he'll be on his own.

Excellent, there's time for me to make our favourite dinner for two, spicy shepherd's pie with sweet potato mash.

An hour and half later and the pie is ready to come out of the oven, I've polished the glasses and the table is set, but there's no Leeward. I message him again; I've already done it twice in the last half hour but he isn't answering. I wish he would reply because it makes me nervous when he doesn't, I imagine all sorts of silly things happening.

I take the pie out, sit it on the cooker top and cover it with foil, it should stay hot for quite a while, in fact probably better that it cools down a little before we eat it. I grab my wine glass off the table and head to the fridge; there's a lovely bottle of rosé sitting in there. It was a present from my work colleagues when I left yesterday, that and a John Lewis gift card, for quite a large sum, apparently lots of the residents insisted on chipping in too. That's so kind of them.

I'm just ferreting around in the fridge trying to find the wine when the front door opens.

'Hiya, I'm in the kitchen,' I call out. 'I hope you're hungry.'

I don't hear Leeward's reply because I've still got my head in the fridge as I hunt for the wine, but I do hear his familiar footsteps on the wooden hall floor and then the kitchen tiles. They come to an abrupt end just behind me.

'Any idea where that wine is in here?' I ask as I turn around to face him.

He shakes his head slowly. He doesn't look very happy.

'Is everything okay? You haven't had an accident in the car or something?' I knew there was a reason why he wasn't replying to my messages.

He shakes his head again, this time slower than the first time.

'No,' he says, quietly, 'But I did witness one.' He shakes his head and I can see that all the colour has drained from his face.

'Where?'

'On the bypass.' He shakes his head again. 'Just awful. Let's not talk about it.'

'Okay. Are you hungry? I've made our favourite dinner.'

He forces a weak smile and blinks several times.

'Do you mind,' he says, his voice faltering. 'I think I'll just go and have a bath then go to bed early.' Very early, it's not even dark yet.

'Oh, okay. Were your brothers with you? Did they see it too?' I'm asking because in some way, if they were all together, I think it might make it more bearable. I don't know what happened but it's obviously shaken

Leeward.

'No,' he says. 'I was on my own.'

I loosen the foil on the pie to let it cool completely, I'll put it in the fridge later, we can easily have it another day. I clear the table before making myself a cheese and tomato sandwich – not quite what I had planned, but it can't be helped. I have another look in the fridge for my wine, but still cannot find it. I'm beginning to wonder if I actually did put it in the fridge or if it's been left in the bag I brought home from work. I hunt around and find the bag, but there's no sign of the wine.

Have I drunk it and not noticed? Did I imagine it? Did I leave it at work? No, I remember Leeward commenting on what a good wine it was – some special grape – he's far more knowledgeable about wine than I am.

Oh well, I'm sure it'll turn up.

I spend my Saturday evening on my own, my fiancé unconscious upstairs. I've checked on him twice and he's so deeply asleep I wonder if he's taken something; I'm sure we had a few sleeping tablets that Jayne thrust on us when Leeward had jetlag after a business trip to the US. I check his pulse and his breathing, and he's okay.

Downstairs, I flick through the TV channels, so many and so little I want to watch. Then I flick through my phone, googling "accident on bypass". A photo of an horrific crash pops up immediately, the front of the car completely crushed. Two people were killed at the scene, another is critical in hospital. Just awful. The piece says it's a notorious black spot.

Then I notice the date; it happened last Wednesday.

Good God, twice in one week. It certainly is a notorious black spot.

And poor Leeward witnessed the latest one. Just awful.

Two

The week running up to the wedding flies by and Leeward and I hardly see each other. Either I'm out running wedding errands or he's working late or working out.

It's Wednesday and we still haven't eaten the spicy shepherd's pie I made on Saturday. I ring Leeward at work mid-afternoon and am annoyed when he doesn't answer straightaway.

'You took a long time to answer,' I snap.

'I'm at work,' he comes back, equally snappish. I think the prewedding nerves and stress are getting to both of us.

'Oh course, sorry. I was just ringing to see what time you'll be home because we really need to eat that pie I made at the weekend. If not today, it will have to go in the bin.'

'Seven,' he says. 'I have to go, bit manic here. Bye.'

'Bye. Love you,' I say into the void, because Leeward has already hung up.

The sooner we get past this wedding the better; we so should have sneaked off to Vegas, had an Elvis wedding and announced it to the world when we got back. My family wouldn't have minded. Maybe my mum would, a bit, and Dad, it would be mean to deny him the pleasure of walking his youngest daughter up the aisle. Jayne would definitely have complained. Okay, we should have gone for the wedding I wanted, something small and simple.

But we are where we are and it's all happening this weekend. Then it's off on honeymoon, and I'm more excited about that than the wedding and I still don't know where we're going. Given how much Leeward loves all things Lord of the Rings, maybe it's New Zealand. Wow, that would just be fantastic. Imagine it. We looked into it once, five years ago, Leeward had brochures and costings, you can even visit the hobbit village – not that I care so much about that – but New Zealand, I mean, just wow. We didn't book anything, it was just too expensive, but maybe, for our honeymoon… I mustn't be disappointed if it's not New Zealand, anywhere will be wonderful with Leeward.

Leeward rocks in at six-thirty and I'm thrilled that he's early. I pour us both a glass of wine – not my good one, I still haven't found that – while we wait for the pie to heat through.

'How's work?' I ask, dreading the answer because I know he's under a lot of pressure at work.

He rolls his eyes. 'Bloody chaos. We have this event going on this weekend, which of course I won't be attending, so I'm trusting Michael to get some business in. It's just typical the date clashes with our wedding; these are international customers and they could give us a lot of business for the chain, worldwide.' Poor Michael, he's Leeward's assistant and doesn't always come up to Leeward's exacting standards.

'Can't be helped,' I say. 'You weren't to know.' At least, I don't think he was. Leeward has told me about this event so many times, yet every time he mentions it, he acts as though I know nothing about it. That shows just how stressed he is.

'The original date was a month from now. Then it got changed. CEO's daughter's wedding is next month. Fucking typical, doesn't matter that my wedding is this weekend and I'm the one who's supposed to schmooze the clients and get the business. Michael will fuck it up. If he does, he's going, CEO's nephew or not.' He plonks himself at the table while I fuss about checking on the pie and nuking up some peas in the microwave to go with it.

'Me and Mum are getting our nails done tomorrow.' I smile at him and hope it's not too obvious I'm trying to change the subject.

'What about my mum? Is she coming too?'

'No, I don't think she could get the time off work,' I lie. We haven't even asked her; to be honest it never crossed my mind. We're not exactly close, Jayne and I, not like her and Suzi.

'She gets 'em done every week anyway,' he says. 'That looks good, I'm so hungry.' His face lights up as I put the pie on the table.

He eats his in super-fast time, I don't know how he can, it's so hot and I swear that the several days it's been in the fridge has increased its spiciness too.

'That was good. Anything for pudding?'

'Yogurt or ice cream,' I offer pathetically.

'Nah, won't bother.' He looks at my plate. 'And neither should you if you want to fit in that dress on Saturday.'

I smile, but inside I feel really cross about that

remark; there's plenty of room in my dress.

'I gotta go.' Leeward pushes his chair back and stands up.

'Go where?'

'Work. I can't leave everything to chance or in the idiot nephew's hands. Gotta freshen up first, though.' He harrumphs as he stomps upstairs.

I'm clearing the table – having forgone my yogurt or ice cream – when he comes back.

'Sorry I'm such a grump,' he says, putting his hands on my shoulders and kissing the back of my neck. 'I won't be late.' And he's gone.

Just me and the remote control again this evening then.

Friday morning and Leeward's up early, he wakes me with his banging and clanging of the bathroom cabinet doors looking for his electric toothbrush. He does this almost every morning, as if someone has hidden it overnight, even though it's always in the same place. He's found it, I can hear it buzzing.

By the time he switches the shower on I am fully awake and sitting up in bed contemplating my day and admiring my wedding nails – they look amazing. I'm going to Mum and Dad's this morning, and staying overnight, so I need to make sure I take everything I need with me.

I can hear Leeward singing in the shower, that's nice, his voice is deep and dark. I haven't heard him do that before. Hopefully all the work worries are sorted and we can just enjoy our day tomorrow. I listen harder to try to work out what he's singing but don't recognise the tune.

'He's talking,' I muse aloud, straining to hear him. Is

he practising his speech? I can't hear his words but the cadence of his voice suggests he's talking to someone. Is he on the phone? I lean over and see that his phone isn't charging on his bedside table as it usually is. God's sake, he's taken his phone into the bathroom. Bloody work.

'You're awake,' he says, seeing me sat up in bed. He drops his phone on the bedside table.

'Were you speaking to work while you were in there?'

'Could you hear me?' He looks alarmed.

'Yes, no, just your voice.' Maybe he's been arranging some sort of surprise for tomorrow. Oh, I wonder what it could be?

'Yeah,' he says, his back to me as he hunts through his wardrobe before pulling out one of the shirts that I spent ages ironing yesterday, then discarding it.

'What's wrong with that one?'

'There's a mark on the collar. I'll put it in the wash.' He doesn't, just leaves it flung on the chair.

'I never noticed…' I say, sounding casual but feeling irritated.

He doesn't answer, just gets dressed in silence. He's got a good body, all that time in the gym has certainly toned him up and built him up. His shoulders are strong and wide, so are his thighs. I don't think he realises how good he looks, he's so touchy about his lack of height – not that he's short, just the shortest of his brothers – that he doesn't focus on the good bits, the very good bits.

'I'll see you tomorrow, then,' I say as he has his hand on the door knob.

'Yeah.' He looks at me and for a moment I don't know who he is and he doesn't seem to know me either.

'At our wedding,' I offer with a smile.

'Of course.' His face lights up. 'I was forgetting that you won't be here tonight. I'm going to miss you squirming about in bed.' He comes over and kisses me on the cheek; I suppose I have morning breath.

'Not for long. Just one night.' I wrap my arms around his neck but this time it's him who squirms.

'Don't crease me.' Then, in response to my frown, 'Until tomorrow, my love.' And he's gone, no coffee, no breakfast, just down the stairs and out the front door.

I stay in bed for another ten minutes but cannot get back to sleep. Once up, I tidy our room and pick up Leeward's discarded shirt from the chair. After careful inspection – no mark found on the collar – I give it a good shake and hang it back in the wardrobe, putting it in the middle of his shirts so as not to arouse suspicion. I washed and ironed fifteen of Leeward's shirts yesterday – he seems to be wearing two a day at the moment what with going back to work most evenings – and I've no intention of making more work for myself.

Mum helps me pack everything into her car, there is *so* much.

'It is just the one night you're staying,' Mum says, laughing.

'I know. Sooo muuuch stuuuff,' I yell out, throwing my arms about. 'I'll be glad when tomorrow comes.'

'Do you know where you're going for your honeymoon yet?'

'No.' I pause. 'Do you? Has he told *you*?'

'No, no, not a word. Anyway, even if he had I couldn't tell you, could I?'

28

'He's told you, hasn't he? Where is it? Is it New Zealand? I hope it's New Zealand.'

'He hasn't told me.'

'I hope it's New Zealand.' I watch Mum to see if her face gives anything away, but it doesn't.

'New Zealand's a long way to go for two weeks,' she says.

'I suppose.' I hadn't really thought about that. 'Doable though, isn't it?'

Mum just grimaces her answer and shrugs.

'Or Canada, that's not so far. Always wanted to go to Canada.'

'That sounds nice.' Mum stuffs the last of my bags into her boot.

'Are you sure he hasn't told you?'

She smiles. 'Quite sure.' Then she winks; she's teasing me, isn't she? 'All I know is what you've told me, that you're leaving at stupid o'clock on Monday morning.

'Yeah, that's all I know too.'

Grimmy is in her usual place in the corner of the kitchen, watching with her hawk eyes as we bring everything in from Mum's car.

'How long are you coming for, then?' She growls from her chair, like a dog that has just been woken up.

'Just tonight.'

'Brought enough with you?'

'I bet I've forgotten something,' I mutter, grabbing some bags and taking them upstairs to my childhood bedroom, where my dress is still hanging on the hook behind the door.

'I'm having my hair done today,' Grimmy says when I come back for more bags.

29

'No, it's tomorrow, with the rest of us. Paula can fit you in, she doesn't mind.'

'No. Today,' Grimmy says, glancing at the clock which is rapidly ticking towards her lunchtime.

'No, it's tomorrow morning. She's coming at six.' Six. Six! Because for some insane reason I agreed with Leeward that the wedding would be at twelve noon, even though there's Mum, Grimmy, the bridesmaids, oh, and me, all to have our hair done tomorrow morning.

'No, today.' Grimmy glances at the clock again.

'Mum?'

'What's that?' Mum has been ticking things off a list and not paying attention.

'Grimmy says she's having her hair done today.' I raise my eyebrows, waiting for Mum to correct Grimmy.

'Oh yes. We rang Paula. She doesn't mind.'

'Oh. Right. Okay.' I think of Paula dragging her hairdressing stuff right across town twice in two days. I know she's a mobile hairdresser, but I think it's a cheek. And she's got two small children she'll have to make arrangements for. Twice.

'She says you can pay her all in one go tomorrow.' Grimmy smiles at me, a rare exposure of her dentures.

'Thanks.'

'She's coming at one,' Grimmy adds. 'Here. Not at mine. I don't want all that mess in my home.'

I glance at Mum who just smiles her usual non-combative smile.

'She's perming it for me.' Another Grimmy smile. 'And colouring it. What colour should I have? Blue, pink, brown?' Now she grins.

'Whatever *you* like, Grimmy. It's your hair.'

'It's your wedding. Should I go blue to match the theme? It's only a rinse. She says it'll fade out in a few washes.'

'Blue. Why not?' I picture Jayne's face when she sees Grimmy's hair, she'll be annoyed she didn't think of it herself, unless, of course, she has. Jayne is fond of a striking colour, I've seen it purple, black and red in the last year alone.

'Probably blue then. Is it lunchtime yet?' Grimmy sighs.

I wonder why the day before my wedding has turned into the Grimmy hair show.

Paula is a patient soul, Grimmy changes her mind about her hair colour three times. In the end she goes for nothing, yes, nothing, aka natural white, the colour of any sane nonagenarian.

'Maybe I should have gone for the blue,' Grimmy says as Paula is packing up her hairdressing paraphernalia. I watch Paula freeze mid-air.

'No, Grimmy, it looks good as it is,' Mum soothes. 'You don't want to look silly.'

Grimmy considers this for a moment. 'Yes, you're right. There'll be plenty there to do that.'

Mum and I exchange glances, Paula supresses a smirk and we all busy ourselves with other things rather than rise to Grimmy's remark. Mum has made a cake and now that the hair saga – well part one anyway – is over, and she's cleared up, she's going to ice it.

'When can we eat that?' Grimmy calls over. 'All that hairdressing has made me hungry.'

'Later, when everyone else comes round.'

We're having a sort of high tea tonight, with all the members of my family, it's to ensure that everyone knows what they're doing tomorrow; my nephews, the older ones are ushers, my nieces are bridesmaids. Once they've gone home it's early to bed for everyone, because it's early to rise tomorrow.

I haven't slept well and not just because I'm sleeping on my old single bed. My mind is full of everything wedding, everything that must be done before we leave, wondering where my honeymoon will be, hoping that Leeward likes my dress – Mum assures me he will – and hoping that the day is everything that Leeward wants.

When Paula arrives she looks as tired as I feel, but she's cheery and smiley and excited on my behalf. She starts on my hair first, before the little bridesmaids arrive with my sister. I washed and dried my hair myself before I went to bed, because it'll be easier to handle today. I'm wearing it half up and half down in a bunch of twists and curls. I hope Leeward likes it, it's inspired by *Lord of the Rings* meets *Game of Thrones*, his favourite entertainment.

Paula is pulling and twisting and tonging and making sure the extensions stay safely put when my sister bursts into the room and plonks herself down on the bed. Today, we're using one of the spare bedrooms as the hair salon; Mum had enough of the kitchen being commandeered yesterday by Grimmy. It suits me, I don't want this beautifying to be too public.

'Are you on your own?'

'No. They're all downstairs running around like lunatics, I thought I'd let them get it out of their systems.'

'I bet Grimmy's enjoying that.' I think of our great-grandmother wincing as the racing about is accompanied by squeals of delight.

Cat laughs. 'She rang to say she's not coming over.'

'Is she all right?'

'Yeah, Dad went over to check. She just wanted him to make a fuss of her. He doesn't mind, he's not doing anything else. He says he'll put his suit on just before we leave. Mum will get Grimmy when they're ready to go.'

'Okay. Paula's nearly finished me, are you next?'

'No, Mum is. Oh and I've had a text from Jayne,' Cat says, kicking off her shoes and lying down.

'Why?' I feel a little tingle of irritation coupled with anxiety.

'She's sending Suzi round to do your makeup, and mine, apparently.' Cat makes a face that suggests she doesn't understand why anyone needs makeup. It's true that Cat never wears makeup, she is blessed with the kind of skin that just doesn't need it. I'm not.

'Oh. Can you message her back and say there's no need?'

'I did. She's not having any of it, little sis. So it's full on face slap for you and me. We can look like a couple of drag queens.'

'Don't say that. This is my wedding day.'

'Sorry. Didn't get much sleep last night. Neighbour's dog barked all bloody night.' Cat rolls onto her side and plumps the pillow before pushing it under her head.

'There, you're done. I'll just check you and make good once you're ready to go.' Paula steps back to admire her work while I look at myself in the mirror.

'Wow, it's amazing. Thank you.' I hardly recognise myself, and Leeward will love it. I hope.

There's a little knock on the door before my brother, Sam, sticks his head in.

'Wow, look at you, bring on the dragons.'

'What?' Cat snaps, sitting up suddenly.

'You look amazing,' Sam says to me. 'Just like *Daenerys*.'

'Urgh.' Cat falls back onto her pillow at the *Game of Thrones* reference.

'Do you think Leeward will like it?' I hope he does; it was his idea to have my hair super blonde.

Sam smiles. 'Course he will, why wouldn't he?'

By ten-thirty everyone's hair is finished, their clothes are on and I'm being laced into my dress.

'Your waist, just look at it,' Cat says. 'I remember when I had a waist.' She sighs.

'You're joking, aren't you? There's nothing of you.'

It's true, Cat is a sleek size eight on a fat day.

'That's what I mean, I used to have hips, then they slid down my thighs and onto my knees.' She stands back to admire me. 'You look fab.'

'Thank you.'

'Ten minutes,' Sam's voice comes booming up the stairs. 'In the cars in ten minutes. Everyone, go to the loo *now*,' he bellows.

'He's got so bossy in his old age,' I say, laughing.

'Less of the old, he's younger than me.' Cat smooths her hair down; it's dark and glossy and she's had minimal hairdressing done to it. Unlike her face which Suzi has covered in thick foundation. I too have no real skin visible at all; I feel as though I'm wearing a mask. I do quite like the way she's done our eyes though, cat flicks, or something, we'd never have been able to do that ourselves.

'But he's older than *me*,' I snigger.

'Just,' Cat says, patting my dress down. It's true there's just eleven months between me and Sam, he was always my partner in crime, or was it the other way around, when we were kids and especially when we were teenagers.

'How do you think Leeward's brother will react when he sees Suzi at the wedding?'

'I don't think he'll be surprised. Well, *I'm* not. I thought Jayne would do that. She just loves Suzi, that's why she sent her round here to be part of everything.'

'What, so she could drag queen us up?'

'Shut up.' But I can't help laughing, because between the hair and the makeup I look quite unlike myself.

'Five minutes,' my other brother, Mark's voice yells.

A little knock on the door and Dad enters. He looks so smart in his grey tails.

'Everything okay?'

'Of course,' says Cat.

'You look smart, Dad,' I tell him.

'Yes, I'm rather liking the corset effect of this waistcoat.' He pats his belly, clad in dark blue paisley. 'I think you're wanted downstairs now, Cat. Natalia's doing her best to organise everyone but...'

Cat sighs, kisses me good luck and pats Dad's arm on her way out. 'I suppose I'd better go and round up the rabble,' she says, laughing.

Soon, the house is silent, just me and Dad left. We've got another ten minutes before we need to leave.

'You look lovely,' Dad says. 'He's a very lucky man, your future husband. Shall we go downstairs?'

'Yeah, just got to put my shoes on.' I start looking around the room for them. I wish I'd got Cat to find them before she left, bending in this dress is not easy.

Dad waits patiently, a smile on his face.

'Could you check that bag?' I point to a bag on top of a chest of drawers.

'No shoes,' Dad says after peering in. He starts to ferret around in other bags. 'What do they look like?'

'They're cream silk. Pearl encrusted toes.' That's what it says on the box.

He shakes his head.

'They're in a box,' I say, my heart sinking.

Dad glances around the room searching for the box.

'No, they're in a box at my house. I remember seeing them in the bottom of my wardrobe before we left but I don't remember bringing them with me. Oh Dad...'

Three

'Don't panic,' Dad says, trying to hide the sound of his own panic from his voice. 'Let's just think.'

'What?' I snap.

'Are there any shoes here you could wear instead? I'm sure Mum has some suitable in her wardrobe.'

'No,' I snap again, before flopping down onto the bed.

Dad glances at his watch. 'O-k-a-y, if we leave now we can stop off and get them, it's almost on the way, only a slight detour.'

'But we'll be late.'

'Bride's prerogative,' Dad says, offering me his hand and pulling me off the bed. 'Come on. Let's go. Fortunately, your car and driver have been waiting outside for the past ten minutes anyway.'

'I don't want to be too late,' I say as I look for my handbag, then remember that Mum has taken it for me. 'I haven't got my phone, I can't even let anyone know,' I wail, turning into the very thing I didn't want to be, a stressed-out bridezilla.

'Calm down.' Dad's voice is quiet yet authoritative. 'Once we're on our way, I'll text your mum.'

'She never looks at her phone,' I snap, which isn't strictly true, but she does have it on silent all the time and won't be expecting to look at it now. 'Text Cat instead.'

'I'll do that,' Dad says, ushering me out of the door and towards the lovely black limo waiting for us.

In the end it's me who texts Cat on Dad's phone, and tells her what's happening, she replies with a couple of emojis and tells me not to worry; Leeward hasn't arrived yet anyway, but Jayne has and her hair is peacock blue, or it could be green, Cat isn't too sure. She has feathers in it too, instead of a hat.

'I hope Leeward's not still at the house,' I say to Dad once I've relayed the message.

'He won't be, not by the time we get there.'

Now I've got something else to worry about; bumping in Leeward before the ceremony, now *that* would be bad luck.

It's only as we get to my front door, I realise I don't have my keys. I knock hoping that Leeward *is* here, but at the same time not wishing any more bad luck on myself. But it's fine, he's not here, there is no response. Which isn't fine at all.

'Everything okay?' Dad

'All this way and I don't have a key,' I wail. 'We can't get in and I can't get married in these, can I?' I kick my left foot up and show Dad my pink, fluffy slippers.

'No, I suppose not.' His voice is too calm for my liking, far too calm. 'So it's lucky then that because they take up less room in my pocket, I have your Mum's keys.' He jangles the keys in the air, grinning inanely.

'Give.' I snatch them from his hands. It is fortunate that I gave Mum a spare key and only recently too, because I wanted her to drop something off for the wedding – laughably, I can't even remember what – when Leeward and I were at work.

I fumble the key in the lock and fall through the door.

'Let me go,' Dad says, almost pleading. 'Better than running around in all your finery.'

'You'll never find them, Dad. Won't be long,' I screech as I hitch my dress up around my hips and gallop up the stairs.

Dad hovers by the front door as I lumber about in our bedroom, extricate my wedding shoes from their box in my wardrobe and squidge my feet into them. Squidge being the operative word as all these hours in fluffy, unsupportive slippers have allowed my feet to spread. I'm beginning to hate my wedding day.

I hobble across my bedroom towards the door and hear the sound of vibrating. What the hell was that?

Leeward's phone is still charging on his bedside table. He must have left in quite a hurry to leave *that* behind; he rarely lets it out of his sight. I grab it for him and wonder if he's missed it. Maybe that was him ringing himself trying to locate it. As I clomp down the stairs flatfooted, as neither the shoes nor my feet are able to bend, the phone vibrates again in my hand. It's Alfie. I've no idea who Alfie is, probably one of his mates trying to locate Leeward's phone for him. Alfie rings off before I get the chance to answer. Oh well, I'll surprise Leeward with the phone once we're married.

Dad holds the car door open for me and I climb in, relieved and pleased to have my shoes, and Leeward's phone. I feel my stress levels begin to diminish as we start the drive to the venue. We'll soon be on the bypass so that should make up for some of the time we've lost.

'You'll hardly be late at all,' Dad says.

'Good, five minutes is okay, any longer will cause Leeward anxiety, I don't want our married life to start like that.'

'No.' Dad smiles. 'Do you want me to take that or are you going to clutch it all through the ceremony?' Dad says, pointing at Leeward's phone. 'I can put it in my pocket.'

'Good idea,' I say. A message pops up just as I'm about to hand it over and, despite myself, I cannot resist reading it before it disappears. It's from Alfie, again.

Sorry you can't take my calls. Suppose you're at the stupid wedding now, lol.

Stupid wedding? Stupid wedding? Who the hell is this Alfie to say something like that to Leeward on his wedding day? I feel my stress levels start to rise again. Calm down, it's a joke, isn't it?

I pull the phone back in front of me and swipe to open it. Of course, I can't, the phone is password protected. I don't know the password. Think, think, what might it be? I try my birthday, Leeward's, his mum's. Nothing works. I've probably seen him type those numbers a hundred times and taken no notice. I picture his fingers swiping around the screen, trying to visualise it in my head. I try a few more but nothing works. I'll be asking Leeward who the hell this Alfie thinks he is and to have a word with him, I assume he's not at our wedding. Sighing, I pass the phone over for Dad to take it, but just as he holds out his hand another message pops up.

Sorry I can't be there. Hope your best man duties are not too onerous. Don't get off with the chief bridesmaid, lol.

What the…

Hold on, maybe this isn't Leeward's phone. Phew, of course it's not, it must be Kenton's. He must have stayed the night at our place with Leeward. Of course, how stupid of me, this is Kenton's phone and Alfie is a woman, not a man.

Typical Kenton. Poor Suzi doesn't stand a chance despite Jayne's interfering.

I'm just about to hand it to Dad when another message pops up.

Just wanted to say, Lee, that last night was amazing. I love you so much, too. I'm looking forward to building a happy future with you.

What?

Is this not Kenton's phone? Is Lee, Leeward?

My stomach drops and I feel quite sick. I start scrabbling around on the phone trying to get through its security. If this is Leeward's phone what would the pass code be? Think, think, think.

Then I try a lucky guess, 1111. As I try it, I know it will work. I've seen him type this so many times, even if I haven't paid attention, it's gone into my brain. It's *Lord of the Rings* – one ring to rule them all. It works.

I scroll through his messages, his exchanges with Alfie. Months and months' worth. Some are so explicit I gulp. Leeward never says things like this to me. I always think of him as a prude. There is nothing prudish about these conversations.

This must be a mistake. This isn't Leeward's phone. Somehow, he's picked up someone else's. That's it. A perfectly feasible explanation.

Who am I fooling?

I flick over to his gallery, check on his photos, there are plenty of me, and me and him together, but there are just as many of Leeward, or Lee, with another woman, a woman who is not me. Her face doesn't show in any of the photos, just the back of her glossy blonde head, or the side but never her face. Is she being careful or teasing? I keep scrolling, then I find what I dread, the porny pics. I recognise the lower half of Leeward's naked torso instantly, then I see the large, though ultra-toned and cellulite free buttocks of his mistress.

'Stop the car, stop the car,' I screech.

In the rear-view mirror I see confusion in the driver's eyes.

'Are you all right?' Dad asks. 'You've gone very pale.'

'Stop the car. I'm going to be sick.'

'Pull over,' Dad yells, but the driver is already lurching us onto the hard shoulder. We pull up fast, our seat belts locking with the impact. I undo mine and jump out.

I'm still holding the phone, still clutching the evil evidence when I vomit onto the grassy embankment as cars and lorries hurtle past, a few giving me the benefit of a beep and a toot. What must I look like – a bride in all her finery puking on the bypass?

When I've finished I slump down onto the grass, my head on my knees, my dress all around me, my shoes, so pretty with the pearl encrusted toes, peeking up at me.

'What's wrong? Is it something you ate? Are you feeling better?'

I look at Dad. I'm not crying. Not yet. I hold the phone out to him.

He takes it in his hand, looks at it, then at me, then shakes his head.

'It's locked,' he says.

I reach up and stab in the numbers to unlock it.

'Read the messages from Alfie.'

Dad's eyes widen in horror as he follows my instructions. Long seconds pass as I watch him scrolling.

'Jesus,' he says, half under his breath. 'The little bastard.'

'Yeah.' I reach for the phone.

We stay there as the minutes tick away, me on the grass, Dad standing beside me, the driver hovering by the car, careful not to join us, but also careful to keep the car between him and the traffic.

I'm still not crying, which is surprising. I think I'm too shocked to cry. I'm searching my brain for how this can all be a mistake, looking for a solution as though this is a puzzle, a game.

'Why don't you sit down?' I say to Dad.

'I won't. Suit's hired.' He gives me a little smile, a half shrug. The stupid suits that Leeward wanted, all matching.

The driver looks over at Dad and frowns a question. He thinks I don't notice.

Dad coughs a little. 'Do you want to go home?'

I shake my head slowly. I don't think I've got a home any longer.

Dad nods then turns away, faces the traffic; his shoulders go up and down. I hope he's not crying.

A lorry toots its horn then pulls up in front of the bridal car. I imagine how we look to other drivers, a bride on the grass verge, the father of the bride looking anxious. The driver pacing, slowly, patiently. We look as though we've broken down, as though we're waiting for help.

The driver walks up to the meet the lorry driver who is marching towards us. Words are exchanged and the lorry driver leaves, careful not to stare at me, but he can't help casting several glances over his shoulder.

Dad's phone vibrates in his pocket and for a moment I think it's another message for Leeward. From Alfie.

I'm beginning to wonder if Leeward is even going to turn up today. It's very obvious that there's serious stuff between him and this Alfie bitch. But why go through all this? This is the wedding he wanted. I shudder at the cost. He's been distant lately, and I've been preoccupied with the wedding arrangements. Is that why he's strayed? Is he going to humiliate me and leave me standing at the altar? Well, wedding desk to be exact, it's not a church.

Dad turns to me, his phone in his hand.

'It's Cat,' he says. 'She says Leeward and his brothers are there now. She's wondering how long we're going to be.'

He's not leaving me at the altar then. He's there, he's waiting. For me.

Maybe it's all a joke, or a mistake. It's one of his mates. It's a stalker. I think of his responses. The photos. No. No mistake.

I stand up. Straighten my shoulders. Take a deep breath – more traffic fumes than oxygen.

'Let's go.' I stumble down the embankment, heading for the car. The driver opens the door.

'Where to?' Dad climbs in beside me. 'Home?'

'No. Wedding.' I smile at the driver in the rear-view mirror. 'Get us to the venue as fast as possible,' I tell him. 'I don't want to keep my fiancé waiting any longer.'

Dad reaches over and grips my hand, the one that isn't clutching Leeward's phone. 'Perhaps it's a mistake,' he offers.

I force a smile and a nod, even though I can feel the tears pricking at the corners of my eyes, a lump in my throat just fighting to escape. I inhale and exhale through my nose several times.

When we pull up at the venue Cat is hovering outside. She looks more annoyed than concerned.

'Where have you been? Leeward's shitting himself in there. You're fifteen minutes late. I know it's the bride's right to be late but not this much...' She stops, looks me up and down while stuffing my bouquet into my hands. I take it only with my left hand, I'm still clutching the phone in my right. 'Give that to Dad,' she says. 'Is everything okay?'

'I need the phone.' I link arms with Dad and urge him on. The other bridesmaids appear as Cat corals them into position. I look at their dresses and think of how much all this shit has cost.

I used to have my own car.

'You don't need the phone.' Cat makes a grab for it.

'I do.'

I feel Dad wince.

The wedding room looks amazing, no expense spared, flowers everywhere. The music starts, heads turn, a hush shimmers down the room as we hover in the doorway. Jayne's peacock hair-do quivers and quakes in a sea of normal hair.

'Oh my God, your dress is stained at the back,' Cat whispers, and tries to rub at the stain.

'Doesn't matter.' I swipe her hand away.

Dad and I take a fast march up the aisle, not the

sedate one I had imagined. As we draw level Leeward casts me a look of relief mixed with annoyance. Over his shoulder Steve nods but Kenton beams at me, showing off his perfect white teeth. The brothers are standing in height order, short Leeward, medium Steve, tall and elegant Kenton. I give them my sweetest smile and use my bridal flowers to hide the phone, even though I should have handed them to Cat by now, who is hovering on her seat ready to take them. I ignore her.

The Registrar starts to speak as Leeward and I face each other, ready to commit ourselves. We've already agreed that we're going with the standard vows, neither of us wishing to make a gushing, personal speech. I wait while Leeward parrots his out; he really is going through with this. Have I made a mistake? Have I misinterpreted?

I stop the Registrar as she starts to read out what I am to repeat.

'I have my own,' I half whisper.

Leeward frowns. I smile at him, toss the flowers to Cat who performs an amazing one-handed catch, and produce the phone. He looks confused. Of course he does, we haven't pre-agreed this. I unlock the phone. When I start to speak my voice is clear and concise and surprisingly free of emotion.

'*I'm looking forward to building a happy future with you,*' I read.

Leeward smiles at me.

'*Don't get off with the chief bridesmaid, lol.*' I turn to the wedding guests and frown. 'Hardly likely as that is my sister who cannot really stand Leeward.' I giggle as Cat looks aghast.

'What's going on?' Leeward mumbles. He's slow, this boy.

'*Sorry you can't take my calls. Suppose you're at the stupid wedding now, lol,*' I say to his face before turning back to our guests. 'Obviously, I didn't say that.' I smirk before continuing. '*Just wanted to say, Lee, that last night was amazing.* We weren't together last night,' I say to the guests. '*I love you so much too and look forward to sharing the rest of our lives together.*'

Realisation is dawning on my fiancé's face. He makes a half-hearted grab for the phone, but I'm too quick for him, dodging his grab, swiping him out of the way with my free arm and continuing with another message.

'You might want to cover little ears for these ones,' I say, my voice incredibly calm. '*I cannot wait to feel your hard cock inside me again.*'

A gasp goes around the room like a Mexican wave followed by an intense silence. Oh, I have everyone's attention now.

'*When you come inside me it feels like a thousand stars explode.* Yuk! Pass the sick bucket, please.' I smile at Leeward, who just stares at me. Behind him Kenton is open mouthed and Steve looks disgusted. Jayne has her hand over her mouth. Suzi, sitting with Jayne, is suppressing a little smirk. I shift my position slightly to see Mum staring straight ahead, tears brimming the rims of her eyes. Dad has his head down.

'Give me that.' Leeward lunges towards me. I hurl the phone in the air, expecting it to crash to the ground, but, rather impressively, he catches it.

'I think Leeward might be a bit confused about who he is marrying,' I say to the guests. 'Oops, caught out.' I sound so jolly; I don't feel it. I suppose it's the adrenaline that's keeping me going.

Leeward runs out of the wedding room.

47

'Good riddance, you hateful little Gollum,' Grimmy's voice echoes around the room, followed by a few titters which stop abruptly when people realise how inappropriate it is to laugh.

Leeward's brothers march, rather than run out; Kenton gives me a look of apology. Jayne and Suzi follow. All through this no one else speaks, they just let their eyes do the talking.

Once the door bangs shut behind Jayne, I let out a big sigh.

'Sorry you all had to witness that. It seems that my fiancé has been having a very intense affair with another woman for the last six months and I only just found out on the way here. Lucky escape for me, eh?' Do I really mean that? 'Anyway, since we're all here in our finery and there's a lovely meal, not to mention *real* champagne, waiting for us, I suggest we go and party like we've never partied before. I'm begging you all to please stay, because it's all been paid for and Leeward made me sell my car to finance this and I don't want it all going to waste.' I sniff. Oh dear, open the floodgates, here come the tears. Oh shit.

Four

'I think there are only about ten missing, not including Leeward and his crew, of course,' Cat says, attempting a smile at me. 'At least the food and drink won't be wasted.'

'Which is more than can be said for me.' I grab my glass and knock back the contents. All the real champagne is finished now, we're on the white wine and it's really rather nice; Leeward chose well.

We're on the main course and even though I've only picked at my food I have to admit it's all rather lovely.

'You're better off without him. He was never good enough for you.' Grimmy raises her glass at me and judging from her pink cheeks, she has had a few too.

We've rearranged the tables, merging the top table with my family's to make one great big table. I need all my nearest and dearest close to me even if they are looking at me with varying degrees of pity.

My brother, Sam, winks from across the table, he smiles too, but he looks sad for me. Everyone looks sad for me. Mum and Dad have hardly said a word. Grimmy is still revelling in her *Gollum* remark.

I fill my glass up again and raise it.

'Cheers everyone, my lovely family.' I knock back my wine as a few join in. It's all really rather pitiful.

At some point I must fall asleep because suddenly I'm waking up with my head on the table and drool congealing on my chin. When I open my eyes, I can see that all the food has been cleared away. I try to tell myself that it has all been a horrible dream, but I know it hasn't.

'He didn't even deny it or say he was sorry,' I gabble to Cat who's still sitting beside me. She grips my hand in response. 'Hey, where's your dress?' Cat is now in a pair of jeans and a soft top, not the very expensive bridesmaid dress I bought her.

'I've changed, for the evening. The band has just arrived.'

'Evening, already. Right.' I crane my neck to see the band. 'Where are they?'

'They're setting up. The venue is sorting them out. Don't worry, it's not even six yet. Do you want me to help you change? Mum put your bag in your room.'

'I'm not changing.' I stand up, feel lightheaded and grip the table for support. 'This dress cost a bloody fortune and I'm going to get my money's worth.'

'But it's all stained at the back,' Cat says, glancing behind me. 'What is it? It looks like you've shit yourself.'

'It's grass. From the bypass. I haven't shit myself, I've been shit on. By a bastard.' I flop back down into my seat. 'You can come to my room with me though to get my phone. Maybe Leeward's been messaging me.'

'Okay.' Cat stands up, and, after three attempts, so do I.

Back in my room – the bridal suite, what a joke – I hunt for my phone. There is not one message from him. Not one. And not one from anyone else either. I flop onto the super king bed and spread my arms and legs out.

'This is comfy.'

'You could stay here, get some rest. I'm sure people will understand.'

'I'm not hiding myself away. *I* haven't done anything wrong.' I check my phone again. 'Have you got a signal?'

'Yeah.'

'What network?'

'Same as you.'

'Bastard hasn't even called me. Not even a message to say sorry or explain. Oh, here we go,' I say as something flashes up. 'Oh, oh.'

'Is that him?'

'No, it's Kenton.'

'Urgh. What does he want?'

'I don't know. Here, you read it. I need to use the bathroom. I think someone has been sick in my mouth.' I fish my toilet bag out and take it with me.

When I come back, I feel marginally fresher.

'What did Kenton want?'

'He says he's sorry that happened to you and wanted to reassure you that he didn't know anything about it.'

'Urgh.'

'And he's back.'

'Who? Leeward?' I feel my heart race.

'No, Kenton. He hopes it's okay that he's come back. He feels he wants to support you and not his brother.'

'Whatever. Shall we go? The buffet will be out soon and I'm bloody starving. And, I could do with a drink.'

'Coke maybe,' Cat offers. She has the harassed look of a big sister looking after a naughty little sister.

'Yeah, why not?' I grab her arm and link mine through it. 'With lots of Bacardi. Yay. Let's party.'

And, oh, do I party.

I even manage a laugh when someone – one of Leeward's friends – tells me that I'm all over Facebook.

'A video?' I ask, wondering how anyone could be so despicable as to do that.

'No, just a photo and some words. It's quite a good shot of Leeward catching his phone when you threw it. The words are complimentary and sympathetic though.'

'I don't want their pity. Ha, who cares.' I certainly don't, I've had far too many Bacardi and cokes to care about anything, ever again. 'I've always wanted to be a Facebook star.' I haven't and I don't even know why I'm saying it. Then I cackle, like a maniac, and I keep on cackling all the way round the room as I search for Cat, who is hiding out in a corner with the rest of my family. They paste on jolly faces when they spot me coming.

'Band's good, aren't they?'

'Yes. Yes,' everyone choruses.

'So they bloody should be.' I raise a class to them, not that they notice.

'I don't know what they're playing,' Grimmy says. 'I don't recognise any of it. And they're too loud. Do they just play what they like? Are they making it up as they go along?'

Over her shoulder Mum does that nod, the one that means, *typical*.

'No, Grimmy, Leeward chose the playlist.'

'Gollum,' she mutters, letting her top teeth drop a little out of her mouth before sucking them back in and taking a large gulp of cider. I think she might be a little inebriated.

Careless Whisper starts to play and it's really rather good, a soft saxophone belting out the opening notes.

'See, that's what I mean.' Grimmy shakes her head. 'What is that?'

Sam catches my eye and smiles. He's sitting with his youngest asleep on his lap. There's something about this image which catches me at the back of my throat. I swallow it down. I am bloody not crying any more on my non-wedding day. Bloody well not again.

'What about a nice bit of Frank Sinatra?' Grimmy is off again.

'This is George Michael, Grammy,' Dad tells her. 'You remember. You said you liked him.'

'No, I didn't. Get them to play something everyone knows.' She gives me a sharp nudge in the ribs with one of her knobbly elbows. 'Go on, get up there. You're paying them to play what you want.'

I don't really care what they play. Why would I? I don't care about anything anymore. Not. One. Thing.

Somehow, grass-stained wedding dress not particularly obliging, I heave myself up the steps to the stage and get the attention of the band leader. He nods at me to wait until they finish what they're playing.

He has a quick word with the band and they carrying on playing before he turns to me. 'Yeah?' he says, turning off his microphone and sounding suspicious.

Now I'm here I don't know what I'm supposed to be saying.

'Um, my grimmy, sorry, grandmother, well, strictly speaking, great-grandmother, wants you to play something she'll recognise.' I nod over in her direction and she raises a scraggy arm.

'Right,' he says. 'Not sure we know anything from before the second world war.' He does a cockeyed grimace that presses all my buttons, not, it would fair to say, that it takes much.

'Ha, bloody ha. It's my wedding, non-wedding, and I'm paying you and if I remember correctly, I haven't settled the full bill yet.'

Now we're facing each other off while the band are tootling along in the background playing something even *I* don't recognise and I've seen the playlist.

'I know what you can play and I want to sing.' What? I can't sing, I never sing. What the hell is going on?

'Okay, lady,' he says before passing my instructions onto the band, several of whom exchange glances before complying, one even mouthing *Karaoke* with a sneer on his lips.

The band starts to play, I stand at the front of the stage, microphone in hand and get ready for my solo, even though I don't actually know the proper words, so I improvise.

At first I was afraid I'd be on my own
Cos I found your dirty cheating on your mobile phone.
But then I realised as I sat on that grassy verge
That you were just a lying, stinking, cheating, dirty turd

So you ran off, leaving me alone
But not before you picked up that fucking mobile phone
I should have smashed it with my foot
I should have kicked your sorry arse
And you haven't even contacted me to apologise.

So sod off you, Leeward Quinn
See what you're missing now that I am so very thin

I don't need you anyway, you're far too short for me
I won't be the sorry one cos I have my liberty.

Oh no not I, I will survive
I'll be stronger, I'll be better and I know that I will thrive...

After that the words get rather jumbled, I'm just screeching *I will survive* while all the non-wedding guests look on, some in horror, some in amusement, and, I like to think, some in admiration. I feel rather proud of myself and not just because I've sung a brilliant improvised version but also because I sounded pretty damn good, great voice and in tune too.

There are a few mobile phones out taking pics of me. Ha, I don't care if you post those on Facebook. Do it. I just hope Leeward Gollum Quinn sees what he's missing. And Alfie the mistress.

I'm still screeching when the band stops playing. There's a rather undignified tussle over the microphone when the band leader tries to retrieve it. Finally, he succeeds and I bow out graciously, well sort of curtsey to the crowd, my fans. There's a muted round of applause.

Then I step down from the stage.

Only I don't use the steps. I fall. Rather spectacularly. It feels as though I am sailing through the air, graceful and charming in my wedding dress. I finish with a magnificent one-handed handstand.

Ta da.

Cat rushes towards me but it's a smiling and sympathetic Kenton who sweeps me up of the floor and hugs me to him.

'Are you okay?' he asks, his voice full of sickly emotion.

'Yeah, fine.' I shake him off and pull myself up to my full height, which isn't very tall against Kenton's statuesque body.

'I can't apologise enough for my brother's stupid antics,' he says, laying a hand on my shoulder.

'Did he send you to say that?'

'No. No, he didn't.'

'Where is he?'

Kenton looks sheepish. 'I don't really know. I suppose I could guess.' He offers me a little grimace. 'We all went back to Mum's after we left, she's terribly upset by the way, and ashamed of him. Then Leeward just fucked off without a word. He's not answering his phone and he's not at your, his, house. I'm so sorry. You didn't deserve this. You're such a great girl.'

'Ha. Ha.' I shake his hand off me – it's been on my shoulder during his entire trite little speech.

'I don't know what's the matter with him. Why would he want to do that with someone else when he has you?'

'I don't know,' I hear myself slur.

'Is there anything I can do to help you?' Oh, he's so earnest.

'Yeah, you can buy me a drink, it's a cash bar now.'

Kenton escorts me back to my family then asks everyone if they'd like a drink before going off to the bar with a large order. I think some members of my family may be taking it out on him. Grimmy has asked for a pot of tea, the words delivered like a challenge.

'He's got a nerve,' Cat says, voicing what everyone else is thinking.

'It's not his fault. He's as disgusted as the rest of us.'

'Eww, right.' Cat contorts her face.

'He is.'

'Why are you defending him?' Cat sounds angry.

'I'm not.'

'You need to be wary of him,' my brother, Sam, says, leaning over to chip in.

'Yeah, yeah.' I wave my arms about and wince as my left arm throbs a little; maybe that handstand was not as benign as I thought it was.

Kenton comes back carrying a tray full of drinks and Grimmy gives a wicked grin when she sees there's no pot of tea and readies herself to make a nasty comment. She has to bite it back when Kenton steps aside to reveal a waitress carrying another tray; there's not just tea but biscuits too.

'Well done, Kendon,' Grimmy says and I'm not sure if she's deliberately getting his name wrong.

'You're welcome,' he says graciously, 'And please, everyone, call me Ken, I hate Kenton.'

There's a chorus of 'Thanks Ken,' as he doles out the drinks before squeezing a chair in between me and Cat and folding himself into it. Cat frowns and Ken smiles, then turns his attention to me.

I don't really pay him much attention, I'm far more focused on knocking back the two double Bacardi and cokes he's bought me – I asked for them apparently. I'm aware that he's wittering on about Leeward's stupidity again and I can't really argue with that, can I?

After what seems like no time but must be an hour or more the band stops playing and people start to drift away. Ken offers to escort me to my room – my bridal suite – but Cat steps in and bats him away. I'm vaguely aware of unlocking the door to my room and getting into bed as the room starts swaying and the bed is rocking. Sleep cannot come fast enough so this horrendous day can come to an end.

The banging in my head is so loud it actually feels as though someone is knocking on the walls. It's incessant. I groan and attempt to roll over but the pain that racks my body makes me gasp.

'Lauren, Lauren.' Is that Cat's voice? I choose to ignore it, I'm dreaming, aren't I?

'Lauren. Lauren.'

I would open my eyes to check but I know it will hurt, so I don't.

'Lauren, Lauren, are you all right? Wake up.' Cat won't shut up.

'Arghhhh,' I groan, hoping that she'll get the message.

'Wake up, wake up now. Look at me.' Oh stern big sister.

I allow one eye to open; yes, it's Cat.

'Your door was unlocked,' she says. 'Anyone could have come in here. Kenton certainly would have if he'd known.'

'Arghhhh.'

'What did you want?'

What did *I* want? 'Nothing,' I manage. 'What do you want?'

'A good night's sleep,' she snaps. 'You messaged me six times to come and save you.'

'No,' I say. She must have that wrong.

'I've driven right across town, good job I don't drink alcohol, isn't it? So what do you want?'

'Nothing,' I say, closing my one open eye and turning over. 'Owwww,' I howl with pain. The hangover is bad, so bad, the worst I've ever had but the wrist is unbearable. I gasp for breath and wait for the wave of multiple pains to pass.

'Hangover?' Cat sounds most unsympathetic. 'You've dragged me over here for a hangover.'

'No,' I manage, wincing. 'Arm.'

Cat flicks the light on which burns into my eyes even though they are both closed.

'Oh. My. God,' she says.

'What?' I force open both eyes by raising my eyebrows up to my hairline.

'I think that might be broken.'

I look at my wrist and even though I cannot see very well I can see a bruised and swollen joint that is definitely not right. I start to cry now, not just for my wrist but for my sad, sorry life.

'Come on, let's get you sat up.' Cat starts pulling me around and props me up. The room spins. I feel sick.

'Bucket,' I mutter, pointing to the floor beside the bed with my good arm.

'Urgh God. Where did you get this?' She thrusts it under my chin and I perform a spectacular puke.

'Bathroom bin inner,' I say as I spit out the last dregs of vomit.

She snatches the bucket and stomps off to the toilet to empty it, she's gone ages and I can hear the toilet flushing and water running. She's a bit of a clean freak, is Cat.

'Here, you might need this again.' She pushes the rinsed bucket at me before scouting around the room until she finds the fridge and pours me a large glass of water from one of the two complimentary bottles.

I take little mouthfuls and hope I won't be sick again. Cat flumps down on the bed and watches me. We stay like this for ages, me sipping, her watching. She refills my glass twice. I start to feel marginally less awful and I'm not sick again.

'You've still got your wedding dress on.'

'Oh yeah.' I look down to see a nasty brown stain on my chest. 'I think that might be sick,' I say, musing.

'Yes, I think so. Can't see any on the bed or carpet but you pebble-dashed the bathroom. I've cleaned it off.'

So that's what she was doing in there.

'Thanks,' I say sheepishly.

'Let's get that dress off.' Cat leans forward to help me and I yelp like a battered dog.

'No. Can't. Hurts. Arm,' I say between gasps.

'It's broken.'

'Noooo,' I wail.

'Yes, it is. Don't be stupid, you're a nurse, you should know.'

'Oh nooo,' I whinge again.

'What's that?' Cat picks at the pillow behind. 'It's your hair, it's coming out. Far too much bleach,' she says, making another judgement. 'You're going to be bald as well.'

'Thanks for that,' I snap. 'It's an extension, not my real hair.'

'Have your actually got any real hair in there.' She points to my head and I glance around the room until I find myself in a mirror. I do look a proper sight, my face is grey, my dress crumpled and stained and my hair, well, I don't remember the hurricane that obviously hit me.

I slump back on the pillows and sigh. I could cry again, but I'm not going to. It's so bloody pointless.

'You need to have a shower and change your clothes, I'll tie up your hair, then we need to get you to the hospital.'

'It's too early. We can go later.'

60

'I can't,' Cat says, I have things to do. Four kids, remember. Anyway, we might wait less time if we go now.'

'What time is it?'

'Ten to six. Come on.'

I sit up, wincing and complaining and heave myself up off the bed. Beads of sweat gather around my hairline. The dress feels as though it is contracting around me, getting tighter and tighter.

'These laces are hard to undo,' Cat mutters to herself.

'Cut them.'

'It'll ruin it.'

'Like that matters. Please just cut them, there are nail scissors in my toilet bag. And please hurry up, this dress is crushing my ribs. I can't breathe properly.' I pant several times to prove my point.

Cat dashes off to the bathroom, then returns and snips me out of my constricting hell before helping me out of the dress.

I stand there in my underwear feeling stupid and embarrassed. I'm wearing white stockings and a suspender belt with matching bra, all chosen because I know Leeward would have appreciated this ensemble.

Cat looks me up and down. 'That stupid Leeward,' she says, her voice softening. 'He doesn't know what he's missing.' She puts a warm hand on my shoulder. 'Okay, what else do you want help with?'

'Can you just undo my bra and run the shower please. Oh and find my shower hat, I don't want to have to wash this yet.' I stab at my hair with my good hand.

In the end she has to undress me completely and basically give me a shower. I know she's my sister but it's still humiliating. Once I'm wrapped up in several towels, she cleans off the industrial makeup that Suzi applied.

'Bloody stuff,' Cat moans. 'It took me ages to get it off my face too. It's more like paint than makeup.'

'And it was wasted anyway,' I say, managing a little laugh.

Cat laughs with me.

Finally, I'm ready, comfy soft sleeveless top and leggings that I brought to wear to breakfast before putting on something more elegant. Cat has done her best with my hair but it still looks like a bird's nest. A blonde bird's nest.

'Shoes?'

'In my bag?'

'Already looked. Can't find any.'

I think for a moment. 'Oh shit, I don't think I have any.' Isn't this how it all started, my finding out about Leeward's infidelity because I'd forgotten my shoes?

'You'll have to wear these then.' She thrusts the wedding pumps onto my feet.

They look just great with the leggings. The sparkly toes, now a bit grey and grubby, attempt to twinkle at me.

'Are there any biscuits in that fridge?'

'What?'

'My arm is killing me. I want to take painkillers but not without food.'

'Here,' she says, fishing a breakfast bar out of her handbag. 'Have this.'

I munch away while Cat collects all my things up and stuffs them in my bag. She says I might as well check out now and save the hassle of coming back to do it; I think she means save her the hassle.

Once everything is loaded in the car, Cat helps me into the passenger seat. I wince and gasp as she does up the seat belt.

'You're not going to be sick again, are you?'

'I don't think so.'

'If you are, let me know, I don't want *that* in my car.'

'Okay.'

And I'm not sick again as we head off for the joy of an early Sunday morning visit to A&E.

I only have myself to blame, well, no, it's his fault. Gollum.

Five

It's not as busy as I feared it would be in A&E. That said, the waiting room is large and there are more than enough people here especially for so early on a Sunday morning.

We check in at the reception desk and I give a brief explanation of what happened. I must be rambling on because Cat cuts across me.

'She fell over onto her hand.'

'When was this?'

'Last night,' Cat says before I can answer.

'Okay. Name?'

Once I've divulged my name and address, which Cat corrects to that of our parents' after I give Leeward's address, we're told to sit and wait. We file over to the rows of chairs facing the TV where BBC News is playing but with the sound muted. Even though none of it is of any interest to me and I struggle to read the subtitles due to the constant movement of the ticker-tape breaking news, I find myself compelled to stare at the screen, and so does everyone else.

I look down at my feet, the shoes twinkle at me, as if taunting; they're uncomfortable too, so hard and unyielding. What must I look like, my shoes, my hair?

I'm staring at the TV, wincing occasionally and thinking about nothing and everything Leeward, when I become of aware of Cat's nose twitching.

'What?' I snap as I turn towards her. I'm wondering if she's going to tell me I smell like a brewery, not that I can smell anything at the moment, I think last night's excess of alcohol has numbed my senses of smell and taste.

'Can't you smell it?'

'What?'

Cat casts a furtive glance around, then mouths, 'Poo.' It always amuses me that she says poo when most adults would say shit, I suppose it's due to years of being around small children even if some of them are now obstreperous teenagers.

'No, but then I can't smell much at the moment.'

Cat rolls her eyes and slowly spins around to ascertain where this supposed smell is coming from. Her eyes alight on something or someone and that look of realisation dawns. Then her eyes widen. Abruptly, she turns back to face the TV before shuddering theatrically.

As a man in his fifties with fashionable grey stubble saunters past us, his smart navy suit crumpled, Cat leans away from the aisle and towards me.

'It's him,' she whispers.

'No.'

'Yes. We'll have to move.'

'Where? Why?' I really don't want to move, my arm, immobile all the time we've been sitting here is finally less painful and I don't want to remind it that it hurts.

'We can't sit here, we're downwind of him. Come on.'

I glance over at the man who is now feeding coins into a vending machine full of snacks which are definitely not of the healthy variety. He turns and heads back towards us with three packets of crisps. They suddenly seem very appealing; I imagine the taste of salt on my tongue even though crisps are not something I would normally want.

'Why are you smacking your lips?' Cat says, her tone accusatory.

'I'm not,' I say like a child caught doing something she shouldn't.

Crumpled suit man skates past us, apparently not able to pick up his feet. Cat holds her breath and makes no attempt to hide the look of disgust from her face.

'Come on.' She stands up and waits for me to obey.

'Urgh, must we?' I groan as I haul myself up.

As we move away I notice that smelly man is back in his seat in front of the doors which constantly squish open when people arrive or leave, hence Cat's comment about us being downwind of him; the seats adjacent to him and the two rows in front are empty. Cat finds us two seats in the middle of a row far from him and the TV. Now we're staring at the vending machines – snacks, tea, coffee, water, coke – and I find myself craving salt again.

'Do you want a drink?' Cat asks.

'Yes. Please.'

I wait for her to get up and go to the coffee machine, but instead she whips out a bottle of water from her bag.

'Don't slobber on it, we'll share.'

'I can get another one,' I glance over at the machine. 'Or a coffee maybe.'

Cat puts her disgusting face on again. 'Not from a

66

vending machine, God knows how long that stuff has been in there.'

'Not that long,' I say, nodding towards the snack machine as smelly, crumpled man is back feeding coins into it again.

Cat shudders once more and I think I see the start of a retch. She reins it in, ever stoic.

'I can't see it,' I say, nudging her, then wincing as the movement makes my arm throb.

'Can't see what?'

'The shit. You'd think, with the smell…'

'It's definitely him. I can't see it either. I don't want to think about it too much.' We both watch as he slides back to his seat, several more crisp packets in his hands. Cat leans in to whisper into my ear. 'Nappy?'

'Could be. I don't know why I didn't think of that, given where I work.' I snigger. So bad of me. I blame the alcohol abuse. The alcohol abuse is directly attributed to Leeward. I blame Leeward.

Cat frowns and I shut up.

My name is called and Cat jumps up and insists on leading the way. I pick up my handbag with my good hand and follow her.

I feel extremely foolish as I explain how I fell from the stage after my turn at the microphone.

'Karaoke?' The nurse smiles at me.

'Yes, that's right,' Cat jumps in.

'Okay, well it doesn't look too good does it? Lots of bruising. Let's get you x-rayed then we'll see you again. Take this yellow slip and follow the red line.

The waiting room in x-ray is much smaller than in the main A&E. We flop down into the seats and wait to be called. I stop Cat from accompanying me into the x-ray room explaining that they won't let her stay anyway.

It takes minutes and when the radiologist comes back from checking the x-ray, I ask her if it's broken.

'They'll discuss it with you in A&E,' she answers, diplomatically. 'Here's your yellow slip. Just wait to be called again.'

I hold the yellow slip as we head back through the A&E corridors; there are now two trollies with patients on them, looking forlorn and waiting to be moved elsewhere. Thank God, that's not me. A broken wrist, though tedious enough, isn't life threatening.

As I head out through the door to the waiting area Cat snatches the yellow slip from me and puts it in a box on the wall.

'They don't tell you to do that, but if you don't, you'll wait forever.'

'Really?'

'Yes, believe me, this isn't the first time I've been up here.'

'Okay.' She's right, I should have known this, I used to work in this hospital, though not in this department.

We find seats again and I notice that the exclusion zone around smelly man is getting bigger. Cat gags and even I begin to notice the stench of shit. He's dozed off with piles of crisp packets on the empty seats either side of him.

'It's the staff I feel sorry for,' Cat says. 'Having to deal with that.'

'Don't judge,' I reply. 'You don't know what's wrong with him.'

'Okay. I bet I know what's wrong with her,' she says, nodding at a teenager sitting on the floor and being sick into a cardboard bowl. Beside her an anxious adult, her mother probably, holds a spare bowl in her hand.

'Chemo?' I offer.

'Your sense of smell may have gone, by mine hasn't. I know the smell of regurgitated alcohol.' She gives me a half smile, then clamps her lips shut, thus indicating the end of the discussion and that she is right and I am wrong. She's such a big sister!

For the next ten minutes we sit and listen to the sound of the teenager retching into her bowls. I don't look but Cat casts glances over at her whenever the noise gets too much, as do several other people. We're all grateful when the girl's name is called.

My x-ray is on the screen when I go into the cubicle.

'Is it broken?' I ask, fearing the answer.

'Yes.' There's a little smile of sympathy. I know that smile, I do it myself.

'Great.'

'The position isn't as it should be so we'll just put it straight and get a cast on you.' That sounds so innocuous, only I know exactly what that means. And it means it will be painful. She gives me another little smile.

'Do you work?'

'Yes.' I want to say, of course I do, why wouldn't I?

'What do you do?'

I think about this for a second. 'I work in a care home.'

'Ah.'

'She's a senior nurse in a nursing home,' Cat sets the record straight at the same time making it sound as though I am the only qualified person in the entire nursing home. Neither of us adds that I now only work part-time.

'You'll need some time off work then.'

'Yeah.' I nod.

'Okay, if you'll wait again, someone will call you.'

I tell Cat that she is not coming in with me again. I don't have a go at her because she keeps speaking for me, that would just be too ungrateful, I just tell her it's not appropriate.

'Okay,' she says, a faint look of relief on her face.

'Can you have a look in my bag for my phone?'

'It's flat,' she says, once she finds it, before dropping it back in my bag.

'Charger's in there. And there's a socket on that pillar.' I nod just past her knees.

She sighs and gets both the phone and charger out, plugs it in and sits with the phone on her lap, just out of my reach. I'm about to make a grab for it when my name is called.

There's a nurse and a doctor waiting for me in the room. A small conspiratorial look passes from them to me, they will have seen from my notes that I'm a nurse, they will know I know what is to come.

We go through a few inane pleasantries while I confirm my name and date of birth, I glance over at the piece of paper on the desk, my age is underneath my date of birth, 35yrs and 5mths.

'Do you need gas and air?' There's a smile and I glance round the room looking for the tank.

'Do you have any here?

'No, but we could probably source some.' Another smile. The doctor is young and weary looking, I wonder how long she's been on duty.

'No, just do it.'

I take a deep breath as they pull my bones into position. It hurts like hell but I don't shout or scream,

70

just breathe so fast I almost pass out from hyperventilating. Then it's over. The doctor escapes and the nurse starts to slap on a cast, a back slab, just to stabilise it until the swelling goes down, which will probably be the best part of two weeks. She ties my arm up around my neck and tells me to keep it elevated.

'How does that feel?' Cat asks as I slump back down next to her.

'Heavy. And wet.' I give a little shrug. 'But better; it doesn't move now, so it doesn't hurt so much.'

'Did they give you anything for the pain?'

'No.' I laugh. 'I can take paracetamol or ibuprofen. Is my phone charged?'

'No, not yet. Come on, let's go.' She yanks the charger from the wall and stuffs it and my phone, still connected, into my bag, swings it over her shoulder and stands up.

I trot along behind her as she clears the way for me, just as we reach the door, we see the sickly teenager appear, wrapped in a blanket but evidently better. She gives me a sheepish grin. Cat sees it and scowls.

Cat puts me in her car, literally, she folds me in and does up my seat belt. I just manage to wrestle my handbag from her before she closes my door.

As she's driving us home, I find my phone and switch it on, there's enough charge for it to start up and run for a while, but as soon as we get home – wherever that is now – it'll need to be plugged in.

'No messages.' I sigh.

Cat nods as she concentrates on driving.

'None, from anyone. If I didn't know better, I'd say my phone was disconnected from the network.'

'Switch it on and off.'

'That's already happened.'

'Right.' Cat isn't interested.

'I'll check Facebook, see if I am connected.'

'Is that wise?' Cat asks without looking at me, not even a glance.

'Why? Oh God, there's not a video of me reading out Leeward's dirty messages is there? Oh God.'

'No. Not that. Couple of comments about the wedding not taking place, nothing nasty…

'Then what…' But I don't need her to tell me because I've found it for myself; a video of me singing *I Will Survive*, well my version of it anyway. It's not quite how I remember; my words were witty, rhyming perfectly and so, so cutting and very tuneful. In this version I am screeching, and it's mostly incoherent except for the swearwords, which are extremely clear and vile.

Cat says nothing as the video plays out, her face impassive and turned to the road.

'It's had nearly five-hundred hits.' I can't quite believe it. 'And I sound awful, did I really sound that bad? And the swearing, oh my God, it didn't sound like that to me. What bastard filmed that and uploaded it?'

'I don't know.'

'One of *his* friends. Bastard. That swearing…' I hang my head.

'Just a few f-bombs…'

'If only… There were c-words and words I didn't even know I knew. I'll have to emigrate, have plastic surgery, something so people don't know it's me. Or die. That might be easier.'

We're stopped at lights and Cat turns towards me. 'Don't ever say anything like that again. Right. Are you listening? Life is precious. You, of all people, should know that. Promise me.'

'Mmmm.'

'Anyway, it'll soon fade…' The lights change and she pulls away.

'Five-hundred views,' I say, in case she missed it the first time. 'Five-hundred.' I scroll on down. 'And there are comments.' I read a few. Some are typical *OMG*s, but hidden amongst the strangers are comments from my friends at work, sympathetic, sweet messages.

Cat says nothing.

'Oh well…' I toss my phone back into my handbag. 'I won't need to tell anyone what happened, will I? The whole bloody world knows now.'

'There is that,' Cat says, letting the words hang in the air.

'Not much chance of us getting back together once he sees that…'

'What?' Cat snaps.

'Well, after what I sang about him…'

'You want to get back with him after what he did to you?'

I can't answer. I can't say anything because the enormity of what has happened is only just starting to hit me. Me and Leeward, together for ten years and now it's done, ruined in one day, over, finished, no going back.

'He treated you like shit,' Cat says.

'No he didn't,' I say in a small voice.

We pull onto Mum and Dad's drive and Cat gets out and slams her door, before walking around the car and opening mine, she doesn't speak as she waits for me to lumber out.

The smell of Sunday dinner hits me like a warm wall as we go into Mum and Dad's kitchen. My stomach rumbles its appreciation. Grimmy is already sitting at the dining table, waiting. I glance at the wall clock, it's 12.30pm. Grimmy agrees to wait for her lunch until 1pm on a Sunday provided it's a Sunday roast. So good of her.

'I'll leave you to it, then,' Cat says without a hint of a smile.

'Thank you.' *I* smile at her. 'For everything. For saving me this morning and sitting up there, and everything.' I lean in and attempt to hug her, accidently slapping my now rock-hard, though still wet, cast against her in the process.

'Okay, I'll message you later.' She calls a goodbye to Mum who's checking something in the oven and leaves.

'How did you get on?' Mum asks, eyeing my cast.

'It's broken. Got to wait for a phone call later in the week for them to tell me what's next.'

'Ah. Do you need anything?'

I shake my head. 'Oh, Cat's gone off with my bags.'

'No, she brought them in, Dad's just taken them up to your room.'

My room. Oh God, my room. My childhood bedroom.

'I'll just go up and change my shoes.'

I wrestle my feet into my trainers, quite a feat with only one hand. I would prefer to wear my slippers but they're at home – no, not my home anymore – in the bedroom.

I go to the toilet, again a trial with only one working hand as is washing and drying that hand. I stare at myself in the mirror; I look horrendous. Despite Cat's valiant job at cleaning Susi's paint job from my face

74

there are still traces of mascara smeared around my eyes; I look panda-esque, but not in a cute way. But it's the hair really, the blonde bird's nest atop my head, engorged by extensions. I really don't know what I'm going to do with it, it needs careful undoing and a good wash but really, how am I going to do that? I know Mum will help me but I don't want to be a burden, I don't want to be dependent on others for the simplest of things.

I fish my phone out of my bag again and check for messages. None. I suppose people don't know what to say. I go onto WhatsApp and check to see when Leeward was last active on it: twenty-minutes ago. Twenty-minutes ago and he hasn't contacted me. Bastard. I go straight to Facebook and find the video again, some kind soul has posted it on my timeline, how generous. I add a comment that I hope everyone will see.

Would be bride here. Just so you know, I'd had a lot to drink when I performed this as I was rather upset because my fiancé, the man I'd been with for ten years has been having an affair and I found out in the wedding car on the way to marry him. Needless to say, we didn't get married. So, as you can see, I had justification for being upset. Sorry about the swearing, but ask yourself, how would you react? BTW the cheating liar's name is Leeward Quinn.

I tag him in the post, if I'm going to be shamed, so is he. It's all his fault.

Then, just to make sure, I post it on his timeline. He can suffer the same as me.

'What's the matter with your hair?' Grimmy asks as we're sat eating dinner, not that I've eaten very much, despite feeling hungry I don't seem to be able to chew it and swallow it down.

'Grimmy,' Mum admonishes.

'I was just asking why it's like that. It looked very nice yesterday.'

'Grammy,' Dad says, frowning. It always sounds funny when Dad calls her Grammy, it's a mash up of granny and mummy, which makes sense from his perspective. I suppose I'm just so used to calling her Grimmy.

She shrugs and helps herself to the last of the gravy.

I excuse myself before dessert is served, take a couple of painkillers and head up to my bedroom. I flop down onto the bed and pick up my phone. Several messages on Facebook, most kind, offering sympathy, agreeing with me about Leeward being a cheating liar, a few are from friends but most are from strangers.

A WhatsApp pops up. It's Leeward.

Why did you post that on Facebook? Isn't it bad enough you made such a fool of yourself without dragging me into it? There are several angry-face emojis following his words.

No apology, no explanation from him, just an angry message, annoyed because I *dragged him into it*. I'm about to reply then have second thoughts. He can stew in it like I've had to. Ten minutes pass then he messages me again.

Loads of arseholes are posting on my FB page. See what you've done!!! More angry-face emojis. I'm astonished as his nerve, the cheek of him.

I don't reply.

I know you've seen my messages. I can see you've read them!!! Now he's really annoyed with me. Ah, shame.

I smile to myself. It's a small revenge.

Well??? He isn't giving this up.

You brought it all on yourself, I reply, adding several smiley faces.

Bitch, he comes back instantly.

I send several more smiley faces.

He doesn't reply again for another ten minutes and this time his message is cold and calculating.

When you come round to collect your stuff, please post the key through the door after you've locked up.

I'm too shocked to reply.

I cry myself to sleep instead.

When I wake up, snotty nosed and with a thumping headache, hours have passed. I check my phone but there are no more messages from Leeward. Nothing. But plenty more comments on Facebook, and most of them are on my side.

I wonder where it all went wrong. When did he stop loving me? I think back over our years together, I thought we were happy. Maybe we'd settled into a rut after so long together but I thought it was a cosy, lovely rut. I still used to get a thrill when he came home from work after me and he'd walk through the door and smile his crooked smile, one eyebrow raised. I was so looking forward to being his wife.

Where did it all go wrong? And when?

I'm watching TV alone downstairs, it's just after midnight, Mum and Dad are in bed and Grimmy has gone back to her own home across the road. My phone pings. I grab it, then stop mid-air. Is it him? If it is, do I want to have another WhatsApp argument with him just before I go to bed? I hover over my phone for what seems a long time. Finally, I turn it over and read the message.

It's Cat asking if I want a lift to Leeward's to pick up

some more clothes. For a silly moment I think she's been in touch with him, or he with her. But no, when I question, she just says she has some time tomorrow. She has a big car; I'll be able to get most of my stuff in it. I accept.

'Do you think he'll be there?' Cat asks as we head off the next morning.

'I don't know, he's usually at work at this time, but...' What I don't say, won't say, is that we should be on our honeymoon now. New Zealand? I don't even know where we were going. Will he have gone alone? Will he get a refund if not? Were we insured? Surely he bought holiday insurance. When we first got together, when we used to go on long weekends and even proper holidays, we had annual travel insurance, but there hasn't been much point in recent years.

'I hope he's not there,' Cat says.

'Yeah.'

'Because I don't know if I will be able to keep my mouth shut after what he's done to you.'

'Yeah.' I imagine Cat tearing into Leeward. I almost hope he is there; she can be vicious and she'll be far more rational than I am at the moment.

He isn't here. We let ourselves in and creep around the ground floor looking for him. The house is just as I left it on Saturday, before I found the evidence, before I learned the truth. Before my whole life turned to shit.

Cat goes upstairs first, allegedly to use the loo, but I know she's checking to see if he's up there, maybe in bed, possibly not on his own. When she doesn't react, I follow her up.

'What do you want to take?'

'Everything. All my clothes.'

'O-k-a-y.' Cat doesn't sound too sure. 'Is there room at Mum and Dad's for all your clothes?' She means it as a joke, but it's a good point. I've already told Mum and Dad that I won't be going back to Leeward, not that they were surprised.

'They've offered to clear out the attic rooms for me.'

'I see. Yeah. Right. That's cool.'

My brothers had the attic rooms, one each. They're large and currently full of junk, suitcases and the like. There's a small shower room and toilet up there too. The attic was converted when it became impractical for me and Cat to share a room and my brothers to share another. After the conversion my brothers, Sam and Mark, moved up there and Cat and I had our own rooms. My parents have suggested I use one room as a bedroom and the other as a lounge, that way I can have my friends round – I don't have that many friends. It's always been just me and Leeward.

'They've said I can redecorate if I want.'

'Oh, Lauren…' Cat starts and I think she's going to cry.

'I know.' I can't cry anymore, I'm just so exhausted from it, I spent most of the night awake crying.

'Mum and Dad are being really good about it, letting me move back in, at my age.' I give a pathetic little shrug. 'You're all being good. Sam messaged me this morning, and Mark. And you, Cat, you've just been amazing. I do appreciate it, you giving me all your time. I really do.'

Cat looks at me, her eyes narrowed, her mouth half open as though she's about to say something profound. Then, apparently changing her mind, she clamps it shut. She turns and opens a wardrobe door instead.

'I'll get a suitcase,' I say, heading off to the landing

cupboard where we keep them on the top shelf. Only as I reach for the door do I realise I won't be able to get them down with one hand. Not, I discover, that that will be a problem. 'The bastard,' I shout when I open the door. Cat comes running.

'What? What's he done?'

'There should be four suitcases up there, we bought them years ago, you know, when we used to have holidays. Two large, two small, they matched. They're gone.' I turn and march back into the bedroom, yank open Leeward's wardrobe doors. All his work clothes are still there, all those shirts I ironed, hanging in neat lines, but his new holiday shirts, short-sleeved and patterned, are gone. I start pulling open drawers, knowing instantly how many clothes he's taken with him because I know only too well the contents of these drawers because it's me who washes, irons and puts away his things every week. 'He's gone on my bloody honeymoon,' I yell.

'But why take *all* the suitcases?' Cat asks, realising only after she's spoken the words what the answer must be.

Six

I turn and tilt my head to one side. I smile at Cat even though smiling is last thing in the world I really want to do.

'Because,' I say, 'He's taken her on my bloody honeymoon, hasn't he?'

Cat goes back to the bedroom and flops down on the bed in shock. She shakes her head. 'Surely not.'

'What other explanation can there be? He doesn't need four suitcases, does he?'

'Well, maybe he thought he'd use the baggage allowance up. Since it was all paid for. He does like to get his money's worth. Anyway, you don't *know* he's gone on your honeymoon.' Cat really is clutching at straws.

'He's gone and he's taken her. I'm telling you, he has.' I flop down next to Cat and we sit in silence for a few minutes. Each of us lost in our own thoughts. I'm secretly hoping there's a better explanation and he hasn't gone off on my honeymoon, I'm trying to find some good in this, but I'm struggling.

There's a click of the front door and Cat and I jump up off the bed together. We listen, Cat alarmed and me grateful. I recognise the sound of a key in the front door. Leeward hasn't gone anywhere. He's still here. He hasn't gone on my honeymoon with her, because if he had they would be long gone by now because the plane was leaving at dawn this morning.

We wait, almost holding our breath while the door is opened and Leeward comes in, closing the door behind him. He must know we're here because Cat's car is on the drive. I tiptoe across to the window and look out. Yes! Leeward's car is now parked behind Cat's.

'Hello?' a voice calls up the stairs.

'Who's that?' Cat mouths to me.

It isn't Leeward, the voice is darker and richer than Leeward's.

'Kenton,' I hiss, before storming to the top of the stairs. 'What are you doing here?' I yell down at him.

'Um, bringing Leeward's car back,' her offers, sounding pathetic.

'Right.' I stomp down the stairs as fast as my broken wrist, which throws me off balance, will allow. Cat is close behind me.

'Bringing it back from where?'

He shuffles a bit and looks over my shoulder at Cat.

'Because he took them to the airport, didn't you?' Cat spits.

Kenton is blushing, his face flushed with embarrassment beneath its usual dark olive colour – I've never seen him blush before.

'Well?' I'd fold my arms except one of them is tied around my neck, so I cross my good arm over it.

'It was all arranged, before…'

'Well, thanks for that, Kenton.'

'Look, I'm sorry. I didn't want to have any part in it, but as I said, it was all arranged before. And he couldn't get the money back, so he went.'

'With her?'

Kenton looks down at his shoes.

'I'm so sorry. I've told you already that I think he's a bloody idiot to do that to you. I don't agree with him and I can't make excuses for him either, but he's still my brother. Even if he is a fucking idiot.' He turns his next question to Cat. 'Would you desert Lauren if the situation was the other way around?'

'It's not though, is it? Because Lauren wouldn't do that, would she, Kenton?'

'Please, call me Ken.'

'Oh shut up.' Cat barges past Kenton and yanks open the front door. 'I've got some IKEA bags in the car, I'll bring them in to pack your stuff, Lauren.' She marches out leaving the door open in her wake.

'Look, I'm so, so sorry.'

'What's she like?'

'Who?'

I stare at him now, narrowing my eyes. 'Alfie?'

'Nothing compared to you,' he comes back too quickly, so smooth and well-practiced.

'Huh, really.' Cat is back, her arms full of crinkly, blue IKEA bags. She nudges Kenton out of the way and starts up the stairs. 'You'll have to excuse us,' she says, 'We're busy. Come on, Lauren.'

'Where did they go?' I ask, because I have to torment myself further.

Kenton shrugs and looks away.

'Don't pretend you don't know,' Cat calls from halfway up the stairs.

'New Zealand,' his words are muttered into his chest as he keeps his head down.

'Fab,' I say, fighting back the tears that, so far since

we've been here, have not manifested. I turn to go upstairs.

'I'm sorry,' Kenton offers again.

'You keep saying that,' Cat yells down at him. 'Why don't you fuck off out of here now, we've got work to do.' Cat is mad, she must be, because she rarely swears. In fact, I think she's sworn more in the last few days than she has in the last year.

'Can I help?'

It would be very useful if he could stay and help, because dragging those full bags back down the stairs and into the car is going to be all on Cat, and Kenton is a big, strong man.

'No. Fuck off,' Cat shouts while I say nothing. 'And move that fucking car off the drive and out of my way too,' she adds.

Two hours later and all my clothes are packed and in the car. Cat has a fine sheen of sweat across her forehead. She catches me staring as she swipes at it.

'Won't need to bother with the gym today,' she says smiling. 'That's my workout done.'

'I do appreciate it.'

'I know you do. What are sisters for, eh?'

'I suppose that's what Kenton meant.'

Cat narrows her eyes at me. 'Don't make excuses for those pair of shits.' She takes my good hand. 'Come on. Let's see what else you want.'

We wander through the house, I take a few things from the kitchen, things that I've bought myself or with Leeward. I have to admit that there isn't much of me here; now I look with cynical eyes, this house is all Leeward. His taste, his style, right down to the black leather sofas, the black furniture, the darkest grey venetian blinds, so dark they might as well be black and the dark blackout curtains he insisted on. Even our bedding is dark grey striped, not the floral that I wanted.

'This is his house,' I muse. 'There's nothing of me here.'

'Well, maybe, but you deserve a share. Is there anything else you want to take? Surely after all these years…'

'No,' I cut in, turning to leave. 'Can you get the key off my key ring? He wants me to post it back through the letterbox after I've locked up.'

'I don't think so,' Cat's voice is super indignant. 'You need to be able to come back if you want. You can't just submit to his demands. Arrogant bastard.'

'It's okay. I want him to have *this* key back. I know him. If I don't, he'll change the locks and I'll never get back in. Mum has a spare that he doesn't know about.'

Cat's smile is pure wickedness as she grabs one of Leeward's best carving knives and uses it to prize the key from the ring.

'Oops, I think the tip's bent.'

'Surely not?'

'No. You're right, it's too good to bend. Shame that.' She flings the knife in the sink and we leave.

Mum helps Cat unload the car and carry my IKEA bags up to my room while I pick up the odd little thing and try to help. I feel so useless.

'We're going to make a start on clearing out the attic rooms tonight,' Mum says in her best cheery voice.

'Thank you.' I sound pathetic.

'You go on in, I've made a plate of sandwiches, they're under the glass dome, go and help yourself,'

Mum says to me before turning to Cat. 'Are you staying for lunch, Cat?'

'No, thanks. Stuff to do,' she says, hauling the last of the bags out. 'And I want these bags back, please,' she says to me.

I nod my agreement.

This is what my life has come to and all contained in half a dozen old, crumpled IKEA bags.

'Yes, they're so useful,' Mum says, cheery voice again.

'Yep, you can pack your whole life into them,' I say as I head back indoors.

Grimmy, who has already had her lunch because it's well past noon, is dozing in her chair in her corner of the kitchen. I'm careful not to wake her by clattering a plate out of the cupboard or lifting the glass dome. I don't really want to face any of her opinions or questions. I take my plate and a glass of water – two journeys of course – to the far end of the room and slump down on the sofa.

As I munch through the sandwich, completely unaware of what it is or what it tastes like, I start to make a mental list of all the things I must do. And soon, before Leeward thinks of them. Number one: finance. I need to separate my money from his, not that I have much, but I certainly won't be paying any more of *his* household bills.

'Cake and a coffee to follow?' Mum asks when she comes in and sees that I've finished; she washes her hands as she speaks.

'Yes, please.' I pick up my phone and pull up my banking app. It's astonishing how quickly I am able to cancel so many direct debits. I must remember to email the utility companies and tell them Leeward is now going to pay those bills. Other than our joint savings account, now empty bar £7.63, we do not share a bank account. I pay for gas, electric, water and council tax; we share the food bills, taking it in turns to pay. I sometimes think I pay more than him because it's me who will stop by at the supermarket and pick up things midweek.

Leeward pays the mortgage, I have no idea how much that is, but I do know that he struggled to pay it before I moved in – he'd even had a lodger for a while, but that didn't work out because the lodger was too messy and stole Leeward's food from the fridge. But that was ten years ago, so surely the mortgage payment isn't big now, compared to his salary, I mean. The house is just a three-bed semi, though I suppose it is in a fairly expensive area. I've no idea what it's worth, I add *discovering house value* to my mental to do list. He also pays the house insurance; he's pointed out on many occasions that he pays the bills that keep a roof over our heads. I usually counter than I pay the bills that keep us warm and watered. I used to think it was playful banter.

'Oh, just remembered…' Mum trots off to the utility room and returns with a giant bouquet of flowers. 'These came for you.'

I get up and extract the card from the flowers.

'Aren't they lovely?' Mum says. 'Do you want me to put them in a vase?'

'Yes. Please.'

I'm shaking as I fumble to get the tiny envelope open. Has Leeward changed his mind? Has he come to his senses? Is he about to apologise, beg my forgiveness, beg me to come back?

Am I mad? He's gone off on my honeymoon with

his mistress.

When I finally get the card free it drops to the floor, face up. I don't even need to bend over to retrieve it, I can read it from standing up.

I'm so sorry. I had no idea what he was doing. I am here for you. Ken xx

Kenton. What the hell is he playing at? Of course, he sent this before this morning's little altercation.

I pick the card up and drop it and its envelope in the bin.

'Who are they from?' Mum asks.

'Kenton.'

'Oh.'

'Yeah.'

I slope off back to my sofa and sit down, pick up my phone so that I can start emailing the utilities but before I've even clicked into my email a message pops up from Kenton.

L, I hope we're still okay after this morning's clash, K. xx

I really cannot reply to that. He's my enemy's brother, of course we're not okay. Another message pops up.

Please don't think bad of me. I had no idea they were going together til I turned up. I thought you might have made up. I thought you might be going. xx

That's a big fat lie, even if he didn't know she was going he could be pretty damn sure that I wasn't. I don't reply.

I've told Leeward what a damn idiot he is. I hope you and I can still be friends. K, xx

Thanks for the flowers, I reply. As far as I'm concerned that's an end to our messaging, I'm not answering his other points, why should I? But Kenton isn't put off and I can see he is already typing his reply.

L, Obvs I know they can't make up for what happened but I hope they cheer you up just a little bit. K xx

He's still online and no doubt waiting for my reply. I've said thank you, I've been polite. That's it. I switch my phone off and take a big bite out of my cake.

By the next morning I've informed all the utility companies that Leeward is now the bill payer and I've transferred the pathetic £7.63 from our joint savings account into my current account. Mum and Dad have made a valiant start on the attic rooms and are asking me what colour I want them painting.

Oh. My. God. I'm moving back in with my parents on – what appears to be – a permanent basis.

I've emailed my boss at the nursing home, not that I needed to tell her about the wedding fiasco – she witnessed it for herself, but I do have to inform her about my wrist and that I won't be back for a while. She's very sympathetic and, I think, secretly relieved that I only work part-time now. She tells me not to worry, all I need is a doctor's certificate and I'll be able to reclaim my holiday back too. Not that I know what I'm going to do with all my *free* time.

I'm going to have to beg and grovel to get a full-time job there, but I can hardly do that at the moment. I suppose I can always leave. I don't want to. I love working there, I love most of the residents. Some of them have been there for years; they're like a second family to me.

I don't want any more change in my life.

I've had no more messages from Kenton, which is a relief; at least he's had the good sense to let it be.

'Good morning,' Grimmy says as I enter the room; she's in her usual corner and her teeth are on display

89

which means she's smiling and not being snidey.

'Morning.' I feel I should go over and kiss her cheek but she's not that sort of granny, well great-granny and I can't bear her flinching every day. I stuff a couple of slices of wholemeal in the toaster.

'Your dad's at work and your mum's popped out for some bread. Someone's eaten all the white.' There's a toss of her head and a slight roll of her eyes. I feel she's accusing me.

'Don't look at me, I hate the stuff.'

Grimmy doesn't respond to my statement but instead changes course. 'Heard from Gollum yet?'

'No. And I don't expect to.' Which, of course, isn't true. 'And please don't call him that.'

'Speak as I find.' She shrugs as though that makes it all right.

'Well don't, it's mean.' I can't quite believe I'm talking to her like this. We've always pussy-footed around Grimmy, well, to her face anyway, apart from the Grimmy thing, which she obviously doesn't notice.

'That's better,' she says, grinning. 'That's the spirit we want to see. You're going to need it with Gollum.'

I shake my head and shudder. Having clumsily buttered my toast, I slope off to the sofa, as far away from Grimmy as the room allows.

Mum bursts in carrying her shopping.

'Morning, Lauren.' She gives me a big smile, it's simultaneously cheery and sad; she's feeling my pain. 'I've got your bread, Grimmy. You don't need to fret about your lunch now.'

Lunch? I check my phone; it's 11.30am. I hadn't realised I'd slept in, mainly because I didn't think I'd slept at all.

I finish my toast, grab myself a drink, tell Mum I

don't need any lunch and slope back off upstairs. I suppose I should shower and get dressed, but it's such a trial with the cast, trying to keep it dry, trying to wash myself with only one hand. And my hair, oh what a mess, it really needs sorting out.

I message Paula, see when she can pop round and help me. I could ask Mum but I need these extensions sorting out and I need a proper hairdresser. The extensions that haven't fallen out are pulling on my scalp, or at least, that's what it feels like. She comes back straight away and says she can come this afternoon.

I go into Facebook, something I've resisted doing since the vile video incident. Lots of people have posted on my timeline, most offering me sympathy, though, inevitably there are a few nasty messages from stranger trolls. I don't care, it makes no difference. I consider deactivating my account, but not before I go onto Leeward's. I imagine him posting pictures of New Zealand, of her, of them together. I feel sick at the thought.

Fortunately for us all, he's deactivated his account. Probably couldn't take the abuse even though he bloody well deserves it.

I give serious thought to having a shower before slumping back against my pillows and closing my eyes. I'm not asleep of course.

I wonder what Leeward's doing now, with her? It'll be the middle of the night, they're probably in bed. Him and her. I've gone over and over this in my mind and what I don't understand is, if he wanted to be with her why was he marrying me? It makes no sense. How long has it gone on, their sordid little affair, because that's what it is – he was engaged to me. Even though he never gave me a ring – because it would be nice to have diamond wedding rings instead, he said – he still asked me to marry him. We were having the wedding of his choice, not mine. It was what he wanted; he was so enthusiastic about our wedding. So why was he with her? Why was he staying with me if he wanted her? I don't understand. I just don't and this is what kept me awake half the night.

Have they gone to Hobbitland, or Hobbiton, as Leeward always corrects me? I torment myself by clicking on the Hobbiton website; I know it's only a film set, and I know I wasn't that interested in the films but now I really want to visit Hobbiton. It looks so cute.

I wanted to see New Zealand.

I wanted to go on honeymoon.

I wanted to marry Leeward.

It's all my fault, I should have gone ahead with it and sorted it out later. I've probably pushed him into Alfie's arms. He was going to finish with her once we were married, I'm sure of it. She was chasing him, pursuing him, it was all her. Just a stupid dalliance that we could have recovered from. Or maybe it was all her, a fantasy on her part, all one sided.

Is it too late?

Could we still get back together?

Am I mad? Those texts were not one sided. Far from it. He was as complicit in their affair as she was.

I hope he's okay.

I pull him up on WhatsApp and type, *L, Hope you're okay. xxx L*

I delete it before I can send it. Then retype and press send without giving myself time to chicken out. It's not unreasonable to send such a message, is it? We've been together for ten years. I still care about him; I hope he still cares about me.

After a few minutes I check to see if he's read it. He hasn't. It's the middle of the night.

I stumble into the bathroom and switch the shower on. I wrap an Asda bag around my cast – a cheap one, the type you're not supposed to buy – and tuck it into the cast so that it doesn't get wet. I hook my hair up and dodge the water once I'm in the shower. The sooner this hair is sorted out the better.

I check my phone when I get back from the bathroom; he's read it, but he hasn't replied. I sit and stare at my phone, he's online but he's not typing. Maybe he's only just received it. Maybe she's right there, looking over his shoulder so he can't reply yet. Maybe he's considering his reply.

He goes offline.

I wonder where he met her? At work? Was she a client? Did she pursue him, wear him down? I know he's not to everyone's taste but he has an allure that some women – me especially – find so attractive. He's not good looking in the conventional sense, he's certainly no match for his brother, Kenton. Oh, but, his eyes; his eyes are to die for, an unusual inky blue, they seem to burrow deep into your soul when he turns them on you. He has a wonky smile, not his teeth – they're perfect, just his lips, the way they curl more on one side than the other. I love it. I know not everyone does. The first time I brought him home – one of those raucous Sunday teas with my whole family – I overheard Grimmy asking Dad if Leeward had had a stroke. She's a scream, is Grimmy. Not.

I've always liked his body, it was as though everything was packed in tightly, because he wasn't as tall as his brothers. As though all the maleness was somehow condensed making him more masculine than most men. Now, after so many months at the gym, that's even more the case.

Maybe that's where he met *her*.

'Paula's here,' Mum calls just as I've struggled my way into leggings and a t-shirt. Just pulling them up one-handed is a trial; ditto for knickers too. I haven't bothered with a bra; I'm so skinny that I've hardly got any breasts anyway.

'Oh, poor you,' Paula says but doesn't ask how it happened because she has, no doubt, seen the video like the rest of the world.

I plonk myself on the dining chair that Mum has set up by the patio doors overlooking the garden so that Paula can tackle my hair under Grimmy's gimlet-eyed stare.

'Do you really want me to take them all out?' Paula asks after a few minutes of rooting around in my bird's nest, lifting up the extensions and apologising whenever I wince.

'I think so. I can't really cope with them.'

'Some of them are well secured. Why don't I just take out the loose ones, the ones that will fall out anyway.'

I sigh. 'I really can't cope with them. They're so heavy they're making my head and neck ache.'

'Normally they wouldn't be removed so soon after they've been put in. The ones that are stuck well are so close to your scalp. I'm going to have to put keratin solution on and heat up the glue to get them out. I suggest we just remove the loose ones and let the others grow down a bit. Maybe I could give you shorter haircut, that would help with the weight.'

I think of my hair, its length now down to my waist, the platinum blond highlights, so many of them that I look blonde all over.

'Shave my head,' I command.

I hear Grimmy cackle.

'I'm not doing that. It might seem like the solution now, but it really isn't.' She puts her hand on my shoulder, squeezes gently. 'Listen, let me work on it. I promise it will be so much more manageable. Obviously with your wrist and everything, you haven't even been able to undo your,' she falters, 'Wedding hair,' she adds, evidently deciding to be brave. Or brutal.

'Okay,' I say, the fight going out of me. 'Do whatever you think.'

Three hours later, with the back ache from leaning over the bath so that Paula can wash my hair starting to subside, I study myself in the mirror. I have a short bob. It's still very blonde and it's still far thicker than my normal hair due to half the extensions still being in place, but I have to admit it's a stunning transformation and a vast improvement.

'That should be a lot easier for you to manage,' Paula says, starting to pack away her stuff. 'What do you want to do with these?' She holds up a handful of long, blonde hair extensions.

'Bin 'em.'

'They're real hair,' Paula says. 'Must have been expensive.'

'They were.' I smart at the memory of how much they cost and think of how Leeward pleaded with me to grow my hair and add extensions. 'But I don't want them.' I watch Paula's face as she weighs up how tactful it would be to ask for them. I save her the angst. 'You take 'em. You might be able to find a use for them.' I smile as she stuffs them into her bag.

Grimmy, who I thought had dozed off in her chair suddenly speaks. 'I'll pay for your work, Paula,' she says.

'No, Grimmy, you can't.'

'It's in lieu of a wedding present.' She fixes me with her stare, daring me to argue. 'Rather give it to you than him.'

'Okay. Thank you,' I mutter. 'Much appreciated,' I say as Grimmy rustles around in her handbag for her purse.

'When do you get a proper cast on?' Paula asks once she's been paid.

'When the swelling goes down. A week if I'm lucky, but probably nearer two.'

'It'll be better though, then. So much lighter. My gran had a purple one when she broke her wrist.' Paula smiles, I don't because hearing about her gran's cast doesn't make me feel any happier.

After she's gone, I go and lie down on the bed, fall asleep surprisingly quickly and only wake when Dad knocks on the door to show me the paint he's bought for the attic rooms.

'Pale blue,' he says, smiling. 'I hope that's okay, since you said for us to choose.'

'It'll be great, Dad,' I say, like I give a toss.

'Good, I'll make a start this weekend.'

I smile my biggest smile because my family are trying so hard to help me and I'm just being miserable. I know they understand but God, *I'm* sick of me, so they must be.

Leeward evidently was.

No, he wasn't. He was going to marry me.

'Tea's ready,' Dad says as he leaves the room. I pull myself up, sort myself out and go downstairs where I can hear animated chat and laughter in the kitchen.

'Cat.' I feel genuinely pleased to see her.

'Lauren. How's the wrist?'

'Oh, you know.' I wave it about like a lobster claw.

'Hair looks amazing.' She walks around me to get a better view. 'So much better. Definitely more you.'

'Apart from the colour.' I smile and don't add that the colour was all Leeward's idea.

'It'll grow out.'

'When it does, I'll have it cut short, very short. Are you staying for tea?'

'Yes. I come for tea every week while Nat's at her dancing class. It's near here, so saves me going back and forth. I get to spend some quality time with my family.' She places exaggerated emphasis on the last sentence. 'Even Grimmy,' she adds quietly, turning her head towards me.

'I heard that,' Grimmy says, plonking herself down at the table. 'I'm not deaf.'

Cat doesn't reply, instead pulling up a chair.

'Lasagne,' Mum announces, placing it on the table.

'My favourite.' Cat laughs. 'Mum always cooks my favourite when I come for tea.

'Yes, every damn week,' Grimmy grumbles.

No one responds.

During tea we talk about things that have nothing to do with me or my nearly wedding. I even laugh at one of Cat's stories about her boys. It sounds like chaos in her house, but fun. When she suggests that I come round tomorrow I realise that I've hardly been to her house for years. I don't even know why.

Yes I do. Leeward doesn't like Cat.

At Cat's the next day we sit in her garden drinking orange and lemonade with sprigs of mint.

'This is lovely,' I say.

'Yeah, I find it refreshing. The mint just sets it off.'

'No, I mean sitting here with you in your lovely garden.'

'Grass needs cutting, Paul usually does it on Saturday mornings.' I see her wince when she realises what's she's said.

'Oops,' I say for her and manage a laugh.

'Sorry.'

I shake my head. 'I have something for you. Oh, and the girls.'

'Have you?'

After rummaging in my bag, I find the bridesmaids' gifts. I pass Cat the brooch, still in its pretty silver paper and tied with a blue bow.

She opens it and her eyes light up.

'Oh but…' she starts.

'No but. I can hardly take it back. Anyway, you went above and beyond in the maid of honour stakes, you've more than earned it.'

Cat considers this for a moment or two. 'You're right. It's lovely. I can put it on my jacket.'

'Yeah, that's what Mum said.' I smile just to let her know I'm pleased she likes it and, moreover, will wear it. 'Can you give these to all the little bridesmaids.'

'Okay.'

'I messaged him…' I say suddenly, letting the words hang in the air as I take another sip of my drink.

'Why?'

'I don't know.'

'Did he reply?'

'No, but he's read it.'

Right then, right on cue my phone pings. I grab it as Cat sits with her eyebrows raised in question.

'Kenton.'

'Oh.'

I read out his message. *I know you probably don't want me to pester you what with everything that's gone on between you and Leeward, but I just wanted you to know that I'm here for you. Any time. Day or night. If I can do anything, and I mean anything, just message me.*

'Cheeky bastard,' Cat echoes my thoughts. 'Now reply nicely.'

'What?'

'Reply nicely. There will be things you do need to know and if Leeward isn't communicative, a spy in the camp will be useful.' She gives me a wicked grin.

'You are so bad.' But I'm already composing a gushing response. 'I must try not to punish Kenton for what Leeward has done.' I'm serious too.

'Absolutely,' Cat says, her face devoid of any expression.

'Stop it.' I laugh, too much.

'That's good. Seeing you laugh.' She leans over and pats my knee.

'Haven't had a lot to laugh about. Still don't.'

'No. Okay. I think you can have a month.'

'What?'

'A month to wallow in self-pity then you have to pull yourself together, sort your life out and move on.'

'Just like that.' She's joking, isn't she?

Cat shrugs her big sister shrug, the one she used to use when I fell over when we were kids, it was usually preceded by *stop making a fuss, you're okay.*

She's tough is my sister.

'We were together for ten years. I feel like he's died.'

Another shrug.

'I know you never liked him. Any of you.' I'm annoyed now.

'He never liked us. I think that came first.'

Did it? Is that true?

'I can't talk about it now.' I stand up, my intention is to leave but I remember I can't drive and even if I could I no longer have a car.

'A month,' Cat says, grabbing her car keys.

Seven

December

I needed to wallow for slightly longer than the month Cat allocated me. In the end it was my final trip to the fracture clinic that made me realise that I really didn't have such a hard life, although I still have my down days.

I was there to get my cast off, the lightweight fibreglass one that replaced the hideous plaster back slab put on in A&E. I was so relieved to see it gone, no more itching or smelling. I will never forget the odour of stale cheese mixed with vinegar that emanated from under the cast. I sat in the waiting room smiling to myself as I waited to see the doctor for my final signoff.

The little old lady who came into the waiting room smiled at everyone, and I do mean everyone. She was small and frail looking, she reminded me of Grimmy though not as old. She still had the plaster back slab on *her* broken wrist, which meant her break was probably less than two weeks old. A nurse walking past stopped on her way through.

'Mary, how are you? How have you done that?'

'Just tripped on a step,' Mary answered, her beaming smile making it sound like she'd won the lottery.

'What's happening with Sally?' The nurse's face took on an air of genuine concern.

'We've had a carer in twice a day, so that has helped, though not for the first 72 hours.' Mary laughed.

'Oh, I'm so sorry. You're still so jolly, I don't know how you manage to keep smiling.'

'You have to,' Mary said, laughing. 'Otherwise you'd just go under, wouldn't you?' Another smile.

'I suppose so. Where's Sally now?'

'Coming in with my niece. They're just in the shop downstairs. Bit of a day out for Sally.' The smile vanished temporarily to be replaced by a half grimace. 'Ah, here they are.' She turned, as we all did, to see Sally and the niece fighting their way in through the heavy door, Sally's large wheelchair, complete with neck brace, making the job difficult.

The nurse ran over to help and stopped to say hello to Sally.

I looked at Mary, old and frail. Hers looked like a hard life.

By comparison, I'm very lucky.

I pulled myself up after that. Mostly. Except on the dark days when I couldn't stop crying.

Leeward never replied to my message, nor the subsequent ten or more I sent late at night or after I'd had a glass or two of wine. Maybe he was too ashamed of what he'd done. Maybe he was just mad at me because I humiliated him on our non-wedding day.

Kenton messaged me weekly, short friendly messages asking how I was. I always replied. More than once I asked him how Leeward was. He usually just replied with a curt *he's fine*. Whether he'd been instructed not to say anything to me or whether he just didn't want to talk about his brother, I don't know.

I mentioned it to Cat.

'Course he doesn't want to talk about Leeward. He's not interested in Leeward.'

'Why not, they're brothers.'

Cat laughed louder. 'Honestly, you can be thick sometimes. He lusts after you. I think he always has.'

'No. No. You're wrong.' Wasn't she?

'I've seen how he looks at you. That time when I dropped your Christmas presents off at your place and he was there. He couldn't take his eyes off you. And remember Leeward's surprise 30th birthday party, he followed you around like a pet dog. And, of course, now…'

I let what she'd said sink in. I thought about it.

'Oh my God. No. Maybe.' Yes, I think Cat has a point.

'He's just waiting for a respectable amount of time to pass before he moves in on you.'

'Shut up.'

I went back to work after six weeks. My colleagues were tactful and didn't mention what had happened, although they all knew, several of them had been there and witnessed the spectacle and those who hadn't had seen my singing performance on Facebook. Most of the residents either didn't remember or had never seen Facebook, which is just as well.

Only one, Mr Porter, Archie, brought it up.

'Well, girl. What's all this I've been hearing. That man of yours let you down?' He shook his head. 'He must be mad, missing out on a nice girl like you.' His words were followed by one hell of a coughing fit. It was late October by then and the winter coughs and colds that always claimed a few residents were starting their rounds.

'Are you being treated?' I asked rushing to his aid. He was old, even older than Grimmy but he didn't have her physical stamina, though, to use his words, he still had all his marbles.

'Yeah, bit of cough mixture. That other nurse sorted it, girl. So, what about this man of yours?'

I sat down and told him, not the full story, not the porny phone messages or my sweary song, but the gist.

'Bloody fool,' he said afterwards. 'Bloody idiot. You deserve better.'

Afterwards I went off to check his notes, see what he'd been prescribed, then I called the GP to get him some antibiotics because I didn't think a bit of cough mixture was going to help that cough. I was probably overstepping the mark but patient care came first.

Archie is probably my favourite patient, he's been there as long as I have, probably longer. He's a cockney, born and bred and still sounds like one even though he moved out of London more than fifty years ago. He still uses the odd bit of rhyming slang, apples and pears, titfer, boat race, little things like that, but only when he's having a bit of fun with us. You can have a laugh with Archie.

He has a friend, Miss Lawrence, Florence. Florence Lawrence. She prefers Flo – understandable really. She's another cockney, younger than Archie, the two became friends when she moved into the home five years ago. They spend time together reminiscing about London, a London that disappeared long ago but is still fresh in their minds.

So here we are: December. The run up to Christmas. I'm still working part-time, I've been promised the next full-time vacancy whenever it comes up, but who knows when that will be. I kick myself daily for giving up my great job so willingly. I cover every sickness and holiday and so am earning a bit extra but it's not the same as a proper full-time position, I can't rely on it. I can't get a mortgage with it.

It's fun at the nursing home at this time of year. We play all the old Christmas songs; the residents love it as much I do. In the afternoons we put a Christmas movie on for those who like to watch them. We've had *White Christmas* with Bing Crosby on four times already; it's our most requested, though I prefer *It's a Wonderful Life*.

I'm still living with Mum and Dad. It's not so bad. No, it's good, I really cannot complain and they refuse to take any money from me. I have the whole top floor to myself and that includes a shower room. It's like a mini flat really, and I get all my meals cooked, even though I offer to help frequently, but Mum is quite territorial about her kitchen, something I hadn't realised before.

I save every penny I can. I have managed to buy a little car, a twelve-year-old Volkswagen Beetle which I know Leeward would not approve of. It's my two-fingered salute to him, not, I suspect, that he's aware of it. He is being very non-communicative but I have managed to find out from Ken – he insists I call him Ken otherwise he won't answer me – that Leeward is moving after Christmas. It was like getting blood out of a stone but he let it slip when I went for a drink with him. Okay, I know I probably shouldn't, but he kept asking and after all, he was my nearly brother-in-law. We've been out a few times now. You should see the way heads turn when I walk into the pub with him, all the women gaze at him and then stare at me with envy. This never happened with Leeward. Anyway, we're agreed we're just friends.

Now I have my car my savings are going towards a house deposit. Comfortable as it is, I cannot live at Mum and Dad's for ever; I don't want to be one of *those* even though Cat says there's nothing wrong with it.

'That's because you want me to be the spinster sister who looks after her parents in their old age,' I say when we discuss it.

'Yep, that's true.'

I'm nearly thirty-six and I've promised myself I must be out of here by my birthday. That's the end of April so I don't have much time.

'Any luck at work?' Cat asks.

'No permanent full-time, if that's what you mean. But I am earning just as much with all the extra shifts.'

'Won't count towards a mortgage.' She leaves the words hanging in the air.

'I know.' I don't need her to rub it in.

'Maybe you should look elsewhere after Christmas.'

'Yeah. Maybe.' I don't want to. I love where I work. I don't want any more change in my life unless I initiate it.

'Ken says Leeward's moving.'

Cat's eyes light up. 'Oh, is he indeed? Now is the time to get some money back from him then. He can obviously afford it.'

'Ken says he's doing a part-exchange.'

'What? Is that so he can cheat you out of what's rightfully yours?'

'I don't know that I'm entitled to any.'

'Maybe not legally, but morally…'

'I know.' Do I? He won't speak to me. He won't answer my messages which so far have been civil and polite, he won't take my phone calls. 'Dad is talking to a solicitor friend of his.'

'Good. Let's hope he comes out on your side. Where's Gollum moving to?'

'Some new-build. Ken was vague.'

'Was he?' She manages to put so much into those two words that I flinch. She's implying that Ken is complicit, she's implying that Leeward is buying a giant new house that I have helped fund; she's merely echoing all the thoughts that have gone around and around in my head since I found out about his move.

I arrange to see Dad's solicitor friend on my next day off. His offices are tucked away down a side street in town.

'Hello, Lauren,' he says after the receptionist has ushered me into a meeting room. 'I'm Linus.' He extends a hand and we shake. We shuffle around the table in the middle, it's modern and minimalist, not how I imagined a solicitor's office to be, not that I've ever had need for a solicitor before.

'Thanks for seeing me,' I mutter, thinking this is pointless.

'Your dad has given me some info, but why don't you tell me all about it.'

'I don't know where to start really…' Yet somehow I vomit out verbal diarrhoea for over twenty-minutes. I give him all the gory details; I don't seem to be able to stop myself. It's odd, because I've never told the story, the whole story to anyone before, not even my family, although, of course, they've lived through it. I feel strangely better when I've finished.

'Shame you didn't have a joint bank account,' Linus says.

'Well, only the savings one.'

'Needed to be current. Show evidence of monies you paid in and mortgage payments coming out.'

'It's useless, isn't it?'

'Not entirely. You could take him to court, you could sue him. You'd have to provide evidence of what you paid for and how it impacted on household finances. But, it could go either way. You say you don't know how much the mortgage payments were?'

I shake my head. Why didn't I? Because it didn't matter; we were going to be together forever. I trusted him.

'They could be very high, we don't know, of course we'd find out. He could claim that you were nothing more than a lodger…'

'We were getting married,' I cut in.

'Prior to your wedding, I was going to add.' Linus smiles at me. 'We could go to court and you could lose and it would have cost you more money.'

'Yeah, that's what I thought. I don't have the money to waste on fighting him.' I didn't want to waste my *life* fighting him either.

'We could try a letter. Bluff him. It may not work. Legally this is tricky ground, but morally he owes you.'

I'm stunned when I see a message from Leeward pop up on my phone. He must have received the letter over a week ago and I'd resigned myself to getting nothing when he didn't respond immediately.

10k is all I can give you.

I don't reply because I'm at work but when I get home I show his message to Mum and Dad.

'It's his opening gambit. Or, at least, that's how I see it,' Dad says.

'What should I say? Should I accept? It's better than nothing. It's more than I ever thought I'd get. I wasn't expecting anything. I thought he'd ignore it.'

'Ring Linus,' Dad says.

When I do, he gives me advice which makes me both nervous and excited.

I accept Leeward's offer of ten thousand pounds and tell him it is a start but I am thinking more like thirty thousand. I'm careful with my wording, as instructed by Linus, making it clear that I am definitely taking the ten thousand no matter what.

He doesn't reply for over an hour. I can imagine his face turning red with anger, the way it did if someone cut him up on the road. In the end after some toing and froing we settle on twenty, which I think is fair. He says I have to wait until he sells his house to pay me. He doesn't know that I know he's part-exchanging it. I send a two-word reply.

Thank you.

I refuse to feel guilty. This was all his doing, his fault. Booking the wedding of the century was his fault, ruining it was his fault. Persuading me to give up my job was his fault – well no, it was my fault for being weak – but it was his idea. And he had effectively thrown me out of his house and made me homeless, where would I have gone if I didn't have such generous parents who could take me in? He didn't care.

If I add up all the things I've paid for over the years, the things that have enabled him to pay his mortgage, it would be far more than he's giving me, not to mention losing my car and my half of our savings on the wedding *he* wanted.

I won't feel guilty.

Just sad.

I remember when it was good between us. The fun times. When I look back over old photos, the ones floating in the cloud downloaded from all my old phones, I see two, happy smiling people with their whole future in front of them.

In my more honest moments I look back and can see when the cracks started to appear. And it was long before our wedding. He never used to work late or stay away on business, he did everything he could to get back to me, then slowly he began staying away, working late. It's easy to spot with hindsight but at the time I was too busy living my daily life to notice.

Maybe he was too.

We used to be good together.

'You should go round there before he moves,' Cat says, mischief in her eyes.

'I don't want to. I don't want to see him. Anyway, I don't want to do anything to make him backtrack on the money he's agreed to give me.

'I didn't mean when he was there.' Cat grins.

'What?'

'You've still got that key, haven't you?'

'Oh yeah, well Mum has.'

'Well then, we could sneak round one day when he's at work. Park around the corner, saunter up to the house…'

'Hang on,' I cut in. 'We, did you say we?'

'I couldn't let you go on your own. It might be too traumatic for you.'

'Cat,' I snap, but I'm half considering it.

'Just saying. You never know, there might be things you want…'

He gives me my money two days before Christmas but I know he hasn't moved because Ken has told me. I can't quite believe it when he sends me a message to say the money's left his bank account and I burst into tears when I check to find it in mine.

'This is going to be the best Christmas ever,' I hear myself saying in true soap-opera-disaster-soon-to-follow fashion. I immediately move the money into my savings account, just in case there's some way he can recall it, even though I know there isn't. I've never had so much money all at once before.

'Leeward's gone on holiday again,' I tell Cat on Christmas Eve when we're having a nice meal and a few drinks because tomorrow I am working from noon.

'Oh lucky him, two holidays in three months. When was the last time you went on holiday?'

'I don't know.' I sigh. 'I suppose I could go anytime I like now he's paid me off.' Though I'm hoping the money will be a house deposit once I get a full-time job.

'Where's he gone?'

'Seychelles.'

'On his own?'

'I didn't ask, anyway I don't think Ken would tell me.'

'How long for?'

'Back New Year's Day.'

Cat turns to me and her eyes sparkle, or maybe that's just how it looks to me because I've had far too many glasses of wine.

'What are you doing the day after Boxing Day?'

'Nothing. Watching crap TV with Grimmy,' I add,

laughing.

'Good. Keep the afternoon free. We're going on a visit.'

'No.'

'Yes.' She nudges me and I almost spill my wine.

'No.'

'Yes.'

'Okay.'

Christmas Day in the nursing home is nice. Especially for me, no one is seriously ill and I'm doubling as a care assistant this afternoon. Many of the residents have been taken home by their families for the day, though not so many on this floor, the dementia floor. I'm here until six, then downstairs after that. Christmas lunch has been served in the day room and everyone is settling down to either watch TV or sleep, just like everyone else in the UK on Christmas Day.

Several of the residents cuddle their toys, mostly teddies. So many here have retreated into childhood, some even think that visiting husbands and wives are their parents. It's so sad and could really get you down but all the staff try not to dwell on it because really, it helps no one.

'Where am I? I need to get out of here. I haven't committed any crimes. I'm innocent.' Ben is only forty-five, he has an early onset form of the disease and thinks he's in prison. It must seem like that.

'Yes you did, you're a murderer.' Enid seems to take such pleasure in tormenting people. I wonder what she was like before she became ill.

'No, I didn't. No, I didn't.'

Now Carla is joining in. Carla used to be a teacher and talks in the rhythm of chanting times tables.

'You are a naughty boy.

Go sit in the corner.

Hands on your head.

We're giving out the milks.'

'I think I'm going to have to create a distraction,' Stella, the care assistant, tells me. 'Shall we have some music?' she shouts so everyone can hear.

Ben looks confused, Carla stops chanting, others nod their agreement, Enid sneers.

'Not that Bing Bossy crap,' she yells. Could she really have been this nasty before?

'Big band and dancing. I love a summer dance.' I don't know the name of the man who says this, I don't think he's been here long.

Stella puts some Frank Sinatra on before she turns off the TV. Frank's voice seems to sooth everyone, including me.

Then Ben gets up. He moves to a space in the day room, tottering a little on the vinyl tiled floor, Stella and I both jump to catch him before he falls, but he rights himself and starts to dance. He's enjoying it, a brief respite from his prison, even though the dancing is more line dancing than big band.

'I'm thinking of having lamb chops for tea,' Jean says, plonking herself down beside me. Jean is sweet-natured and has been here for years. 'What do you think?' She holds up two paws ripped from someone's – maybe her own, but probably not – teddy.

We're told to correct the residents when they misunderstand something, to try to make them understand, but as I look into Jean's eyes, bright with excitement at the prospect of lamb for tea, I nod and smile. 'Good idea.'

'That's what I thought,' she says, tucking the paws

into her pocket before joining Ben on the dance floor.

After tea – not a lamb chop in sight – I make my way downstairs. Archie greets me in the corridor.

'My favourite nurse, I didn't know you were on, girl. How's that grandmother of yours, still going strong?'

'Yes, she is, thank you.' I often tell him about Grimmy and her antics, edited highlights anyway and he always asks after her. I have told Grimmy about Archie too because she grew up during the Blitz in London, so I know they'd have something in common, but she says she's not really interested in the past. I smile at Archie. 'What are you up to?' I don't want to ask if he's been out with his family in case he hasn't.

'Just waiting for the family.' He coughs, his body shaking with the effort. 'They won't be long. Six, they said.' I hate that we can't clear his cough.

They'll be late, I think, because that's how it is, but to Archie and the other residents ten minutes late means they've all been killed in an horrific crash.

The door buzzes and a group of people, including children, tumble in. There are presents and balloons, they've really made an effort. I recognise his daughters, and assume the others are their adult children, the small children must be Archie's great-grandchildren.

'Here they are.' Archie marches forward to greet them and I smile a welcome over his head, then I melt away and head for the office.

I check the paperwork, get ready to do my rounds with the evening drugs trolley and wonder what my family are up to. Then I wonder what Leeward is up to on his exotic holiday.

Has he taken *her*? Stupid question.

On the day after Boxing Day I climb into Cat's car and

feel like a naughty kid. We're dressed in dark fleeces and dark leggings, her idea.

'Have you got the key?' she asks, starting the engine.

I wave it around. 'Hope he hasn't changed the locks.'

'Oh, don't say that. It'll spoil our fun. Do you think he has?'

I shrug. In a way, I hope he has, I feel guilty and I haven't even done anything yet.

We pull up around the corner and walk the short distance to Leeward's house, it's nearly 4pm and already twilight, soon it will be properly dark. It was Cat's idea to wait until now so the neighbours would be less likely to see us.

'His car's here,' Cat says. 'That's not a good sign.'

'Ken took him to the airport.'

'Did he say anything about *her*?'

'He never says anything about *her*, he's discretion itself where she is concerned.'

As we approach the front door his security light blinds us.

'That's new.'

Cat knocks on the door and rings the bell several times.

'What are you doing? I've got the key.'

'Just in case. You never know, he might have someone house-sitting or something.'

'Yeah, and what are we going to say if he has?' I can't think of anything plausible.

'Open the door,' Cat says. 'There's no one here.'

I put the key in the lock and turn it twice. Nothing happens.

'He's changed the lock.' I feel relieved. We can go now. I pull the key out.

Cat snatches it from me, rubs it on her fleece and pushes it into the lock. She turns it twice and leans into the door with her shoulder. It springs open.

'Just the damp,' she says, grinning.

And we're in. It's darker inside the house than outside. We stumble into the lounge.

'He's drawn all the curtains,' I say, flicking on the light switch.

'No, people will see us. Use your phone light.' Cat reaches over and switches off the light.

'No need. They're blackout curtains. Leeward insisted on them.' I flick the light switch back on.

'Good old Gollum.' Cat grins.

'Don't call him that.'

'Shush. Come on, let's explore.'

Nothing has changed really, same furniture, same carpet, same everything. What did I expect in less than four months? In the kitchen I go through the drawers.

'Looking for something?'

'Yes, I bought a really good can opener, I don't see why he should have it. Cost a fortune.' I'm feeling mean, meaner than I did before we got here. I shouldn't feel so mean; he's just given me twenty grand. 'Can't find it,' I mutter. 'Should have taken it the first time.'

'You weren't really in the right frame of mind.' Cat yanks open the dishwasher door. 'This it?' She holds up my expensive can opener.

'Yes. Is it clean?'

'Yes. We'll have that.' She whips a plastic carrier out of her fleece pocket, shakes it open and drops the can opener into it.

We grin at each other.

'That'll mess with his head. Anything else?'

I look around the kitchen, opening more drawers

116

and doors. I shake my head.

'We could take one of his remotes,' Cat says as we go back through the lounge and she picks up the one for the Sky box. 'We could stand outside and change channels.'

For a split second I'm tempted, then I shake my head and Cat drops the remote control.

'Shame,' she says. 'It would have been fun.'

I glance around the room, there's no obvious sign of her. I wonder if she has moved in or if they are waiting until they move into their brand-new home to live together.

There's no sign of me either, no sign that I lived here for ten years.

I start up the stairs, my heart beats in my chest, I feel anxious but determined.

In the third bedroom, a box room really, the one he uses as his study, everything is neat and tidy.

'Hey, we could change his password.' Cat points to his laptop. 'Do you know his password?'

'He never bothered with one.'

'We could give him one.'

I shake my head. I suddenly realise I'm not here for revenge. Why am I here? Would I have come if Cat hadn't urged me on? I can't blame Cat; *I* kept the spare key.

The spare room is sparse, the one we kept for guests, bed always ready. Not that we had many, Ken once or twice after he'd had rows with girlfriends, I can't even remember which ones. I wonder how Suzi is? Does he still see Suzi? Of course not.

'Did I tell you that Ken has asked me to his work New Year's Eve party?' I know I haven't.

'No. The cheek of him. You should go. Imagine

how much that'll wind up Gollum.'

'Yeah.' I laugh. I've already agreed to go but not because I want to get at Leeward. Why then? Maybe I just like the attention.

I'm stalling outside the bedroom, our old bedroom, my old bedroom. What if it's full of dresses and shoes, hairbrushes and makeup.

'Come on.' Cat pushes past me, opens the door, flicks the light on. 'Phew, smells a bit musty in here, I don't think he's moved his lady friend in yet.'

I step over the threshold, remember this room, remember this life.

'Hey, didn't I buy you that vase?' She points to the chest of drawers and the swirly blue vase. She strides over and picks it up, sniffs it. 'It's had flowers in it. I suppose he had to do something to cover the pong when he was being the love hobbit.'

I laugh. How can I not? But I'm irritated by her flippancy.

She pulls a face. 'Want it?'

'Absolutely,' I say, almost absentmindedly as she stuffs it into her carrier bag.

'That'll mess with his head.' Cat sniggers to herself. I think she's enjoying this too much.

I'm studying the room, looking for signs. I approach the wardrobes and Cat stands back. We exchange a glance.

I close my eyes and pull open the door to the wardrobe that used to be mine.

'Nothing girly,' Cat announces.

I allow myself to look. 'He's got more clothes. New ones.'

'See, he isn't short of money, is he? How many new clothes have you bought?'

'None. I'm saving up.'

Cat raises her eyebrows at me, doesn't say 'see' again, doesn't have to.

'And you were feeling guilty about the twenty thousand.'

'No, I wasn't.' Maybe I was, just a little.

'Yes, you were.'

I look though his clothes, pull out a brown leather short coat. 'This can't have been cheap.'

'Try it on.'

'No.'

'Go on.'

I pull the coat on over my fleece, cross it over and tie the belt.

'You could wear that. It's a bit big, but looks cool wrapped over like that.' She giggles. 'In the bag?' She holds the carrier open.

'Stop it.' I take the coat off and hang it back up. 'Come on.' I turn to leave then suddenly think, supposing he's swapped wardrobes, supposing her stuff is in the other one. I yank open the door, my hand shaking. Phew, just more of his clothes, old familiar ones.

'Want to go?' Cat says, putting a hand on my arm.

'Yep.'

We stand in the hallway looking around, checking no lights are left on.

'I have to,' Cat says, dashing back into the lounge, grabbing the Sky remote.

'No.'

She stops, holds the remote up, studies it. 'You're right, what am I thinking? I'm a responsible mother of four, I'd go mad if one of my kids did that.' But she doesn't put it down. 'I'm just going to hide it instead.'

She whams the remote so hard under the sofa that we hear it hit the wall behind.

'Did you always dislike Leeward so much?' I ask once we're safely back in the car.

'To be honest I've never been that mad on him but he made you happy.' She looks at me. 'Then he made you very unhappy, so now I hate him.'

'I don't.' Liar, liar.

'No, well you should.'

'I think I'm moving on like you told me to. You should too, Cat.' I really don't know who I'm kidding.

'Okay.' She starts the car. 'How long do you think he'll hunt for that remote?' She grins and pulls away before adding, 'And that tin opener. And that vase.'

Eight

April

It's warm and sunny in Mum and Dad's kitchen, the sun's shining through the skylights as we hover around the island, Mum and me.

I'm holding my phone and willing it to ring, or ping a message, anything to show action, anything.

'It's still early,' Mum says, her voice reassuring.

'It's nearly noon.'

'Yes, it is,' a croaky voice pipes up from the corner. 'And no one's started my lunch. I'll have a cheese and pickle sandwich when you're ready, Lisa.'

'In a minute, Grimmy, in a minute,' Mum's light voice calls back.

'I don't have many minutes, not like you youngsters.'

Mum and I exchange looks, our eyes meeting before we both smile. Sometimes it's hard to be sweet to Grimmy when she is so unsweet herself.

'And hot tea this time, Lisa. That last cup was lukewarm.'

Mum gives her a look, a quick, shorthand look I remember from childhood.

'Please,' Grimmy adds.

Mum gets the white bread out and asks me if I want anything.

'No thank you. I'm not hungry, I couldn't eat a thing. You don't think anything's gone wrong, do you? Some problem with the mortgage?' I feel the alarm rising in my body, making my voice quiver.

'No. Why should it? It's just a slow process, that's all. It's always like this. It just takes time.' Mum's voice is reassuring but her words are not. Mum doesn't really know what the process is like now, she doesn't know what can go wrong at the last minute, a mortgage offer withdrawn, funds no longer available; it's over thirty years since Mum and Dad last moved.

'You should eat now in case you don't get the chance to eat later,' Grimmy's sage words croak across the room.

'She does have a point.' Mum pulls a loaf of wholemeal out of the breadbin. 'What would you like?'

It's a fair point, I've been up since before six sorting out my stuff and packing my car, which is now sitting on the drive bursting at the seams. It holds everything I have, including a single blow up mattress we used for sleepovers as kids. Once I spend half an hour pumping it up, it'll be just perfect. I'll be sleeping on it tonight, in my new house. Hopefully.

In the end I have ham, lettuce and tomato, followed by carrot cake washed down with two cups of tea all while I'm flicking through my phone willing some action. All I get is a message from Cat asking if I have the keys yet.

'You managed a lot for someone who wasn't hungry.'

'Shush, Grimmy,' Mum hisses across the room to

Grimmy's corner but it doesn't deter her.

'It's nice to see you with a bit of meat on your bones now. You were far too skinny for my liking after that business with Gollum,' Grimmy says, which is hilarious coming from someone who can't weigh more than six stone.

I pick my phone up again, a pointless exercise, I know. Nothing. Not one thing. I drop it back on the island surface.

'The dog woman is coming at four.'

'It'll be fine.' Mum pats my hand before grabbing our plates and stuffing them in the dishwasher.

'What dog woman?'

'I'm getting a rescue dog, Grimmy. The charity has to make sure my house is suitable before I can have her. They're coming to inspect at four.'

'What? What? You're doing them a favour, not the other way around. You should tell 'em to stick it.'

Mum and I exchange glances again, I find we do that a lot.

'It'll be odd here without you cluttering up the place,' Grimmy continues, changing course. I'm not sure whether she's trying to wind me up or distract me. You can never tell with Grimmy. So unsweet. Whoever coined the phrase *sweet old lady* has never met my great-grandmother.

'Thanks, Grimmy,' I say, just as my phone pings. It's a text message.

Mum's on high alert as I read it. She's watching me, waiting, a smile quivering at the sides of her mouth in anticipation of good news.

I make a sad little face and frown.

Mum lets her mouth drop but doesn't speak.

'It's all gone through,' I shout, at the same time

laughing.

'Yes,' Mum yells.

'What? What's that?' Grimmy mutters.

'I can collect the keys from the estate agent any time I like.'

'Better get going. Do you want me to come?'

I wait for moment, considering Mum's offer. In my mind I had anticipated doing this all on my own, part of my new life, just me, alone.

'No. I'll do it myself. You all come round this evening, after the dog inspection.'

'Okay.' Mum's face is bright and breezy. 'Dad will be home by six, we should be round by seven.' She beams at me.

'Yes. That's perfect. It should give me time to unpack the car.' In truth half an hour will probably be enough time to unpack the car.

'I'll come,' Grimmy says. 'I haven't been anywhere for weeks.'

'You went to lunch club yesterday,' Mum reminds her. 'You were there all afternoon.

'Pah. That doesn't count. It's full of old people.'

'Of course you can come, Grimmy. The more the merrier.' I stuff my phone into my handbag and swing it over my shoulder. 'I'm off. I'll see you all later.'

'Wait,' Grimmy calls as she presses the remote control on her chair and launches herself off it. 'You can see me across the road. The gas man is coming and I need to make myself presentable.'

I don't believe for a minute that she needs helping across the road. She sees herself back and forth as many times as it suits her, without any help at all. She may be ancient but she certainly isn't especially frail.

'Okay. Let's go. But I can't come in.'

Grimmy grabs her handbag and hurls herself, at speed, towards the front door.

'See you later, Mum.'

We're at the end of the path before Grimmy speaks.

'You'll need to come in, I have a little something for you.'

'Can it wait?' I ask, trying not to sound ungrateful. 'I am in a hurry.'

'Two minutes.' She wags a finger at me then gives me the rare benefit of her full denture smile. I am honoured.

Two minutes is also how long it takes us to cross the road and reach the front door of her sheltered housing bungalow. She's lived here for fifteen years or more, ever since Granpa George died. He was the last of her three husbands, I vaguely remember Grandad Michael, her second husband but her first husband died long before I was born, when Dad was still a teenager.

Once inside, she ferrets around in a kitchen drawer before offering me a card.

Oh, Grimmy, thank you.' I start to open it.

'No. Save it for later. When you get into your new place.'

'Oh. Okay.' I push the card into my bag.

'And don't go misplacing it, there's a few pennies in there.' She winks at me. See, sometimes she can be sweet.

'Thank you, Grimmy. I need to get going now.' I kiss the papery skin on her cheek and watch her wince. With her aversion to physical contact, God knows how she managed to bag herself three husbands.

'Are you sure you can't stay another five minutes. The gas man will be here soon.'

'No.' I laugh and shake my head. 'You don't need

me to, do you?' Now I'm worried that she doesn't want a strange man in her house when she's on her own. 'I could get Mum to come over.'

'I don't need your mother. You go. I just thought you might like to meet him. He's young. Like you.'

'What? What?' I sound like her now. 'I don't need to meet him, thank you.'

'You don't want to be on your own forever. It's been a while since you got rid of Gollum. No need to let it turn you off men. Look at me, three husbands and another waiting in the wings if I want him.'

I laugh, she's joking, isn't she? Surely she doesn't want another husband. I cringe at her calling Leeward, Gollum. They all do it now, my family. Even Dad. After Leeward betrayed me with his mistress and it was often just me and Grimmy alone in Mum and Dad's house, she confessed that she never thought he was good enough for me anyway and that I was well shot of him. Good riddance to bad rubbish, she had said, several times. I didn't like it at first, but now I think she's right. I am better off without him. I like being on my own and I'm going to like it even more in my own house. And I'm having a dog, something Leeward would definitely never agree to.

'I need to go,' I say again.

'If you're sure. He's very nice. I met him last week when he came to service the boiler, he's just coming back today to check the radiators again. He's very nice.'

'No. Thank you. I'm not interested.' I wonder if she's engineered his second visit especially for me. No. She wouldn't, would she?

'I've already told him how nice you are.'

'No. Don't. I don't...' I'm lost for words. My nonagenarian great-grandmother is trying to matchmake. God help me. 'Grimmy, just so you know, I'm not looking for a man. Not ever again. Once bitten, twice shy.'

'Don't be silly,' she says as I'm heading out of the door. 'Everyone wants a little special company, a special someone.'

'No, they don't, Grimmy. *I* don't.'

'Well if you're not interested in my gas man, I suppose you can try that tinderbox.'

'Do you mean Tinder, Grimmy?'

'Do I? Probably.' She grins and winks at me. 'Worth a try.'

'Where did you hear about Tinder?'

'I can read,' she says, her voice high and indignant. 'Anyway, Natalia showed me.'

'Natalia? Oh.' I wonder if Cat knows her fifteen-year-old daughter is on Tinder?

'Yes, I'm sure you'll find a nice man on there.'

'I've told you; I'm not interested.' I head for the door. 'Bye.'

I hear her croaky response just I as step outside. 'With an attitude like that you're never likely to find one, either.' I'm not sure if it was meant for my ears, or not.

On the way to the estate agents to collect my keys I think about her words. I am sooo NOT looking for a man. Men, in the romantic sense, are of absolutely no interest to me, whatsoever. Ever. So there. Even Ken understands that we will only ever be friends. We've been out for a few drinks, and a meal, we went Dutch, I insisted even though he argued. Cat says he's looking for more and I should tell him straight. I'm still not convinced. He's been a good friend throughout all this,

Cat says I should be careful not to *use* him, even though it was her who suggested keeping him sweet. I don't think I am using him. We're friends.

Leeward broke my heart. He ripped it into a thousand pieces and he stamped all over it, then scraped it up and hurled it back at me. Metaphorically speaking, of course. I'll never love another man like that again. He was the love of my life and he took his mistress on my honeymoon.

Today is the seven-month anniversary of what should have been my wedding day. Not that I'm counting. There's a certain irony to this being the day I get the keys to my own house.

I find myself parking outside the estate agents without any recollection of the journey from Grimmy's to here because I've been so consumed with thinking about the past.

Stop it.

I must only focus on the future now. The future is bright, the future is…oh shut up and get the keys.

In the estate agents' office there's only one spotty youngster sitting behind a desk eating a sandwich – egg by the smell of it. I gag. He looks up and raises his eyebrows in question.

'Hello there.' I give him my friendliest smile. 'I've come to collect the keys to my new house. My solicitor has just informed me everything has gone through.'

He tilts his head in a way that makes him look like a cross between a puzzled cat and a giraffe – he's got a very long neck. He carries on chewing before finally speaking.

'Name?'

'Lauren Nokes.'

He tilts his head back into a normal position and checks something on his computer.

'And the property address.'

'Um,' I have to think for a moment, how ridiculous is that? '13 Westmoreland Road,' I say, triumphantly.

'Postcode?' He stands up and heads towards a big locked cabinet.

'Um. Err.' It's not good. I cannot remember. If he had asked me for the address and postcode of Leeward's house I could rattle that off without even thinking about it. 'Sorry, it's gone.'

'ID?' He's unlocked the cabinet and is now rattling a bunch of keys with a label on them.

'Oh, yes.' I scrabble around in my handbag for my purse and, after what seems a long time with him just standing over me shaking the keys to my new house, I fumble my driving licence out and show him.

I watch as the little shit sniggers at the photo. Yeah, well, it wasn't my best look. In the photo I have long blonde hair, parted in the middle, flowing down my shoulders, just how Leeward liked it.

'This really you?' he asks, eyeing my short, dark brown, pixie cut. After all those years of bleaching I've embraced my natural colour. It's great and I love it, wash-and-go hair; shower, thirty seconds with a hairdryer, bit of product on the ends and I'm ready.

'Yes.' I snatch for my licence but the little shit moves too quickly and swipes it away from my grasp. He narrows his eyes and continues to scrutinise the photo and my face. Then he stomps over to the photocopier and makes a copy.

'Okay,' he says finally, handing my licence back. 'If you can just sign this form.' He whips out a piece of paper with my name and the address of the house. 'Just

129

to say you have received the keys,' he says pushing a cheap ballpoint pen at me.

I sign and hand him back his pen as he simultaneously drops the keys into my hand.

'Thanks,' I say, without a hint of gratitude or a smile.

Calm down, I tell myself once I'm in my car. Don't let anything or anyone spoil your day.

This is Independence Day. I feel there should be a fanfare now, a big orchestral theme tune picking me up and carrying me into the future. But there isn't, and the radio in the Beetle doesn't work anymore, either.

Westmoreland Road, no longer a road, more a close, not a through road. The council closed it off years ago when they built the *new* through road, which means it's just perfect.

I turn into the quiet street, only forty houses, twenty on each side. Built in the 1920s, number thirteen is on the left-hand side, last but one in a short terrace. When I first viewed it, it was the scruffiest house in the street, and the most dilapidated. I was lucky, the refurbishment had only just begun and I was able to influence how it was done. Now its red brick and stucco frontage blends perfectly with its smart neighbours.

I pull up onto the drive, which, like the rest of the houses on the street is actually the front garden, paved over. It's great, because there is comfortably room for two cars parked side by side. There's parking and a garage at the back too. Such a luxury in an old house. Leeward's house was modern, it had all the latest gadgets, but, two cars parked on the drive meant tandem parking. I've lost count of how many times we had to move one car to get the other out. Not my problem now. Nor his, apparently, as he too has moved, no doubt cosying up with his mistress.

I take a deep breath, grab my handbag and get out of the car. I stand back and take a good look at the house; everything is clean and freshly painted, new windows, new roof, new guttering. It's like a new house but better, because many of the old features have been retained: coving, picture rails, the original doors.

And it's all mine. I don't have to share it with anyone. I can do as I please.

Take that, Gollum.

Not that he'll ever know it, or see it.

My hands tremble as I put the key in the front door lock. I'm nervous. God knows why.

Inside, the smell of fresh paint and new carpet envelops me. I love it. I kick off my shoes and wander through the hall and into the kitchen as I inhale all the aromas of my new home. A bouquet of flowers, a bottle of prosecco and a card sit on the kitchen worktop. This little haul is from the developer, wishing me good luck and hoping I will be happy in my new home. I will. I've made my mind up to it.

I pull Grimmy's card from my handbag, smoothing it out as I do because it's bent from being in there for an hour or more. I open it. A new home card pops out, with Grimmy's spider-scrawl handwriting wishing me a happy home. Then I notice the tiny envelope stapled on the back, inside a gift card. I'm stunned when I open it.

I pull out my mobile and ring her immediately, waiting for ten rings, imagining her stumbling to the phone – or maybe she's gone back to Mum and Dad's.

'Hello,' Grimmy's voice croaks.

'It's me, Lauren. I just wanted to say a great big thank you for the gift card. I'm so thrilled. It's so generous of you. Thank you so much.'

'Is it enough?'

'It's very generous.'

'I mean is it enough to buy a sofa?'

'Oh yes, yes. Thank you so much.'

'That's all right then. I need to go now. Bye.' She puts the phone down.

I don't tell her that I've already bought a sofa using a *four years, no interest* payment scheme. I really wanted two sofas; two will sit so well either side of the fire place in the lounge. But I couldn't afford a second one. Now, thanks to Grimmy's generosity, I can. See, she *can* be incredibly sweet sometimes.

Grimmy knows I've struggled to get every penny together to buy this house. The twenty thousand from Leeward plus my savings have been my deposit. But it was securing my full-time job again that enabled me to get the mortgage. My replacement decided she didn't like working full-time, it interfered too much with her family, her children, she also didn't like the extra responsibility. She came back after Christmas and made her announcement, so we've swapped jobs. It's worked out really well for both of us.

According to Ken, Leeward is settled in his new home too. Ken, ever tactful, won't tell me where the new house is. He asked me if I really needed to know. Of course I don't. And I've moved on!

I wander through the rooms stroking the doors and walls, rubbing the carpets and floors with my bare toes, running the taps, flushing the toilets. The house is small compared to Leeward's old house. Here there are just two bedrooms and a bathroom upstairs; downstairs, a cloakroom, a lounge and a kitchen/diner, the original tiny kitchen having been knocked through into the dining room – for modern living as the developer put it. Everywhere is clean and fresh and lovely, and a little bit bland. The walls are neutral because I couldn't decide how else to have them.

I pull several paint charts from my bag. Over the last few days I've decided that I am going to have feature walls in some of the rooms, mainly the bedrooms and the sitting room. I'm going to paint them myself, really, truly putting my stamp on my home. I've never decorated before, Leeward always had the professionals in to do his, he even chose the colours – shades of grey – suggesting that I didn't have an eye for style. Cheeky bastard.

Two hours later I've unpacked the car, nipped to the supermarket for some essentials, including tea, coffee, milk and, more pertinently, cutlery and a dinner service. It has four of everything, mugs, dinner plates, tea plates, bowls. It's flowery and blue, and bright and cheery and Leeward would never have had it in his house, which makes me smile.

Now, as it approaches 4pm, I'm waiting for the woman from the dog charity to arrive to inspect my house. I recall Grimmy's words and a little part of me agrees with her, it is a cheek, then I remember that they're rehoming these dogs and they have to get it right, some have already been neglected or mistreated, they can't chance that happening again.

The knock at the door makes me jump, even though I'm expecting it. When I open the door the woman who stands before me is the same one I saw at the dog charity. Same wild hair, same orange jumper covered in dog hairs. She has an air of abandonment about her; she's super-smiley and says *super*, a lot.

'Lauren,' she says, grinning.

'Hi, err...' What the hell is her name?

'Bev, from Dogs Are Home,' she says, as though I don't recognise her at all. And, I have to go with it, because I couldn't remember her name.

'Hello, hello.' So good I have to say it twice. 'Please come in.'

She steps into my empty, spotless hallway then follows me into the kitchen/diner, also empty and spotless apart from the dog basket and bowls I bought last week and have put in pride of place near the radiator.

'I've just moved in. Today,' I say when she blinks her puzzlement at me.

'Ah, I see.' A great big smile. 'Super. And you're waiting for your furniture. Super.'

'Yes,' I lie. There is no furniture apart from my new *on credit* sofa which will be delivered later in the week. But at least the kitchen's fully fitted with everything, cooker, fridge, washing machine, and the floors are all new and lovely. What more could a woman want? Or a dog.

I can't afford anything else until I get paid at the end of the month. I have enough to buy food and some paint for my feature walls and that's it.

Bev marches over to the French doors and peers out onto the garden. It's not exactly enormous. There's a patio, a bit of lawn, and a stoned area, then there's the garage and parking. She turns and frowns at me.

'Garden's not very big,' her voice goes up at the end of the sentence.

'No. But it's enough for, you know, a dog to do its business.' When did I get so coy about pee and poo? I see it all the time at work. 'And, of course, there's a

134

great big park at the end of the road, which is where we'll be going every day.'

'Ah, is there?' She looks as though she wants to be pleased.

'Would you like me to show you?' I can tell she isn't convinced.

'Would you mind? I do have to be sure and I don't know this area at all.'

'Sure.' I grab my keys and lead the way out.

We walk to the end of the road, turn left and there they are — the gates to paradise, their green paint may be fading but the foliage behind is vibrate and abundant.

I turn to walk away but Bev ventures towards the park. I hope she isn't expecting me to show her the exact route I plan to walk the dog. She keeps going and I have to follow her through the gates and on into the expansive greenness.

'Super,' she says, taking it all in, the bandstand in the distance, the little kiosk, the joggers' path, the benches, the enormous ancient trees. 'How big is it?'

'Um.' How the hell do I know? Think, think. 'About half a mile across and maybe a mile long.' I'm guessing, I really have no idea, I just know it's big. 'Plenty for a dog to run around in.'

'And dogs are allowed?'

'Oh yes, as long as you scoop their poop.'

A big smile spreads across Bev's face. 'That's just super,' she says as she turns to go back to my house.

Once inside she pulls some crumpled paperwork from her bag and starts ticking boxes like fury. I watch, fascinated as I am approved to be a dog owner.

'Sheba, wasn't it?' She turns to me and for the briefest of moments I don't know what she means.

'Sheba, yes.' Sheba is the dog's name, a cute little black terrier cross. I don't know what she's crossed with but she's so sweet, there's a lot of Westie in her, though her legs are too long and perhaps a bit of Jack Russell. It was instant attraction as soon as we set eyes on each other. I'll be changing her name though, I hate Sheba. I've thought about what I will call her and I like Shadow or maybe Shade. I imagine us taking long walks around the park, her with her brand-new tartan lead and collar, me in my new walking boots – I should be able to afford them when I get paid.

'Tomorrow, then.' Bev is talking to me and I've been so taken with my little daydream that I haven't been listening to her.

'What's that.'

'Ten am. I won't be there but they'll be expecting you. Super.'

'I'm sorry.' I shake my head.

'You can pick Sheba up at ten, tomorrow.'

'Oh, but I was thinking maybe the end of the week. You know, after my furniture arrives.' Liar, liar. Although the sofa will be here by then, not that Sheba will be sitting on it.

'Dogs don't need furniture. You can put her out in the garden when it's being brought in.'

'But I…'

'It needs to be tomorrow at the latest. Space is at a premium at Dogs Are Home.'

'Oh but…' I wanted to paint and settle in a bit first. 'My furniture's coming then.' Liar. So many lies I'm starting to get confused.

'Ah, well. Just a moment.' She whips her phone out and makes a call and because this happens in front of me, I know exactly what she's saying and I can't think of a way to stop it. 'Okay,' she says, when she's finished. 'If you go now, they'll be ready for you. Super.'

'Okay,' I hear myself meekly agree, but my face is obviously giving me away because Bev looks at me for a moment.

'That is, if you still want her.' Suddenly the super smile is gone.

'Yes, yes, of course I do.'

'Super. They're expecting you soon.'

And she's gone and I'm collecting my bag and the aforementioned tartan lead and collar and going off to collect Shadow – that's definitely what I'm calling her.

At Dogs Are Home they *are* waiting for me, smiles on their faces and Shadow already on a lead – it's not tartan.

'You must be Lauren,' the man says.

'Yes. I am.'

'Great, just a bit of paperwork and she's all yours. Sit, Sheba.' He pulls gently on the lead.

I sign some forms and, just when I think I can escape he asks if I have any questions. I haven't, and I feel a bit lacking, because he's asked me lots, including if I have enough food. We've swopped their lead and collar for my new one which seemed to disappoint him because I think he was looking for a sale. But I *have* been coerced into buying a doggy car travel harness, which I can barely afford but, apparently, it's an essential. It's all in a good cause, I tell myself and any profit is going to the charity.

'Okay, Sheba, are you ready to go with your new mummy?' the man asks Shadow. I cringe at the mummy reference.

Shadow behaves impeccably, climbing into the car and sitting calmly while I connect the travel harness to the seat belt. She even lies down before I've started the car.

'Well done, Shadow,' I say over my shoulder.

It's a shame she doesn't stay there.

We've barely got to the top of the Dogs Are Home drive before she starts howling. A quick glance in my mirror and I can see that she's on her hind legs, front paws on the back of the seat and howling out of the door window. So much for the restraining qualities of the harness, though I imagine she'd be in the front without it.

'Shadow, sit,' I command, to no effect. 'Shadow. SIT.'

Again, my command, even with its authoritative tone makes no difference.

'Sheba, down,' I call in one last ditch attempt to calm her. And, of course it works. Maybe it's going to take her a while to learn her new name. 'Well done, Shadow,' I say.

Nine

'Reminds me of the house I lived in with my first husband, your real great-grandad,' Grimmy says, shuffling her way in and heading straight for the kitchen. 'Garden was a lot bigger though. It's tiny. That grass already needs mowing. Do you have a lawnmower?'

'Um, no.' I hadn't even thought of it. Leeward always had a gardener who came every week in the summer and once a month in the winter. He said it was a justifiable expense – one I realise that I helped fund. I realise I'll have to add lawnmower to my growing list of things I must buy.

'Don't worry, I have an old one that should do this little lawn. You can have that,' Dad says.

'What's this?' Grimmy says as, with caution, Shadow eyes Grimmy from the safety of her basket.

'This is Shadow, everyone,' I say, introducing my dog.

Dad bends down and strokes her under the chin. Mum pats her back, Shadow lifts her head to appreciate the attention then licks Dad's hands.

'They're a tie, dogs,' Grimmy says. 'And unhygienic.

What is it?'

'She's a terrier cross, probably westie,' I say.

'Crossed with what?'

'I'm not sure, maybe Jack Russell or …'

'A Heinz then.' Grimmy turns away from Shadow and starts looking around. 'Is there anywhere to sit in here?'

'Not yet.' I hadn't thought of that when I invited them round. I have the kettle on and teabags in the cups, but no chairs.

'Don't worry, Grammy, I have your garden chair in the car.'

I don't know if Dad always has her garden chair in the car or if he thought of it especially.

'What's a Heinz? I ask, wondering if I've misheard Grimmy.

'Heinz. 57,' she says, as though I should know.

I look at Mum and Dad.

'57 varieties,' Mum says quietly. 'Like the Heinz range of foods.'

'Oh, right.'

'A mongrel,' Grimmy snaps. 'They didn't have any of this cross nonsense in my day. Where's this chair then?'

Ten minutes later we're sitting in the lounge, Grimmy in her chair, Mum, Dad and me on the floor, Shadow has joined us, resting her head on Dad's lap.

'Have you taken her out for a walk yet?' Dad asks, patting Shadow. I think he's fallen in love with her and it's reciprocated.

As kids we had lots of pets, including two dogs, but after the last one died, which was long after we'd all grown up and left, Mum and Dad haven't had another one.

'Yes, just before you came.' We'd had a very brisk march around the park as time was definitely not on my side.

'Such a tie, dogs,' Grimmy says again. 'Aren't they, Lisa?'

Mum nods her head in agreement and smiles.

'What will she be like when you're at work?' A sensible question from Mum.

'Okay, apparently, she's used to being left on her own during the day. The only reason she ended up in the dog's home was because her owners emigrated and didn't want to take her with them. She's not damaged or been abused. And I'll pop home in breaks whenever I can.'

'That's what they all say,' Grimmy mutters.

'No, she seems fine. Anyway, we'll find out tomorrow, I'm off to B&Q to buy some paint and obviously I can't take her with me.'

Dad gets up and wipes the new-carpet fluff from his trousers, he's still wearing his work clothes.

'I could pop round occasionally and let her out in the garden,' Mum says.

'Could you? That would be brilliant.'

'Just make sure it's not at noon, Lisa, that's my lunchtime,' Grimmy instructs Mum.

'Do you want that putting on the wall?' Dad nods at my TV on the floor, the one I bought for the attic rooms in their house where it had rested on a large chest of drawers. 'I could do it this weekend.'

'Yes, please.' Perfect timing, I should have finished the painting by then.

'Let's see upstairs then,' he says.

'I'll stay here, Lauren. Them stairs look steep,' Grimmy announces from her garden chair throne.

141

'Okay.' I lean in closer to her. 'You'll be pleased to know there's a downstairs toilet, so that'll never be a worry when you visit.'

'I'm not incontinent,' she snaps back, quickly followed by, 'When are you getting this new sofa?'

'Later this week. You'll have to come round again to see it.'

'I'll still need a high chair,' she says. 'I expect it'll be too low for me.'

She has a point there, something I hadn't considered.

I give Mum and Dad the obligatory tour, they laugh at my blow-up bed. I have lovely new bedding but I haven't had time to make the bed up.

'Lovely wardrobes.' Mum pulls open one of the fitted wardrobe doors where I've already hung all my clothes. 'When are you getting a bed?'

'When I can afford one,' I laugh.

'We could get you one as a present.'

'No, you could not. Don't even think of it. You've given me the biggest present of all by letting me stay at your place for nothing so I could save. So absolutely not.'

'But Grimmy's buying you a sofa,' Mum says.

'I know and that's too much but she's already paid for the gift card.'

'She can easily afford it,' Dad says, laughing. 'And we can easily afford to buy you a bed.'

'No. Please. No.'

'Okay,' Mum says, 'Okay.'

Dad laughs.

After they've gone I wonder if, after a night's sleep on the child sized air bed, I might be swallowing my pride and accepting their offer of a new bed. I hope not. I want to be independent. I realise I've spent far too long relying on other people, on reflection I think that Leeward did a lot of my thinking for me – which I now find really rather pathetic. Anyway, what I can't afford I will have to go without or wait for. I'll truly appreciate it then.

I let Shadow out into the garden, she spends a long time sniffing around, then pees in all four corners. The garden is fenced on all sides so I don't have to worry about her escaping. When she comes back in, I fill her water bowl and settle her for the night before going upstairs to make my bed and climb in. It's only nine-thirty, but I'm exhausted.

I am sound asleep when I am woken by howling. I groan. I've got a dog who howls in the night.

Except it's not night. It's daylight outside. In fact, it's bright daylight outside, the sun is streaming in through the windows. I need curtains. The builder put up curtain poles for me as part of the deal, but I didn't even think about curtains until I came to bed last night and had to creep around under the sill to get undressed. I wonder how much curtains will cost?

Shadow's howling increases.

I grab a sweatshirt, pull it on over my pyjamas and run down the stairs and burst through the kitchen door. I find Shadow howling at the patio doors, desperate to go out.

Only after I've let her out do I see that it's after nine already. Poor dog has gone almost twelve hours, and so have I. I check to see that she hasn't peed all over my kitchen, but she hasn't.

I let Shadow wander in and out of the garden as I have my breakfast and get dressed. It's a treat to use my new shower knowing I'm the first person in it. Everything about the house makes me smile. Everything is and will be to my taste, my choice.

Shadow is asleep in her basket when I leave for B&Q. I have a list a mile long and I just hope my credit card can afford it.

I'm gone an hour and a half and when I return Shadow is pleased to see me, jumping and barking and licking my hands. It's nice to have someone so happy at my arrival. She even seems to respond to me calling her Shadow, after all it's not such a leap from Sheba, is it? I let her out into the garden and promise her a walk once I've got a coat of paint on the lounge feature wall.

I've spent an absolute fortune in B&Q. Not only did I have to buy bedroom curtains that I hadn't budgeted for, but also a step ladder. Otherwise I won't be able to paint the top of the walls, or put the curtains up. Those two items alone have trebled my original budget, and I had to buy a dustsheet, another unbudgeted item. Oh well, it'll all be worth it. I hope.

After a quick cup of coffee, I don my overalls – well, Dad's cast offs, but they are the proper thing; white dungarees complete with paint splats. I can even spot the paint they used in the attic rooms they painted for me. I roll up the legs, pull on an old pair of socks – Leeward's, ha ha, wrap my head in a scarf, spread out the dustsheet and crack open the paint.

Almost three hours later and I've got one coat on. It seems to have taken a long time what with the cutting in and being careful not to get paint on any of the other walls. I stand back to admire my handiwork – my first paint job. I love the colour though it definitely needs another coat but I can't do that for quite a few hours.

My stomach rumbles so I grab a quick sandwich and feed Shadow who's circling my legs. I think she wants that walk I promised her and, by the look of how grey it is outside now, it had better be soon. The sky has changed from bright blue and clear to solid grey and murky.

I run upstairs to grab my boots, forcing them on over Leeward's old, thick socks. In the hall I pull on my coat over the dungarees, yank off the headscarf and fluff up my hair a bit. I attach Shadow's tartan lead to her collar. She looks adorable even if I don't, but I'm only going to be half an hour at most and it's so dingy outside that no one will see me.

Once in the park Shadow's excitement is evident, her tail is wagging and her ears are up. She starts to run and that's when I realise that I'll have to run with her as I'm too scared to let her off her lead in case she runs off and doesn't come back. Yesterday's walk had been a very sedate affair, but she'd probably already had a big walk by the time I picked her up from Dogs Are Home.

After just a few minutes I'm sweating and puffing and panting. As we pass another dog walker, he winks at me. I look away and decide I won't be making eye contact with anyone else. There are far more people in here than I ever expected. Dare I chance letting Shadow off her lead? Happily, and suddenly, she spots a tree that takes her interest and spends a few minutes sniffing it, which gives me some time to recover. I'm so hot I want to take my coat off but then my paint-splattered dungarees will be on full display and I'll have to carry my coat as well as cling onto Shadow's lead. Maybe I'll just unbutton it to let some air in.

Shadow is off again and I'm struggling to keep up, my coat flapping around me. I hadn't realised I was quite so unfit and the effort of keeping my head down isn't helping either.

Mercifully she stops again for another sniff. But this time it's not a tree, it's another dog. A tiny little thing that holds its head up, refusing to be cowed by a bigger dog.

'What's your name?' A male voice, deep and seductive, asks, while a large hand pats Shadow's head.

'She's Shadow,' I answer, trying to control my puffing and panting and pulling on Shadow's lead to encourage her to walk away while forcing myself not to look at the man.

'She's got some energy. I saw you racing with her when you were right over the other side of the park. Can't she be trusted not to run away?'

'No,' I say, gulping air. 'I've only just got her.'

'You need to get one of these.' He thrusts his hand under my nose and shows me his lead. 'It's retractable, saves you having to run a marathon.' I glance at the tiny dog and wonder if it really needs a retractable lead, it looks as though it couldn't run anywhere fast.

Mentally, I add another item to my ever-growing shopping list.

'This little one is new too, we only got her recently,' the man continues. 'This is only her second walk. Her name is Daenerys.' He rubs his dog's ears.

'Daenerys? From Game of Thrones?' I don't succeed in keeping the note of derision from my voice.

'Yes. I know, but what can I say? My partner chose it.' He laughs and his laugh is so infectious I can't help but smile along with him and finally, I look into his face. This conversation has gone on too long for me not to.

He's very attractive and a pair of piercing, smiling

blue eyes meet mine. My stomach does a little flip. He reminds me of Thor as played by Chris Hemsworth; I don't know how many Thor films there are but I know Leeward has made me sit through them all several times each. This guy even has Thor's sexy beard and shoulder length hair. And he's wearing brown leather, even that reminds me of Thor's breastplate.

I wish I wasn't wearing the painting dungarees.

'Our dogs seem to be getting along well,' he says, his voice a sexy growl.

'Yeah.' I can't look at the dogs because I can't take my eyes off him. I'm letting myself slyly appraise him and hoping that he isn't doing the same to me. He's big; tall, with big shoulders and dirty-blonde hair. My stomach does another little flip. Shame he's got a partner. Who knew dog walkers were so attractive? Except me, I'm definitely not at my most attractive today.

'No doubt we'll meet again if you live locally?'

'Yeah,' I manage again, smiling and pulling my coat across me and holding it closed. 'Better get on. Come on, Shadow.' Shadow takes no notice, so I yank on her lead. 'Bye, Daenerys.'

'Bye to the both of you,' Thor says, laughing and pulling his little dog along beside him.

After I've walked away, under the pretext of checking on Shadow who is very reluctant to leave her new friend, I allow myself a quick glance in Thor's direction. Wow, what a man. What a shame I look such a mess. In future I must always make an effort with my appearance when walking my dog.

No, I won't. I am NOT looking for a man.

Shadow finally comes to heel and after her encounter with Daenerys doesn't seem quite so energetic. We carry on walking, albeit briskly, around the park. I'm taking in the greenery, which looks almost olive coloured under the dark grey sky. It is definitely going to rain. Right on cue a heavy raindrop lands on my nose. I pull my hood up and put my head down, urging Shadow on.

Bang.

I've walked into someone.

How stupid am I?

I see the phone in his hand. So, he obviously wasn't looking where he was going either.

'Sorry,' I mumble at the same time as he does.

Hang on, I recognise that voice.

'Lauren?' he says.

'Leeward,' I squeak. 'What are you doing here?' In my head I'm imagining that he has found out about my new house and is now stalking me.

'Taking a walk,' he says. 'What are *you* doing here?'

'Walking my dog. This is *my* local park.' So take that, Leeward Quinn. I have a dog because I can do whatever *I* like now.

'Oh yeah, cute.' He glances down at Shadow who is now sitting at my feet. 'What is it?'

'It's a Heinz,' I spit, sounding just like Grimmy.

'A what?'

'Oh never mind.'

We then stand for a few seconds. The silence is awkward. I feel angry and sad at the same time. I almost forget what he did to me, his betrayal with *her*; I remember the good times, the fun we used to have. And looking at him now it's easy to remember why I fell in love with him, he looks amazing, obviously still going to the gym. I hear a long sigh come from Leeward.

'So why are *you* here? In this park, I mean.'

'Look,' he starts. 'I've moved.'

I don't reply. I don't admit I already know or that Kenton tells me everything.

'Anyway, this is *my* local park too,' he adds.

I feel sick to the core. I don't even know what he's doing in the park, he would never go out for a walk with me. Please don't let us be neighbours, please don't.

'Where have you moved to?' I ask, despite not wanting to know even though I *need* to know.

He points to the opposite side of the park and names the road, the relief washes over me and blots out most of what he is saying, all I catch is new build.

'What about you?'

'Other side,' I say, vaguely pointing in the general direction of my new home. I don't name the street or give him any more information.

'I hope you're okay, now.'

'You what?' I can't believe what he's just said. Why do I get the impression he thinks I've been ill, a madness even, and that's what caused our break up? Stop it, Lauren, you're being neurotic.

'Your wrist…'

'Oh that, yeah it's fine.'

'How's work?'

'Fine. How's your work?'

'Same old, same old.' He smiles and it incenses me.

'What, still working late and staying away overnight at every opportunity?'

'Oh, L-a-u-r-e-n,' he says, followed by another sigh.

Over his shoulder I can see Thor striding towards us, his little dog tucked under his arm. He's going at quite a pace. Perhaps he can see the antipathy between me and Leeward, sense the animosity and he's coming to rescue me. Just throw the hammer, I think, throw the hammer and take Leeward out.

'Hey again,' Thor says as he reaches us.

'Hi,' I simper.

Leeward turns around and smiles at Thor.

'Finished your calls?' Thor asks Leeward. 'Only it's going to lash it down in a minute.' These two know each other? Ah, is this another lodger to help pay the bills in the new house.

'Um, yeah.'

'Supposed to be a day off and he has to take work calls. What are you like, Lee?' Thor rolls his eyes at me in a jokey way. Lee, Thor just called him Lee; I was never allowed to call him Lee. Maybe he just does it and Leeward can't stop him. 'Hey, you two know each other. What a small world. Do introduce us.' Thor turns a megawatt smile on us both.

'Yeah, this is Lauren,' Leeward's voice isn't much more than a mumble.

Thor holds his hand out to shake mine and as I offer my own clammy little mitt, it's enveloped in a big, warm, bear paw. Such big, strong hands.

'I'm Alfie,' Thor says in his deep, rich voice.

'Alfie?' My voice is a squeaky mumble. 'Alfie?' I turn to Leeward. '*The* Alfie?'

'We'd better go now, rain's starting,' Leeward says, dodging past me and urging Alfie away.

He's right too, the drops start to fall thick and heavy now. I don't move. I just stand there watching the two of them marching away. Alfie so big and Thor-like and Leeward scampering along to keep up with Thor's giant strides and so, well, Gollum-like. Back to their lovely, new-build on the other side of the park. Their own little, or probably big, love nest.

I pull my phone out of my pocket.

Ten

I'm on the phone to Cat before I've even got out of the park. Once I'd pulled myself together, closed my mouth which was hanging open in shock, I couldn't march home fast enough, even Shadow knew better than to mess with me.

'And, and,' I'm ranting, 'He, Alfie, the Thor god, didn't even know who I was. When Leeward, who Alfie is allowed to call Lee, by the way, introduced us, he didn't even flinch, not a flicker of recognition. Nothing. He's never heard of me. Leeward, no, Lee, was cringing, but Alfie, no, he was just fine. I don't think he even suspects who I am. I don't think he even knows Leeward had a fiancée. What do you think, Cat? What's your take on it all?' I've reached my front door and now I'm fumbling with my key while trying to keep my phone to my ear and not let go of Shadow's lead.

'Are you sure that's Alfie? I mean…'

'Yes,' I say, bursting through the door and letting go of Shadow who bolts for the kitchen and her water bowl before I can even remove her lead. 'I asked him, I said, "Is this *the* Alfie?" and he said "yes."'

'Oh. My. God.'

'Yeah. Quite.'

'What's he like?'

'I've told you, he looks like Thor, you know, as played by Chris Hemsworth. You do know what *he* looks like?'

'Hot. Very hot.'

'Yes, exactly. And Leeward looks the hottest I've ever seen him, really buffed up and gym fit.'

'I bet that's where they met.' As Cat drops this bombshell, I just know she's right. The timing fits perfectly. 'I wonder if they met *at* the gym,' Cat muses. 'Or if Leeward started with the gym because they'd already met?'

'I feel sick. Don't say any more.' It had been Leeward's idea to improve ourselves for our wedding, he at the gym, me on a perpetual starvation diet.

'Okay.'

I take a few deep breaths and shrug myself out of my wet coat.

'You still there,' Cat asks, gently.

'Yes. Yes. Just, you know…'

'Did he look…gay?' Cat's voice is tentative.

'No. He looked hot; I've just told you. They both did. And I look like crapola in my painty clothes.' I bend over to take my ankle boots off. 'Oh SHIT, oh SHIT,' I shout.

'What? What's wrong?'

'I'm wearing odd boots. For fuck's sake, how did that happen?'

There's a silence on the other end of the phone. It goes on too long. Far too long, the silence so solid that Cat must have her phone on mute.

'You're bloody laughing, aren't you?'

A snort comes out of the phone followed by a

'Sorry.'

'It's not funny.'

'No, of course it's not.'

'It bloody isn't.' But even I can see how it might seem to someone else.

'Perhaps they didn't notice.'

'I bet they bloody did. Lee,' I say his name in a whiny, silly voice, 'Never misses a thing and Alfie was bent over by my feet for ages talking to Shadow and stroking her. He definitely saw.'

'Oh.'

'I took a photo,' I say, 'Of them walking away. I don't even feel guilty or creepy now because they're probably having a good snigger about my boots.'

'Send it, send it to me.'

I think for a moment. 'No. I'll show you when I see you.'

'Send it. What's the matter with you?'

'I don't want it getting out there.'

'And you think I'd do that?' Cat sounds cross.

'No. Not you. No, of course not. But, you know, once it's out there in the ether, who knows where it might end up.' I'll never get over the video of me screeching that awful song, I'll never forget that and I will never let something like that happen again. I've never found out who posted it, even though the poster's name was all over it, he/she didn't seem to exist. Cat had said they'd obviously closed their account; I think they probably only created it to post that video. I will never get caught like that again.

'It'll only be on my phone.'

'No. Come here. You haven't seen my house yet anyway.'

'I know and we're due to come at the weekend, I

can't wait that long. I'll come tonight between dropping Natalia off and picking up the boys from football practice. I have a spare fifty minutes. Seven okay?'

'Yes. Sounds good. I even have wine.' Just the one bottle I treated myself to at the supermarket before I realised I'd have to spend so much money on everything else.

'A whole bottle just for you?' Her voice is censorious.

'Oh yeah. Maybe not.' I'll save it for another day. Sometimes I completely forget that Cat doesn't drink, sometimes I wish she would, if only to keep me company.

'Um, Cat,' I say, remembering what Grimmy had said about Natalia. 'Did you know that Natalia's been on Tinder?' I hold the phone away waiting for her to screech.

'Oh, yes. Well, no she's not. She was just showing it to Grimmy.'

'When? Why?'

'Oh, I forget.'

'No you don't.' I already don't like the sound of this. I wish I'd kept my big mouth shut.

'Christmas, I think. I'll see you later.'

'No, wait. Why was Natalia showing Grimmy Tinder?'

'Grimmy just wants you to be happy, that's all.'

'I am happy,' I snap.

'Yeah, that's what I told her. See you later.'

So Grimmy has everyone involved in finding me a man even though I've told her I don't bloody want one. Not everyone needs three husbands!

Cat has my phone in her hands and is scrutinising the

photo carefully and has enlarged it to get a better view.

'I wish you'd send this to me. I could put it on the computer and get a better look.'

'No. And that's exactly what I mean. Put it on the computer, make another copy. Then what?'

'Nothing. I wouldn't do anything.'

'Yes, but supposing one of the kids innocently uploaded it to Facebook or Instagram.'

'They wouldn't,' Cat says, shaking her head and frowning. 'But I get your point. Can't you put it on *your* laptop so we could see it better?'

'No, because that's another copy, isn't it?'

'Yes, but yours. Do you think you're being a bit paranoid?'

'Probably. But if it ever got out, they'd know where it came from.'

'He is hot, though. What I can see of him, that is. And tall.'

'Yeah, like Thor.'

'Not,' Cat says, 'That that excuses your ex-fiancé's behaviour.'

'No, it doesn't.

'They do look quite comical. Giant Thor,' she affects a very deep voice quickly followed a high-pitched one. 'And tiny Gollum.'

'Don't call him that and he doesn't have a squeaky voice.'

'Did he have to run to keep up with Thor?'

I snigger. 'Yes, a bit.'

Cat laughs too much for my liking. 'I wish I'd seen it. You should have videoed it.'

'Enough. Stop it. Imagine how I feel?'

'Mmm. Better or worse?'

'Confused. And upset. I did everything he ever

wanted me to do, I changed my bloody appearance for him, had blonde hair and dieted myself away, even Grimmy commented on how thin I was, but what he really wanted was a great big man.'

'Well, you couldn't change into that, not without surgery.' She snorts again.

'It's not funny.'

'You'd laugh if it wasn't you.'

'Would I laugh if it was you?'

Cat shrugs.

'And they've got a dog, I was never allowed a dog.'

'No. I'm surprised Ken hasn't said anything to you about Alfie and Lee, especially with them living so close to you.' Cat grins.

'Sparing my feelings, I think.' Ken has been very forthcoming with details of house moves and holidays but has never discussed Alfie, even when I've pressed him.

'Is Leeward gay?' Cat asks.

'Duh, what do you think?'

'Well, he was with you for a l-o-n-g time. Did you notice anything?'

'Maybe I turned him gay.' This conversation is not good for me, not good at all.

'He's probably bi,' Cat says, with confidence. 'That's it. He's probably fought his feelings for years. Been mixed up and confused. That's why he always had that scowl on his face.'

'He did not.'

Cat shrugs. 'Okay. Well it doesn't matter now, does it? You're free of him. Thank God you didn't go through with it. Thank God you found his phone. Imagine if you'd married him? It would all have come out eventually. That Alfie is far too big to hide forever.

157

You would have been Leeward's beard.'

'His what?'

'You know, a beard, a wife to hide the fact that he was secretly gay.'

'Really? Does that still happen? People don't need to be secretly gay, or bi or whatever Leeward wants to be.'

The sense of what Cat's said hits me. I've spent the time since meeting them in the park trying to put their faces out of my mind. I've managed another coat on the lounge walls, cleared up, had a shower and washed my hair, dressed in clean clothes, even though my pjs were calling, and done anything and everything to distract myself – all with loud music playing.

'He never mentioned my hair,' I say softly.

'Maybe he didn't notice.'

I think about this; I had my hood up the whole time we were talking. But my hood is wide and it's very easy to see my hair.

'He did. He definitely did. I suppose he doesn't care anymore, about me, I mean.'

'Lauren, I think he always cared more about himself than y... anyone else. Anyway, show me this house of yours, I've only seen the hall and kitchen so far.'

'And you haven't even met Shadow.' I open the door to the garden and call her name. She doesn't come running, in fact she ignores me, even though she can see me quite clearly.

'Cute little garden,' Cat says, peering over my shoulder.

'Too small, according to Grimmy.'

We both laugh at that.

'Shadow,' I shout again, but she still ignores me. 'Shadow.' Nothing. 'Sheba,' I say between gritted teeth and in she comes and makes a beeline straight for Cat.

'Hello, Sheba,' Cat says, making a fuss of her.

'Shadow. It's Shadow.'

'You need to tell her that.' Cat laughs again.

'I have. I am. Come on.'

I give Cat the tour and when we get back into my lounge she admires my paint job, telling me she's very impressed.

'I have some chairs and an old kitchen table you could have until you can afford your own.'

'Have you?' I love Cat's taste, anything she's had, even old, will be lovely.

'Yeah, they're in the garage. They were Mother-in-law's.' Probably not so good then. 'Do you want them?'

'Yes, please.'

'We'll bring them over at the weekend. When's your sofa coming?'

Cat has only been gone three minutes and I'm considering going to bed early so I can get an early start on painting my next room when there's a knock at the door. I wonder what she's forgotten. I fling open the door, laughing.

'What did you…'

It's not Cat.

It's Ken. With an enormous bouquet of flowers, a bottle of champagne and a box of chocolates in his arms.

He sees me looking at his gifts, shock on my face coupled with confusion.

'Housewarming gifts,' he says. 'I have a card too.'

'Oh. Thank you. Come in, come in. I thought you were Cat.'

'Oh, are you expecting her?'

I'm about to lie, I'm about to say yes, any minute.

Why? I like Ken, we're good friends. But given the timescale of her leaving and him arriving, he probably saw her leave. I wonder if he was waiting for her to go, he knows her car, it was on my driveway, next to mine.

'No, she's just gone, I thought she'd forgotten something.' I'm glad I'm not in my pyjamas.

'These are for you,' he says, rather unnecessarily, pushing everything from his arms into mine. I step back and take the items individually.

'Thank you.' I feel self-conscious as I lean up to kiss him on the cheek. He turns his head at just the right time and our lips brush. I step back and bustle towards the kitchen with my presents.

I busy myself finding and filling another vase, opening the card he's also given me, putting the champagne in the fridge and opening the chocolates.

'Would you like a coffee to go with that?' I ask as Ken takes a creamy truffle.

'If you're making one.'

I'm not. But I will. I'd rather go to bed. Alone.

'Thank you so much for my lovely presents. That's so kind of you, especially after the day I've had.' I watch his face to see if Leeward has told him about our encounter in the park.

'Oh, what have you been up to?'

I tell him about my trip to B&Q, my painting, my walk in the park. He doesn't react when I mention the park.

'Oh,' I add, smiling. 'And I met Alfie too.'

Ken blinks several times, he looks flustered, not a reaction I've ever seen from him.

'Alfie?'

'Yes, you know. *The* Alfie. I know you've met him because you took them to the airport for my honeymoon, and probably *their* other holiday? And well, they've been together ages, so I know you've met him.' I arch my eyebrows at Ken and wait for his explanation.

'Err, yeah.' He looks sheepish.

'Why didn't you tell me?'

Ken laughs, not a funny laugh like Cat's had been, but an ironic one. 'Maybe I was trying to spare you further heartache.'

'I was always going to find out, wasn't I? Eventually.' I'm making his coffee, though none for myself.

'I suppose so.'

'Especially as they live just across the park. I'm sure you realised how close we are.'

'No. I honestly didn't. If you remember you only messaged me your address last week. I didn't know where this place was, I had to put it in my satnav.'

'Okay.' I believe him. And, if I'm honest I'm being mean. He's been a good friend – or at least I think he has. And he's turned up with gifts tonight. 'What have you told Leeward about me?' I hand him his coffee.

'Nothing.' He sounds indignant.

'Not told him I was buying a house?'

'Absolutely not.'

'But you told me about his new house.'

'Yes, so you knew he had money enough to pay you some, because obviously Alfie had a house to sell too and they've bought the new one between them.'

'Okay.' I pick up the box of chocolates and head into the lounge. 'Come and see my handiwork,' I say, smiling.

'I'm sorry, Lauren,' Ken says as he follows me into the lounge.

'How long have you known?'

'I found out on your wedding day.'

'My non-wedding day,' I correct.

'We all did. He had to come clean when Mum really laid into him.'

'Wow, I didn't know your mum cared that much about me.' I feel rather touched. It doesn't last.

'Well, to be honest it was more about her and her outfit, the wedding party, the whole thing. She was furious with him for cocking it all up.'

'Oh, she didn't care about me then,' I laugh. I'm not bothered how Jayne feels about me, certainly not now, and, if I'm honest, not before.

'Has the whole family met Alfie?'

'No. Only me and I got tricked into it with the airport run. Steve and Sian aren't interested in anyone but themselves, which is fair enough, Sian is about to give birth, I mean literally. She went into hospital this afternoon; I'm just waiting for the call to say I'm an uncle.' He looks excited.

'Oh, that's nice.' It is too. But it should have been me having a baby soon. I try my hardest not to feel envious but it's difficult. 'You didn't say…'

'No. It seemed as though it would have been rubbing your nose in it.'

'Yeah. I see that.' I can see it from his point of view. He's been piggy in the middle. I don't know why he's bothered really. He could have not ever seen me again. That would have been perfectly reasonable.

'Mum hasn't spoken to Leeward since that day. Not one word. She won't speak about him either, if I mention him, she cuts me dead.' He's saying this because he expects me to be pleased. Sadly, and with only a modicum of guilt, I have to admit I am.

'And they've got a dog. I was never allowed a dog.' I snap this at Ken as though it's his fault.

162

'Don't you have one now?'

'Yes. Yes. She's in garden again, she loves it out there. You can meet her before you go. Anyway,' I smile brightly, putting an end to all talk of Leeward and his lover. 'What do you think of my handiwork?' I wave my hand along the wall like a game show hostess showing off the prizes.

'Great colour. Good job.'

'I'm doing feature walls in all the main rooms.' I head for the door then stop; do I really want to take Ken upstairs? I hesitate. That accidental kiss is still playing on my lips and on my mind. Also, ringing in my head are the alarm bells that Cat set off months ago when she said that Ken is just biding his time before he makes his move on me.

Ken is waiting, watching me during my inner deliberation. I smile, then lead the way upstairs, suddenly aware that he's following me and has a perfect view of my backside.

'When are you getting a bed?' He half laughs on seeing my single air bed; it is completely swamped by my king size duvet.

'When I can afford one.' I usher him from my bedroom and show him the bathroom and spare room which is completely empty. One of the joys of having nothing when you move into a new place is not having lots of clutter from your previous life.

No baggage, I think, smiling to myself.

I march down the stairs at speed, glancing back to see Ken trailing behind me.

'I'll get Shadow.' I open the back door and whistle, not very well, for her. Her ears prick up and she comes running. Perhaps that's better than calling her. 'Hello, Shadow,' I say, emphasising her name. 'Good girl. Meet

Ken.'

Shadow gives him a cursory look, sniffs, then lopes over to her basket and drops into it.

'Cute dog,' Ken says, without approaching her or attempting to make a fuss.

Ken glances at his watch – very expensive and sooo him. 'I'd better make a move, promised I'd pop in on Mum.'

'How's Suzi? I ask, not without malice.

'Yeah, good, I think. I'm not with her, if that's what you mean.'

'Oh no. It's just when you mentioned Jayne, well they were good friends, weren't they? Jayne even brought her to the non-wedding.'

'I don't know,' Ken says, his tone dismissive. 'I was thinking,' he starts, 'I could take you out for dinner. To celebrate your moving here.'

'Oh yeah. We could go to that pizza place we went to a couple of months ago. Such good value.' We had a great time, and it was only ten pounds each including a small lager.

'Err, I was thinking somewhere a bit classier. My treat. What about Saturday?'

'Saturday? Um. Okay.' I didn't mean to say that.

'Great. I'll pick you up at seven. Wear something,' he pauses, 'Dressy.'

'Okay.' I feel oddly obliged to comply, otherwise our friendship over these last months has been nothing but me using him to get information – although that hasn't been quite as successful as I thought it had given how he kept the biggest secret of all.

'Did you know Leeward was gay?' I frown at him, wondering if he had spotted it long ago.

'No. No idea. Anyway, he says he still likes women,

just likes men more.' He stops, then adds, 'Not all men, obviously.'

'Just Alfie.' I watch Ken's face. 'More than me.'

'It's his loss, Lauren. He was always punching above his weight with you.'

I laugh. I can feel my face colouring with embarrassment, then I decide to press for more information.

'How long had it been going on?'

Ken sighs. I can tell he really doesn't want to talk about this or be drawn into it.

'Do you know when they met? And where?'

'You see,' he starts, 'This is part of why I didn't want to say anything. I become a part of it and I don't want to be.'

'But, do you know?'

'Yes, they met at the gym when he started to go to get buff for your wedding.'

'How ironic.' Cat was right.

'Yeah.'

'He still goes by the look of him.'

'Yeah. I'd better go.' He smiles and leans in to kiss me goodbye and this time I ensure that our lips do not touch.

I'm beginning to think that Cat might also be right about Ken. And he's certainly waited it out. And waited until I'm out of my parents' house too.

The voice in the back of my head, the rational-irrational one, poses a question: *Would it really be so bad to be in a relationship with Ken?*

What would Leeward think?

Eleven

I'm up early the next morning to get the first coat of paint on feature wall in the spare bedroom. Then I take Shadow out for her long walk around the park. I still don't have the retractable dog lead as suggested by Thor, but I have ordered it online – another charge to my credit card. It should arrive tomorrow.

I am very careful not to walk Shadow at the same time as I did yesterday. I don't want to chance bumping into *them* again, although from what was said, Leeward had only taken one day off – not that I can be one hundred percent sure of that – so avoiding going at the same time decreases my chances of bumping into them.

The park seems to be busy again today, more dog walkers – I exchange pleasantries with them today because I actually look okay; I've changed out of the painting dungarees and fluffed up my hair. I've also made sure that my boots match.

It's nicer weather today, warm with no ominous clouds in the sky. I pass a couple of women pushing their babies and wonder if Leeward's brother and his wife have had their baby yet. I didn't even know Sian was pregnant. I have to admit that I don't know Sian very well at all, Leeward wasn't that close to his brother so we didn't see them very much. Ken was always more favoured in our house than Steve.

That could have been me, I think, having a baby. It should have been me.

When I check the time on my phone, I realise that we've been out for over an hour. We've been round the park twice and Shadow is now walking nicely to heel, mainly because I think we've used up her energy. And mine. I turn to head back but it seems I've indulged these thoughts too soon. Suddenly Shadow's nose goes up and her ears twitch and she's racing along with me galumphing along behind her – most inelegant. I really don't want to run anymore; I'm exhausted from jogging with her around the park. The sooner that new lead comes, the better.

She's heading for the bench where a man is sitting with his dog, Shadow's speed is increasing and her tail is wagging with excitement. I grip her lead and try to rein her in, and eventually, just as we reach the bench, I get control of her and pull her to heel.

The man on the bench doesn't even notice me as I put myself between him and a straining Shadow. His dog – a twin for Shadow but a grubby white instead of black – lies between his feet, looking forlorn and sad, its lead a piece of string. I glance at his face as I drag Shadow past, he looks awful. His skin is pale and blotchy, his hair unkempt and his bloodshot eyes stare aimlessly into the distance. Oh dear. He's on something.

'Spice,' Cat says with conviction later, when I tell her on the phone. She's rung to check on my decorating progress – allegedly – but also to see if I've seen any more of Thor and Gollum.

'Spice. Possibly.'

'Yeah,' she says, 'You know that one that leaves the user catatonic. Sounds just like your man.'

'I know what it does. It was his dog I felt sorry for, looked so pathetic and on a piece of string.'

'Yeah.' She tuts her disapproval. 'How's your decorating going?'

'I'm going to do the feature wall in my bedroom tomorrow, then the one in the kitchen-diner the next day. Oh, and my sofa's definitely coming tomorrow. I had a text. It'll be between eight and one.'

'Cool. Though I hate those big time slots they give you. Have you ordered another one yet with Grimmy's voucher?'

'Yes, online on my phone. It'll be six weeks though. Oh, and I should be getting the internet soon too.' And not before time, I took a chance and ordered it before I'd even moved in.

'It's all coming together and we'll bring that furniture around at the weekend. I was thinking Saturday about six.'

'Yes. Great. No. Wait. I'm going out on Saturday night. I have to leave at seven so I need to get ready.'

'Ooo, where are you going?'

A part of me doesn't want to tell her.

'Just out for a meal.'

'On your own?' She doesn't miss a thing.

'Um, no, with Ken. It's his treat to celebrate me moving into my own house.'

'Oh yeah. You need to be careful with him. I have told you this before.'

'I know, I know. But…'

'But what?'

'He's very attractive. Would it be so wrong?'

'I'm going to let you work that answer out for yourself.' She's using her big sister voice. 'Have to go, catch you soon. Oh, we'll come Sunday morning instead.'

'Not too early,' I say. Why do I feel as though she's hoping to catch me out?

I'm up, showered and dressed well before eight. I can't chance the sofa people turning up early and catching me in bed. Of course, I know by being ready so soon that they won't come until one.

I've finished the first coat of paint on my bedroom wall, tidied up and now I'm almost twiddling my thumbs while Shadow paces around impatiently, wanting to go out. Her retractable lead still hasn't arrived and I hope it comes before I take her out which will be immediately after the new sofa arrives.

I make my lunch and eat it, while keeping a listen out for the door, for evidence of a delivery lorry, for anything.

And, of course, the sofa arrives just before one. They bring it in, position it, unwrap it and ask for my signature in what seems like seconds. Once they're gone, I sit on it, lie on it, roll around on it. I love it. I imagine how it will be even better in this room once the second sofa arrives. Shadow comes into the lounge and sniffs the air and then the sofa, walking around and around it with a mischievous glint in her eyes. She finally comes to a stop and hovers in front of the seat next to me.

'No, Shadow,' I say, my voice as firm as I can make it because I know she's planning on leaping up here. 'Not for you. No.'

She tilts her head to one side, turns tail and trots off to the kitchen where I can hear her scrabbling around. I'm about to get up to see what she's up to when she returns with her tartan lead in her mouth.

'Clever girl, Shadow.' I pat her and rub her chin. 'Clever girl.' The lead had been on the kitchen worktop, hence the scrabbling. 'We'd better go then.' I stand up and hope I'm not going to regret not waiting for the retractable lead.

Once in the park Shadow really goes for it, dragging me around behind her. At this rate I'm going to be super fit. We get around the park twice in record time and she's ready to go again. I pull her back; I've had enough and I want to get another coat of paint on my bedroom wall and then sit on my new sofa and watch TV.

I pull Shadow towards the entrance and, though reluctant at first, she complies. Her tail wags and I think she's pleased to be going home.

Stupid me.

Spice man is sitting on the park bench again with his dog at his feet.

This time Shadow will not be deterred and bolts towards them. At the same time, Spice man's dog leaps up in anticipation of Shadow's arrival and I'm dragged along in Shadow's wake.

We reach them and despite my efforts to prevent it, Shadow and the other dog are soon entwined, wrapping themselves around each other, Shadow's tartan lead entangling itself with the string.

'Shadow,' I shout, to no avail.

Spice man looks up at me and I think he smiles, not that it lasts long.

I look down at Shadow and the white dog and they

look like a furry yin and yang sign, each with their nose to the other's tail, and their bodies close together.

'Shadow,' I shout again. No reaction.

'Sit, Betty,' Spice man says, sounding shockingly coherent for someone on Spice.

Betty duly sits.

Shadow does not, instead bouncing around like a mad thing and definitely not a dog who's been on a very long walk.

'If you can get your dog to sit, we can untangle their leads,' Spice man says.

'Shadow, sit,' I say, imitating his tone. No reaction from Shadow. I try again to no avail.

'Okay,' he says. 'This makes it tricky with your dog moving around so much.'

He's right, and Shadow is super excited and is now jumping around with her tail wagging making funny little barking noises, which I've never heard her do until now.

'If Shadow would just calm down,' he says, gently pushing on Shadow's rear end.

I swallow hard. I hate doing this.

'Sheba, sit,' I mumble. And Sheba sits. Little traitor.

'That's better.' He starts to untangle his string from my tartan lead. 'I thought your dog's name was Shadow,' he says, mocking me.

'It is. Or at least I want it to be. But she's a rescue dog and was previously called Sheba.' At the mention of her name Sheba tilts her head at me and I swear she smirks.

I don't know why I'm explaining myself to a druggie tramp who spends his days sitting on a park bench.

'And did you want to call her Shadow because she's black?'

171

'What?' Did I? Oh my God, he thinks I'm racist. 'No, no. It's because she darts in and out of the shadows.' Oh, how pathetic does that sound?

'Good, because that would be like me calling my dog, Whitey.' I swear he smirks but there's a bit of defiance there too.

I glance down at his dog, white isn't really how I'd describe her, more grubby, more off white, more creamy. 'Creamy.' It's out of my mouth without me realising. Creamy, isn't that what the Australians used to call mixed race Aborigine and white children? I'm sure I remember it from that film with Hugh Jackman and Nicole Kidman. Oh God, I am a racist.

Spice man looks at me and blinks several times. Maybe he's never seen that film and doesn't make the connection. Then he shakes his head. So maybe he has seen it. 'There you go,' he says, handing my lead back to me with a sigh. 'Hey, don't I know you?'

'I don't think so.' Oh my God he's seen me screech-singing on Facebook.

'You look very familiar.'

'I walk the park every day and you sit here every day, maybe that's where you know me from.' Why am I being so nasty? What's wrong with me? I can't blame him for Shadow's antics or my casual, unintended racism. And if he has seen me on Facebook, it's not his fault. 'Sorry,' I say. 'That was mean of me.'

He looks at me through his bloodshot eyes, looks me up and down even. 'Yeah. Well. I do know you. It'll come to me.'

'Thanks for untangling,' I say, pulling Shadow to heel and striding off.

I feel mean when I get home. Did he deserve that? Have I allowed myself to believe he's a drug addict when he may not be? Who knows why he sits on that bench? Not me. Does he sit there all night too? They lock the park at dusk, does he hide? Is he there through all weathers? Am I getting carried away with my assumptions?

Too many questions. I'll avoid him tomorrow. Whatever his problems are he doesn't need me being nasty and judgemental added to them. I'm supposed to be a caring professional. Then I remember his comments, and decide that he was just as judgemental as me, if not more so.

And when he remembers me from Facebook, he'll certainly judge me then.

I'm beginning to think going to that park is fraught with problems.

There's a knock on the door and when I answer it, it's my new retractable lead being delivered. Would it have helped today? Or would it have made the tangling situation worse?

'And as for you, you little traitor,' I say to Shadow. 'Just so we both know; your name is Shadow. Right. Shadow. Shadow, sit,' I command. And Shadow sits.

Another coat of paint on the wall and an evening in front of the TV – which will definitely be better once it's on the wall – lolling around on my lovely new sofa. I've even retrieved the rest of Ken's chocolates and am indulging myself as I stuff them into my mouth. It's only as I finish the last one – I'm going to feel sick later – that I notice Shadow has settled herself next to me on the sofa and gone to sleep.

'No,' I mutter, more to myself than Shadow. 'I don't want dog hair all over it, it's new.' Who am I kidding?

'I saw Spice man again today,' I tell Cat when I talk to her the next day. He's always sitting on that bench so seeing him in the park is almost unavoidable. Cat's rung to see how much I'm enjoying the new sofa.

'Give him a wide berth.'

'I did, I do. But Shadow has other ideas, she's attracted to his dog.'

'The one on the string?'

'Yes. They're like twins, in different colours. She belted over to them again, but I did manage to stop her getting too close, which was just as well, unlike yesterday when their leads got tangled up.'

'Oh yeah.' Cat says, but I don't think she's really listening, her voice has that air of disinterest about it.

'Yeah, he was crying, and I mean really crying, great bit sobs, snot and all. But silent. Amazing that.'

'Eugh. Probably the Spice.'

'I don't think he is on Spice, or anything else. He just looked so sad, well, no, heartbroken. I felt sorry for him. And mean.' He seems to be able to make me feel mean every time I see him.

'You don't know what he's on. It's not normal to sit and cry in the park, is it? Keep away.'

'I will.' But there have been times since September when I've cried in public, admittedly I've attempted to be discreet about it, but it has happened. Maybe, he just couldn't rein it in, or maybe he doesn't care.

'Still on for your date with Ken?' Cat says, pulling me back to the here and now.

'It's not a date, just dinner, with a friend.'

'Does he know that?'

'Of course he does.'

'I mean,' Cat continues, 'I know you're single and so he is, but do you really want to get involved with your erstwhile brother-in-law?'

'He wasn't my brother-in-law. Not officially, anyway.'

'Splitting hairs.'

'Look, not that you need to concern yourself, but I'm sooo not looking for a man. I've just got my independence, my own place, my own mortgage even, everything. I'm not looking for a man.' I'm not. I don't need a man.

'Good. Only the other day you didn't sound so sure.'

'It's just dinner.' It is. 'Did I tell you I bumped into my neighbours? They were on holiday when I moved in but they're back now, lovely, semi-retired couple. They said they'd pop in and let Shadow out if needs be when I'm at work.'

'That's handy.'

'That's what I thought.'

'What about the other side?'

'Oh, young couple with a toddler. Just said hello and nodded at them when I've been taking Shadow out.

'Anyone else?'

'No, not really. I think they're all out at work during the day.' It's true I haven't seen anyone else; the street is like a ghost town.

'Oh, got to go. We'll see you Sunday morning, bright and early.' She ends the call before I have a chance to reply.

When Ken arrives to pick me up it's with another bouquet of flowers and another box of chocolates.

'Wow,' I say. 'You're spoiling me.' And making me fat because I don't have the willpower to resist chocolates.

'Nothing is too good for you.'

I smile. I don't know what to say. I don't want him to say things like that to me.

'You look lovely,' he says, blatantly appraising me.

'So do you.' He does, male model lovely – I feel quite frumpy next to him – and he smells divine, better than me which is annoying because I'm wearing my favourite perfume and a dress I felt very pleased with, but now...

I climb into Ken's lovely two-seater car, expensive and elegant, just like him, and lean back in my seat. When he starts the engine there's an impressive roar; it feels as though we're preparing for take-off.

'I hope you like Italian.' How does he manage to make that sound suggestive?

'I do. It's my favourite.' He must know this, I'm sure I've said it in front of him. Probably moaned about it because Leeward hates Italian so we never went to an Italian restaurant together. His preferences were steakhouse, Chinese, Indian. And I do love pasta, definitely my favourite Italian dish, and I have been known to devour a whole pizza to myself given half a chance.

Once in the restaurant we're shown to the perfect table and it's obvious from the way the waiters talk to Ken that they know him. I bet he brings all his girlfriends here.

I study the menu, unable to choose between the many pasta dishes available. I'm frowning as I debate with myself; shall I have fettuccine al salmone or penne al gorgonzola or ravioli de pesca or...

'Let me choose for you,' Ken's liquid voice interrupts.

'Oh. Um.'

'Please. I know the menu well and I can definitely

pick the perfect dish for you. Let's skip starters so we have plenty of appetite for the main.' He smiles sweetly and I feel my stomach flip.

'Okay,' I say, wondering if this is a good idea.

He mutters something to the waiter, which I don't catch then turns his attention back to me.

A bottle of wine appears on the table and Ken pours us both a glass, his tiny, mine large. That's when I realise he's expecting me to drink damn near the whole bottle because he's driving and has already poured his quota.

'I can't drink all that,' I say, sounding ungrateful.

He smiles. 'Don't worry, we can take it with us.'

I don't think I like the sound of that either.

He raises his glass, prompting me to do the same. 'To Lauren, her new home and her happy new beginning.'

'Thank you.' Now it's my turn to smile sweetly. I am grateful, this is a nice gesture but I can't help remembering Cat's warning about Ken's intentions.

Our meals arrive. I stare at mine for too long.

'All right?'

'Yeah.' No. There is no pasta. None, not one tube of penne or piece of ravioli, nothing, just a big slab of meat and some vegetables and fried potatoes. I love veg, of course, but this is an Italian restaurant, what's the point if you don't have pasta. Whiney, ungrateful bitch. I smile a little too brightly and pick up my knife and fork.

'You'll love it. Veal. Melts in your mouth. I almost always have this when I come here.'

'Cool. Do you come here often?'

He makes that face that suggests he's thinking about his answer before laughing. 'Most weeks.'

With his numerous girlfriends, no doubt. I wonder if he chose veal for Suzi, for all of them?

What do I care?

'Yeah, usually during the day,' he continues, 'Business lunches, always impresses the clients.'

'I bet,' I say, cutting a tiny slither of my veal, which isn't my favourite choice of meat, in fact, I tend to prefer fish, but I don't feel I can say anything without sounding ungrateful. Why didn't I just refuse his offer to choose for me? Just because he's paying doesn't mean he can dictate what I eat. I pop the veal into my mouth. Oh God, he's right, it does melt in my mouth.

'Gorgeous, eh?'

'It is.'

'I meant you.'

'What?'

He looks at me, assesses my reaction, smiles. 'Just joking.' Then he laughs just as a waitress comes over to fill up our drinks.

She lets her eyes linger on Ken. I wonder if she knows she's licking her lips. He refuses a top up and so do I as there's nothing to top up, I've only taken the tiniest sip of wine so far. I ask for a jug of water and two glasses, she looks to Ken for approval. Damn cheek.

I agree with Ken that the meal is good, very good, because it is. I don't whinge about the absence of pasta and, in general I am gracious and charming. But I can't help feeling a little uncomfortable, manipulated even, especially when Ken suggests we share a pudding, he even has one already picked out.

'Oh, not for me,' I say, as pleasantly as I can. 'I'm full up from all that meat, lovely as it was, I'm stuffed.' I know stuffed doesn't sound very elegant, but I don't care.

'No problem.' He lifts up the wine bottle and moves it towards my glass.

'Oh, no more for me,' I say, putting my hand over the glass just as he pours. 'Oops,' I manage as we watch the red stain spreading across the white tablecloth, and I stain a napkin as I wipe the wine off my hand.

'No probs. We'll take it with us.' He puts the cork back in and plonks the bottle down.

'Would you like coffee?'

'No, thank you. Caffeine keeps me awake.'

He grins and, I think, he flashes his eyes. It's such a subtle gesture that it could be my imagination. Is this how he charms the ladies? Right on cue the waitress arrives – where's our original waiter, that's what I want to know – and, as she's asking about our order, I'm sure she winks at Ken.

'Just the bill,' he says, smiling at her and I'm sure I see her dip as her knees go weak. I know he's good looking, well, more than good looking I suppose, but really, what a way to go on.

Once we're in his car, and I have my seat belt on, Ken thrusts the wine bottle at me. It's two-thirds full and although I had more in my glass than Ken, I didn't drink it all.

'It's a super wine that,' he says, as I nurse the bottle on my lap.

'Yes, it was, very nice.'

'But you didn't drink it all?'

'God no. I don't want a hangover in the morning.' I try to keep my voice light, but I'm actually a bit annoyed with him. I feel as though he was trying to get me drunk. 'I've got an early start.'

'Have you?' He starts the great, roaring engine.

'Yes, Cat and Paul are coming round early tomorrow with some more furniture. I'm getting a table and chairs.'

'Cool. Maybe next time you could cook for me.'

'Maybe.' I smile. Yeah, and it will be pasta, pasta and pasta, masses of it.

As we pull up outside my house I already have my keys in my hand, having fumbled them out of my bag while juggling the wine bottle.

'I'd invite you in, but I've got this early start,' I say, watching Ken's face drop.

'But it's barely ten.' He pulls up his sleeve and shows me his rather lovely watch resting on his rather lovely wrist. God, he is so attractive.

He's Leeward's brother.

He leans in to kiss me goodnight and I make sure we exchange cheek kisses. I yank open the door and leap out as quickly as I can.

'I'll message you about that meal,' I say, sounding jovial. Then I stuff the wine bottle into the door pocket.

'You take it,' he says.

'No, I won't drink it. It'll get wasted. I don't really drink much.' Liar, liar.

'Oh. Ah.' I know what he's thinking, that after the wedding escapades I've become some boring teetotaller who can't handle the hangovers, but he couldn't be more wrong. I didn't dare drink too much wine, because I really cannot trust myself around Ken.

'Night.'

And I'm gone, inside my house and leaning against my front door just as Shadow comes bounding out of the kitchen to greet me.

Twelve

Cat and Paul arrive just after eight in the morning. I'm up and dressed, waiting for them. I answer the door with a great big smile on my face.

'You're up early.'

'You said you'd be here bright and early.'

'On your own?' she asks, looking beyond me.

'No.' I wait for her to react, which she does by frowning and narrowing her eyes. So predictable. 'Shadow's here of course.'

'No...?'

'No.' I shake my head and step aside as Paul brings in the first of the chairs.

'I think that's a good thing.' She pauses. 'Assuming that he didn't stay overnight and skipped off early.'

'I'm not going to answer that.'

'Why? I'm only looking out for you.'

'It's none of your business.'

'It will be when it all blows up in your face,' Cat snaps, pushing past me to instruct Paul as to where to put the furniture.

After they've finished I'm relieved to see that the table and chairs are really rather nice, certainly much better than I expected. They're wood and in the farmhouse style, the table legs have been painted off-white and there are even cushions on the seats. They straddle the line between shabby chic and naff. I'm going for shabby chic. Of the five chairs, one has arms, like a carver. I lean over and stroke the back of it, it looks very comfortable.

'There were two of those but Mum-in-law kept one for her bedroom.'

'Okay. Tell her thanks,' I say, hoping that if she decides to get rid of it, I'll get it.

'I will, but she'll hardly remember. They've been in our garage a year or more.'

'Why did she give them to you?'

'Lord knows. She dumps all her old tat on us. But I think I might have slipped up with this lot,' Cat says. 'They're better than I remember. Really rather nice.'

'Too late.'

I give my sister and brother-in-law the house tour before we all slump down on my new sofa with a cup of coffee each. Shadow slinks in and leaps onto my lap.

'Shoo, shoo.' Cat leans over and attempts to bat Shadow away.

'She's fine,' I say. 'Leave her.'

Cat shrugs. 'Your problem,' she says before taking a loud and noisy slurp of her coffee.

'I'm just going to go and put the car seats back up,' Paul says. 'Then we'll need to get going, Cat.'

Cat smiles her agreement and waits until Paul is out of the room.

'So, what happened?'

'When?' I tease.

'Stop it. Last night. With Ken.'

'He was very nice and the meal was nice even

though it wasn't what I wanted.'

'What do you mean?'

'Ken insisted on choosing for me. He chose veal, not pasta.'

'Oh no. I think that's a bit creepy.'

'I don't think he meant it to be creepy, but, yeah, I wasn't too impressed. You know how I love pasta.' Watching how her face contorts, I realise I'm going to regret telling her; I really should know better.

'I told you he was after you. He's just been biding his time, waiting until a decent amount of time has passed before he makes his move. Not that seven months is very long at all. You're going to have to let him down gently.' She waits for me to agree and when I don't immediately, she adds, 'Unless you're considering…'

'Maybe.'

'What? No.'

'He's very attractive. Very. You should have seen the waitress fawning all over him. It was almost comical.'

Cat frowns but doesn't say anything.

'I'll see how it goes.'

'Let him go,' Cat says, standing up.

'What do you mean?'

'You're hanging onto him because it still links you to Gollum.'

'Don't call him that. No I'm not.'

'Ready?' Paul calls from the door.

'Yeah, just coming,' Cat calls back before turning to me. 'Just let him go.'

'You're not the boss of me,' I say, trying not to snap.

'No. I'm not.' She arches her eyebrows. 'You are.' She marches out of the door.

'What's that's supposed to mean?' I call after her,

but she's already outside and leaping into the car. She gives me a big sister half-smile as she closes the door, then mimes eating.

'Ken's been a good friend to me,' I say out loud as I slump back down on the sofa and Shadow puts her head on my lap; she's now lying on the seat.

He has too, taken me out when I felt down, constantly reassuring me that Leeward was the loser. Telling me how beautiful I looked even when I felt ugly. He really complimented my new hairstyle, saying that dark brown and short really suited me. He even feigned happy surprise when I told him it was my natural colour. He's been there to listen while I whined on and on about what a mess my life was. He frequently reminded me that my whole life wasn't a mess, just one aspect of it and that would right itself eventually. And, of course, he played a part in my getting a fair pay out from Leeward when he sold his house. He's always been there for me, and unlike Cat, he isn't judgemental, or, if he is, only in a good, positive way.

No, says a little voice in my head, but Cat doesn't choose your food for you, does she?

Oh, I know he has feelings for me. At first, I could delude myself that he was just trying to make up for his brother's mess, but now, if I'm being honest, I know he likes me. Very much. No man tells a woman she's beautiful as often as Ken does without it meaning something. I can't remember Leeward ever telling me I was beautiful. The best he could manage was 'all right'.

'Shall we go out for our walk, Shadow?' It's nice and early so hopefully we won't bump into *anyone* in the park.

At the mention of a walk Shadow leaps up and wags

her tail.

It's barely ten am when we walk through the park gates and there aren't too many people about; the serious dog walkers have been and gone. I glance over to where Spice man sits every day and smile when I see that he isn't there. Excellent. I'm also pleased that he seems to have somewhere to go at night – even if he does look as though he sleeps on that park bench. The sun is starting to shine, the air smells fresh, and I feel good. I also have Shadow on the new extending lead which means I don't have to run like hell all the time.

I saunter along as Shadow scampers off and comes back and, in doing so, covers a lot more ground than when I run with her so she should be tired out before I am. Yes, I'm enjoying myself.

Life is good.

Even if I do have to go back to work tomorrow.

My parents are coming over later and Dad is going to put my TV on the wall. I think they're bringing Grimmy too, but that's fine because I now have a hard chair she can sit on.

It's all good.

'Hey,' a voice calls from behind me. 'Lauren.'

I hunch up, put my head down and pick up my pace.

'Hey, Lauren.'

'Nooo,' I mutter under my breath. I recognise those deep tones; it's Thor, as played by Leeward's boyfriend, Alfie.

'Hey, can't you hear me?' He's close now, too close.

I glance over my shoulder and feel relieved when I see he's on his own, his tiny dog tucked under his arm.

'Oh hi,' I say.

'Hey. I've been calling you.' He smiles his big smile.

He's wearing the brown leather coat again, the one I so admired on him the first time we met, before I knew who he was. Hey, hang on, I recognise that coat, it's the one I tried on from Leeward's wardrobe, no wonder it was so big. Oh. My. God. So Alfie was living there at Christmas.

'Sorry, I was miles away.'

'It's getting warm, isn't it?' He unbuttons his coat and flaps it about to let some air in. He's built like a brick…no don't think it… bodybuilder.

'On your own?' I ask.

'Yeah. Lee's a lazy lay-a-bed. We had a bit of a sesh last night.' He laughs. It's deep and throaty. 'To be honest I only got up to take this one out.' He wiggles his mini dog about. 'Almost pointless,' he says, laughing. 'Ten minutes and she's exhausted.'

I smile and nod. Lee never laid in bed when he was with me. Quite the opposite, always nagging me if I ever wanted to sleep in.

'I see you got one.'

I shake my head in puzzlement.

'Retractable lead.'

'Oh, yes. I took your advice. So much better, though this is our first walk with it.'

'Don't let it out too much or she'll wrap it around trees and things, that's what this little madam did, didn't you?' He lifts his dog to his mouth and kisses her nose.

'Okay. Thanks.' Now go away.

'How are you settling in?'

'Sorry?'

'Into your new house. You've just moved, haven't you?'

'Oh, yes. Fine. Thank you.' Did I tell him that I'd moved or did Leeward, or Kenton? Have they been discussing me? Has Leeward told him who I am? 'What about you? Haven't you just moved too?'

'Yes, a while back.' His voice is so deep it's almost a growl. He reaches up and pushes his hair away from his face; it's untidy and it occurs to me that he's just leapt out of bed, pulled on his clothes and come out.

I can see why Leeward finds him so attractive.

Get a grip.

'So how do you and Leeward know each other? Did you work together?' Thor smiles as he speaks and shows off his lovely teeth.

'Um, no.' So, he doesn't know. I watch his face as he waits for my reply, so earnest, so honest. 'We're old friends,' I lie. Well, I suppose it's not a complete untruth.

'Cool. We should get together for drinks or something since we're sort of neighbours, and we have our dogs in common.' He looks a little uncertain.

Wow, what an evening that would be.

'Did anyone ever tell you that you look like Thor, as played by Liam Hemsworth?' Why did I ask that?

'I think you'll find it's Chris Hemsworth.' He gives me a cheeky grin. I knew that, I *knew* that. Oh. My. God. If he wasn't my ex-fiancé's lover… What? Stop. Stop now. 'And, yes,' he continues, the grin getting broader, 'A lot of people say that.'

Course they do. Stupid me. Just go away, Thor.

'Is that you?' I ask as we both become of aware of a loud buzzing. I hope it's an emergency and he has to run off now.

'Oh, yes. My phone. He puts his dog down and rummages in his coat pocket, pulling out the phone and reading a message. 'Oops, better go. His lordship is awake and wondering where I am. Come on, Daenerys,

Daddy's waiting.' He laughs. It's deep and throaty. 'See you soon.'

Thank God for that. He picks up his dog and marches off, much as Thor would, taking giant strides.

It's just the little dog that spoils the image.

I wonder what Leeward thinks of being referred to as a tiny dog's daddy?

Taking Thor's advice, I wind Shadow's lead in a bit and carry on with my meander around the park. Shadow can still scamper about and use up her energy and by the time we're almost back to where we started, she's walking to heel and evidently tired. Then her nose goes up.

Spice man is back on his bench, his scruffy little dog between his feet.

I look around for an alternative route, a way of getting back to the gate without passing him. There really aren't any viable alternatives unless I press myself against the bushes on the other side of the path. Shadow wouldn't comply; I'll have to brazen it out.

I march, keeping Shadow on the side furthest from him.

'Morning,' Spice man says as I pass.

'Morning,' I mutter without looking at him, but the little traitor stops in her tracks and, with strength I didn't know she had, literally drags me back so she can exchange sniffs with Betty.

'Hello, Sheba,' Spice man says.

'Shadow. She answers to Shadow now.' I keep my eyes on her so I don't need to look at him. 'Oh, you have a proper lead now.' A brown leather one, no less.

'Yes. I managed to get some of my things back yesterday.'

I glance at him. Wow, what a difference, he actually

looks clean, or at least his clothes do. And, though they look too big for him, they're good clothes, not the mucky tat I've seen him in every day. If he hadn't just indicated that they were his I might have thought he'd been to the charity shop, or someone had donated them to him. His hair is still unkempt, his skin is still sallow, his cheeks are horribly sunken, the kind of sunken I recognise in the very old people at work, when they're just worn out and ready to die. His eyes are still pink-rimmed but in today's clear brightness I can see how blue they are. And sad.

'Cool,' I say. How naff is that?

'Yeah,' he says, patting his dog.

Shadow and Betty exchange sniffs but neither of them is as excited as the last time. Fortunately.

'Have a nice day,' I say as I walk away.

Have a nice day, what the hell is the matter with me? Why didn't I just add, 'Sitting on that bench and being homeless.' Or something equally crass.

The good thing is I'm not likely to see him again because once I'm back at work I'll be walking Shadow early in the morning and in the evening. Spice man can't sit here all day, not every hour the park is open, can he?

Mum and Dad arrive mid-afternoon, bringing Grimmy with them so she can inspect the new sofa, the one she *sort of* bought.

'It's very nice,' she says, her tone stilted. 'Not that I'll be able to sit on it.' She glances around the room.

'Don't worry, I have a better chair for you.' I rush off into the kitchen and return with the carver.

She appraises it, all her thoughts playing out on her face. There's surprise, evaluation and finally acceptance.

There's nothing subtle about Grimmy.

She sits down and, while Mum and I chat and Dad sets the bracket on the wall for my TV, she nods off, snoring gently in the chair.

'Seal of approval,' Mum says, laughing.

'Not quite,' Grimmy says, opening one eye. 'It's hard. What you need is a proper armchair with a remotey like the ones I have at home and at your parents. That would definitely get my seal of approval.' She's talking about her riser-recliners; the one in the corner of Mum and Dad's kitchen and the other in her own house. You press a button and it catapults you from sitting to an upright position in seconds, although it can seem like minutes. Even though the remote controls have their own special pocket in the side of the chairs, Grimmy was forever losing them, once ringing up Dad after midnight to tell him she was stuck in her chair. She's pretty sprightly for her age but she had put the chair in the reclining position and couldn't quite scramble out of it. After that Mum stuck them to the arms using Velcro. 'You can get them made to measure now,' she adds, casting a quick look at Dad, who pretends he's so engrossed in fixing a bracket to the wall that he hasn't heard her.

'Okay, Grimmy.' I really cannot imagine shelling out a thousand pounds on a chair that only Grimmy will sit in and only occasionally at that. Now she's seen the sofa that she's paid for I doubt she'll come round again. Cat says Grimmy's only been to her house four times in the last fifteen years, and then only because a family party was taking place there. Anyway, I don't want an old person's chair taking up room in my new home, I have enough of that at work. *Nasty Lauren.*

She closes her eyes and appears to go back to sleep,

but you never can tell with Grimmy. Mum, Dad and I are careful to keep our voices to little more than a whisper.

'I could have a new one at yours, Lisa,' Grimmy suddenly pipes up. 'Then you can have the old one here, Lauren.'

'Okay, Grimmy.'

Please. No.

Thirteen

I feel mean at the thought of leaving Shadow all day. Even though Mum has agreed she could pop round, she's very busy today taking Grimmy for a hospital appointment, not that Grimmy wants to go because she says all doctors are charlatans. We all think this is to hide her fear that they will find something wrong with her although this is only a check-up after she had a little fall months ago, and she blames that on an errant plastic bag finding its way to the floor and tripping her up. I can't really add to Mum's busy day, can I? Nor trouble my neighbours quite yet.

I'm showered, dressed, breakfasted and making my lunch for work – a lot of cheese and pickle sandwiches and two small Kit Kats, super healthy me, not – while Shadow is sniffing around in the garden. It's early and I'm leaving taking Shadow out for a walk so it's the last thing I do before I go to work. Judging by the garden it's quite fresh outside and overcast, so when I've done everything I need to, I pull on a raincoat and find Shadow's lead.

'Shadow,' I call her in from the garden, but she seems reluctant to come, perhaps sensing that she's going to spend the day alone. 'Come on, girl.' I jiggle her lead; that seems to do the trick.

It's 7.30am and my street is quiet, although several of the neighbours' cars have already gone. It's amazing how I'm noticing this as I haven't consciously been watching the neighbours, or their cars, I'm just aware of their absence. I set off at a pace with Shadow because I have to leave for work at 8am sharp.

We get to the end of the road and turn towards the park. I'm right in front of the gates before I realise that they're not open; the park doesn't open until 8am.

'Sorry, Shadow,' I say, under my breath. Shadow tilts her head and sits down in front of the gates. 'Come on, we'll have to walk the streets.' Now doesn't that sound comical?

After some urging Shadow trots along beside me as we march along and I can't help peering in windows as we go, nosy me. We pass homes where children are jumping around inside, some dressed and some not and I imagine the kind of raucous chaos going on, even remember it from my own childhood. Not that *I'll* ever have to worry about that.

I'm quite enjoying this alternate walk, it sates the nosy people-watcher in me, not that Shadow seems very enthusiastic. I haven't had to rein her in or let the extending lead out at all, though I have had to scoop her poop twice and am now carrying *two* poo bags at arm's length. We're just going down the last road before we turn back when I notice the large house on the corner; I'm sure it used to be a pub. I think it's one of those houses of multiple occupancy now judging by the *Rooms to Rent, Ensuite and Wi-Fi* signs outside. Someone, in the past, has obviously spent a lot of money on converting it as the windows and front door look smart and expensive and the rendering looks new. But, sadly, it has an air of neglect, rubbish strewn around the small courtyard front garden and the inevitable wheelie bins, lined up like soldiers in adjacent gardens, are hurled into the far corner.

Just as I get up close the curtains in the front room open and there, topless, is Spice man. I look away quickly. Did he see me? I hope not.

He is so thin. And pale.

I urge Shadow on and we pick up pace so I can get as far away as fast as possible, just in case he comes after me.

Don't be stupid, why would he?

At least I now know he isn't homeless.

Back home and Shadow looks forlorn and I find myself promising to take her out properly when I get back from work. Her eyes peer up at me from under a furrowed brow then she turns away. I think she's sulking. I feel guilty as hell as I lock the front door behind me and leave for work.

I've been at work an hour and am delighted to learn, during the handover, that no one has died in my absence. I always worry when I have time off that someone will pass away; logically I know that even if I'd been here it's unlikely I could have saved them, but even so, it's always a concern.

Maybe it's the time of year but all the residents seem to be in good health and other than doling out their regular medications I'm in for a quiet day. I do need to visit Elsie on the dementia floor because she needs her diabetic ulcer seeing to, but other than that, it looks like a slow ease into the working week.

'Good morning,' an unfamiliar voice says as I walk

past the day room.

I stop in my tracks and turn back, then go inside the room. A very dapper gent dressed in immaculate clothes is sitting by the window. His shirt is the whitest I've ever seen; his trousers are cream with knife-sharp creases. He wears a snakeskin belt, a neat cream pork-pie hat, and carries a wooden cane with an elaborate carved, bone handle. But it's his shoes that intrigue me, I've never seen the like before: *cream* patent leather.

'Hello,' I say, smiling. 'Who are you visiting? Perhaps I can…'

'No, no,' he interrupts, 'I'm here for the whole cruise. All the way round. Home port to home port.'

'Ah. I see.' So, he's a new resident. 'You look very smart,' I venture.

'Important to dress appropriately for the tropics,' he says, smiling. 'Do you know when they'll be bringing that cup of tea I ordered?'

'No, no. I'll chase that up for you.'

'Thank you, steward, most appreciated. And what lovely weather we're having today.' He turns back to the window and I wonder what he sees, certainly not the dull day I do.

I scuttle along to the kitchenette and ask about his tea.

'Oops, completely forgot,' one of the carers says. 'I'll do it now.'

'What's his name?' I ask, realising I hadn't asked him.

'Albert Evans, but we're to call him Mr Evans,' she gives me a sly smile.

'Okay.'

'He thinks he's on a cruise,' she says, setting up a cup and saucer.

'Better than being in a prison,' I muse. 'He looks very smart, really lovely. Don't suppose it'll last once his clothes have been through our laundry.' I feel sorry for Mr Evans, his clothes are obviously important to him.

'Oh no, we're not to wash them. His family will see to his clothes. They come every day. Four daughters and three sons and numerous grandchildren. There's someone here every day.'

'That's, um, good.'

Two things happen just before lunchtime; I get a message from Ken asking which day he should come for dinner – I didn't think I said dinner, I was thinking more tea; and a request to work late tonight.

I think of poor Shadow all on her own; I really don't want to work late.

'It's only an hour,' Clare the home manager says. 'It's just to cover Cheryl taking her daughter to the dentist.' She looks at me with pleading eyes, they remind me of Shadow's.

'But,' I start, 'I have to…' How can I suggest that my dog's walk trumps Cheryl's daughter's dentist visit? But to me, it does.

'Tell you what, why don't you take two hours for lunch? Would that make it easier?'

'Um, yes,' I ponder. 'That could work.'

Before I leave, I message Ken and invite him for tea tomorrow. He replies with a smiley face and several thumbs up. Now I have one day to work on my *letting Ken down gently* plan. Talk about putting myself under pressure.

Judging by her reaction Shadow is ecstatic when I arrive home in the middle of the day. She jumps all over me, yelping with excitement.

Outside it has warmed and brightened up, so rather than keep her waiting any longer I grab her lead and we head out to the park. I still have my lunch in my bag and I think an impromptu picnic might be rather nice.

Shadow is full of energy and I have to let the lead out a lot so that she can use that energy up. We've been around the park twice and I'm relieved to see that there is no sign of Spice man and his grubby dog. We're just on our third circuit of the park when I spot an exit I haven't noticed before; it's on the opposite side of the park to my house. This is the direction which Leeward and Thor usually head in. Before I know what I'm doing I've reeled in Shadow's lead and we're heading out of the exit. I don't really know what I hope to achieve.

Or why.

We march down a street similar to mine, then turn into another, then another. Then I see it. A new development, only half a dozen or so houses, bright and shiny in the sunlight. They're not big, but they are beautiful, with ample parking, wrought iron railings around neat little front gardens and discreet solar panels on the roofs. I just know that one of these detached beauties is Leeward's; I just don't know which one and because he must be at work, there's no sign of his car. Unless he has a new one. I spot the name of the road and it sounds familiar; didn't Leeward mention it?

I saunter past the row as nonchalantly as I can all the way to the end of the street before I cross over and walk all the way back on the other side. I can actually get a better look from here, especially if I walk Shadow on the kerb side and keep looking at her.

I'm barely halfway down the row when a front door

bursts open and Thor steps out with Daenerys tucked under his arm.

Oh shit.

I yank on Shadow's lead and attempt to hasten our escape before he spots us. I just hope he's getting into his car and not heading to the park.

I'm walking as fast as I can without actually running and I daren't look back in case he sees me; the end of the street is in sight and soon I will be able to turn the corner.

'Hey, Lauren,' Thor's voice is so close but I'm still shocked when I turn and come face to chest with him. 'How lovely to see you.'

'I'm in a rush now,' I snap back. Does that sound as untrue as it feels. And, I now know exactly which house is theirs.

'That's us over there.' He points. 'The one with the blue door. Hey, fancy popping in for a cuppa?'

Cuppa? He said cuppa. Bless him. 'Oh, I can't. Like I said, I'm in a rush. I'm on my lunch break from work, and I've already been around the park twice, just veered off the path for a change of scenery before I take Shadow home and head back to work.'

'Oh shame. Next time. In fact, next time you're passing, pop in.'

Oh God. 'Okay. Thank you.' I smile while at the same time promising myself that there will never be a next time. Never.

'Better get on,' Thor says, turning to cross back over the road. 'Got to pop to the shops before I go to work.' He rolls his eyes in a theatrical way and it makes me laugh.

'You can take your dog to work?' What sort of job is that?

'Yes, the girls in reception take her while I'm running a class. She's no trouble, are you, Daenerys?'

'I wish I could take my dog to work. Where do you work?'

'The gym, in town. You know, Sparks.'

'Oh right. I've heard of it.' I try to keep the emotion from my voice; it's the gym Leeward went to every day in the run up to our wedding. I already knew that the gym was where they met, just having it confirmed from the god's mouth hurts a little.

'Bye, Lauren,' he says, suddenly bending down and kissing my cheek.

'Bye, Th... Alfie,' I correct before making a fool of myself.

'You were going to call me Thor there, weren't you?' He laughs and he's still laughing as he walks across the road. 'Don't worry,' he shouts back, 'A lot of people do it. But I looked like this long before that Hemsworth actor.'

'Come on, Shadow,' I say, scurrying away with my dog, who has been sitting and watching and waiting.

Back in the park we finish our half circuit and head towards our own exit. The bench where Spice man usually sits is empty and in the sun. I still have my lunch in my bag and decide that here and now would be a good place to have my picnic. As I sit down, Shadow settles herself at my feet and closes her eyes, soon she's dozing. I let go of the lead, now full retracted, put it on the ground and put my foot on it.

I check my phone and see that I have almost an hour before I need to be back at work. I close my eyes. Bliss. I can hear the birds singing and smell the grass and I congratulate myself for enjoying a bit of nature. I'm glad Alfie didn't follow me into the park; he's nice, too nice, but I need to distance myself from him. I know that in different circumstances we could probably be friends; as he's already pointed out, we have so much in common. Mostly Leeward. Not that Alfie knows that.

Shadow's lead jerks beneath my foot. She stands up and her snout is up.

'Hey,' Spice man's voice says as he sits down on the end of the bench.

'Err, hi.' Oh shit. Just when I was enjoying a bit of peace and quiet. I finger the lid of my lunchbox, debating whether to stay or go home. I think go home is winning.

'What have you got in there?'

'Um, sandwiches.'

'What flavour?' He looks at me and smiles, he looks almost pleasant. Almost.

'Cheese and pickle.'

'Cool.'

Is he hinting, does he want one? He certainly looks as though he could do with a good meal. At least I now know he's not homeless but maybe Social Services have placed him in there and are paying directly for it and he doesn't have enough money for food. No, they wouldn't keep him so short he couldn't feed himself. Maybe he just wastes his food money on other things.

Spice.

Nasty judgemental cow.

'Would you like one?' I say, lifting the lid and offering the box over.

He looks at me, eye to eye, his are still bloodshot but there's something there, maybe a remnant of what he used to be before the drugs took hold.

'Can you spare it?'

'Sure. Go on,' I urge. It's true there are plenty because I used up the last of the bread, so I've made three when I would normally only eat two.

'Thanks.' He reaches over with his bony, and clean, hand and takes one.

I pick up mine and we eat in silence while Shadow and Betty, now less ebullient than usual, watch us. I'm still only halfway through mine when he finishes his.

'That was good. Thank you.'

'Have another,' I say, pushing my lunchbox at him.

'It's your last one.'

'Please. I haven't even managed to eat this one yet,' I say, half laughing and feeling both generous and patronising.

He takes the sandwich and finishes it just as I finish mine. He pulls a bottle of water, unopened, from his pocket.

'You first,' he says. When he smiles his teeth look clean, and neat and even. Not at all how I imagine a drug addict's teeth should look, all blackened and rotten like they do in those posters you see.

Stop it.

'Thank you.' I reach for the bottle. How can I not? I am grateful it's a new one. Unless he fills it up. But, no, I have to break the seal. I take a drink then pass it back.

He takes a swig then leans back on the back of the bench. 'I didn't realise I was so hungry,' he says.

'Would you like a Kit Kat?' I offer the lunchbox again.

He glances inside, sees that there are two and reaches in.

'You're very kind.' There's an edge to his voice.

He stuffs the Kit Kat in record time and takes another swig of the water. He offers it to me again.

'No, thanks. I'm fine.' I'm not, I'd love a drink to wash down that chocolate covered wafer which I know is sticking to my teeth – I'd normally have a cup of tea at work with my lunch – but I don't want to drink out of that bottle again.

'By the way, I'm Phillip,' he says. 'I think since you shared your lunch, we should share our names.'

'Yeah. Okay.' I don't want to tell him my name, I don't want a lunch friend. 'Lauren.' I smile as I say my name.

'Hello, Lauren. Was that you I saw this morning, walking Sheba, Shadow,' he corrects, shaking his head.

'Shadow,' I confirm. 'She answers to Shadow now.' At her name Shadow puts her front paws on my knees and I rub her ears.

'Cool.' He leans over and pats her and the little traitor drops down and trots over to him and rests her head on his lap. His own dog then does the same. 'It's okay Betty, you're not being usurped.' He pats both dogs' backs.

Usurped. That's a big word for a Spice addict.

Stop it.

'So that was you?' He returns to his question. 'This morning. Holding your dog's dirt bag in front of you.' He mimes my hand held out as it had been this morning.

'Yes. Two poo bags actually. I had to take a different route; the park wasn't open.' I feel the need to explain, I don't want him thinking I was looking for him. Why would he think that?

'Well, you saw where I live, now you know why I spend so much time here.' As he speaks he looks into the distance.

'Didn't look that bad.' Patronising.

'Not that bad. Just one room with my own shower room. But small. The kitchen is shared. Not nice.'

'You don't look like you bother much with a kitchen.' Shut up.

'No. Sort of lost my appetite lately.' He glances at my empty lunchbox on the bench between us. 'Getting it back a bit now, maybe.'

I smile and nod and feel stupid. He looks at me with expectation in his eyes. Say something, say something that isn't patronising.

'Have you been ill?'

He studies me for a long time. Too long. I never mentioned drugs, I never implied anything. Did I?

'I remember where I know you from.'

I brace myself, waiting for him to comment on the Facebook video.

'You work at that care home in town.'

'Nursing home,' I correct, although the difference is too subtle for most people to know or care. I smile my relief that he hasn't mentioned Facebook.

'Yes. Sorry.' He smiles. Is he patronising me now? Serves me right. 'My grandad's in there.'

'Really. Who? I probably know him.' Of course, I know him.

'Archie Porter.'

'I know Archie. Really, you're his grandson? I can hardly believe it.' I really can't.

'Yeah.' He looks away. He looks as though he might start to cry and I don't want to witness that. I can see him gulping back his emotion, his Adam's apple going up and down as he swallows.

'He's lovely, your grandad, such a nice man. It's so nice he has such a big family to visit him,' I gabble.

'Not so big now,' Phillip says, standing up.

Oh God, someone has died. I've put my foot in it.

'I'm sorry,' I say, stuffing my lunchbox back into my bag, picking up Shadow's lead and standing up.

Phillip looks at me and half smiles. 'Don't worry, no one's died. Quite the opposite really.' There's a look of defiance in his face, a dare almost. I'm not going to ask. It's none of my business.

'Better get back to work.' I let Shadow's lead out a little.

'Yeah. Me too.' He gives a bitter little laugh.

'Oh, you work?' It's out of my judgemental mouth before I can stop it.

'Off sick.' Another bitter laugh. 'Until I can sort myself out.' He shrugs.

'Oh. Right.' I nod as though I know what he's talking about and I'm on his side. I am, of course I am, he's coming off drugs, he should be commended. 'Good for you.'

He frowns. Then smiles.

I turn to walk away. 'Hey, Phillip,' I call back. 'I have a friend round tomorrow for dinner, nothing special. Why don't you join us?' What am I doing?

He stares at me for a while before he answers. 'Okay. Thank you. What time?'

'Six.'

He nods.

I give him my address before I scuttle away as fast as I can.

What the hell is wrong with me?

Fourteen

Ken arrives early, my hair is still wet from the hasty shower I took when I came home from work. He glances at it, but wisely chooses not to comment. He leans in and kisses me on each cheek; he smells divine, he looks divine too. I wonder if I am being hasty in my decision to push him away.

He holds another bouquet of flowers and a bottle of white wine. I accept his gifts with grace and wonder if he will take them back after this evening is over, though I still haven't quite worked out what I'm going to say, never mind how.

'This looks very elegant,' he says once we're in the kitchen, indicating my dining table which I've laid with a schmancy tablecloth Mum no longer uses. There's a pile of cutlery and some mats because I haven't had time to set the table.

'Thank you. Would you like a glass?' I hold up his wine bottle.

'No, thanks. Not for me. I'm driving.' Ah, his intention is for me to drink it all. Again. He really isn't very subtle. I put the bottle, unopened, in the fridge.

'I've made a pasta Bolognese. I hope you like it.' I do hope he likes it, but, at the same time, I don't care if he doesn't.

'Oh yes. I'm easily pleased.'

I stir my pan, slowly mixing the meat sauce and pasta together. 'It will be ready right on time,' I say, pointedly. He doesn't reply. 'I saw Alfie yesterday when I was out with Shadow,' I add, and it sounds quite out of the blue.

'Oh.'

'Yes, we took a different route on our walk and I ended up outside their new house. Very nice. Have you been there?'

He hesitates for a moment. Of course he's been there, why would he not?

'Just the once,' he replies.

'Is it as lovely inside as outside? Or is it full of Leeward's dark furniture and blackout curtains?'

'No, it's really rather glamorous. I think Alfie has taken over the interior design. You know, silver mirrors and pale grey furnishings. In fact, I didn't see anything dark at all.' For someone who's only been there once he's very familiar with the detail.

Shadow comes bounding in from the garden and stops in her tracks when she sees Ken. She barks several times at him.

'It's all right, girl,' I say. 'It's Ken.' Shadow gives Ken one final bark before slurping nosily from her water bowl then flopping into her bed in the corner.

A forced smile flashes across Ken's beautiful face.

I turn back to the pasta and stir it some more.

The doorbell goes. Ken twitches. Shadow barks.

'Excuse me.' I smile as I leave the kitchen.

'Hey,' I say as Phillip stands before me. He has Betty

with him. 'Come in, come in.' He looks even more presentable than he did yesterday. I think he may even have attempted a shave.

'Is it okay if I bring her in? Or would you prefer me to leave her outside?' He glances around for somewhere to tie her.

'No, no, bring her in. I'm sure Shadow will be delighted to see her.' As Phillip steps inside, and passes close to me I can smell shampoo or shower gel. He's definitely made an effort.

Betty bounds into the kitchen ahead of us and jumps up at Ken's legs, barking and yelping. He steps back in an attempt to escape her.

'Down, Betty,' says Phillip. Betty immediately stops her antics.

'Two dogs.' Ken bends down and starts wiping the dog hairs from his trousers while Betty slinks off to join Shadow in her basket. They twine themselves together repeating their yin-yang pose.

'Sorry about that,' Phillip says, glancing at Ken before looking at me.

Ken offers a tight smile.

'Ken, meet Phillip, and, err vice versa.' I laugh and sound a bit like a maniac.

The two men nod at each other, I suspect there won't be a great friendship developing here. They're almost the same height, both tall, but there the similarity ends. Ken is super-groomed and fills out his expensive clothes with his muscle and power; Phillip is thin and pale and, although his clothes are fine, they hang limply on him.

Ken looks at me for an explanation.

'Oh, sorry, Ken, I forgot to say I'd invited Phillip too. The more the merrier, eh.' I turn back to the pasta, if I stir it anymore it will be whipped, so I stop and go over to lay the table.

Ken watches me closely; I can feel his eyes boring into my skin. He's probably wondering what I'm playing at; I'm wondering too.

'Perhaps I will have that glass of wine,' he says, his voice deliberately lazy as though to hide his irritation.

'Good idea.' I make my voice as bright as I can. 'What about you, Phil?' Inwardly I cringe. I've just called Phillip Phil, I've offered him a drink when I don't know what his problem is, if it's not drugs, then it's probably drink. What was the phrase he used? *Sort myself out.* Definitely substance or alcohol abuse. And I've really pissed Ken off.

Why did I invite Phillip?

What the hell am I doing?

'Yes, thanks, Lauren,' Phillip says.

I grab wine glasses and pour us each a generous amount and take them over to the table.

'Sit down, please. I'm about to dish up.' I scuttle back to the cooker.

When I come back with their plates, they are sitting either side of the empty seat, my seat.

'I hope you're hungry.' I plonk the plates down.

'I'm starving,' says Phillip. 'This looks really good.'

Ken doesn't compliment my cooking, instead he reaches for the salt and pepper.

'I have some parmesan.' I dash over to get it.

'Just like in a restaurant,' Phillip says, his voice super cheery. Is he trying too hard? Ken isn't trying at all.

I bring my own plate over and start to eat as fast as possible. I gulp my wine too. I am really regretting inviting them both together. Whatever possessed me? Stupid impulse, that's what, and judgemental guilt.

'So how do you two know each other?' Ken puts down his knife and fork and stares at Phillip, waiting for his response.

'In the park,' Phillip says. 'Well, it was the dogs really. They get on so well.'

I glance over at Shadow and Betty, they're nuzzled together, asleep. It's actually a good thing that Betty is here otherwise Shadow would be begging under the table, I don't think Ken would like that.

'So, you met fairly recently?' Ken smiles as he asks, he already knows the answer.

'Yes, just last week. Is there anymore, Lauren?'

'There is.' I stand up. 'What about you, Ken?'

'This is plenty for me, thank you.' He picks up his fork and pushes a single piece of pasta around the plate.

'You can finish it if you like.' I smile at Phillip and hope he agrees because he could definitely do with a good feed.

I pour the remains of the pasta onto his plate and take it back to the table. The portion is almost as big as his original. His eyes widen.

'Don't worry if you can't finish it.' I sit back down and continue eating my own. Ken lays his cutlery on his plate and pushes it away; he's only eaten half.

'So, Phil, what do you do?' Ken smiles across the table.

'I'm a quantity surveyor.'

I almost choke on my pasta. A quantity surveyor. Is that true?

'Self-employed?' Ken is going in for the kill, using just two words to imply that Phillip makes no money, and is self-employed because no one would employ him.

'No,' Phillip replies, his voice normal, seeming not

209

to suspect malice. 'I work for Reynolds. Been there fifteen years.'

'Really? Reynolds?' From his tone I can tell Ken doesn't believe it. Reynolds is the biggest building company in town. They're independent but they build *big stuff*, apparently. I only know this because, when he left university, my brother Sam was desperate to get a job there, with no success. He works for the council now.

'Do you like it?' I ask, dreading the answer.

'Yeah. It's fine. Pays the bills.' Phillip half laughs. I smile back at him and find myself confused. This Phillip doesn't seem at all like the one I met in the park last week. That one was surly, dirty, scruffy, and crying in public. He's certainly cleaned up his act. Maybe he's on a high, or something.

Stop it.

'Where do you live?' Ken asks. This is starting to sound like an interrogation.

'Near here. Rooming at the moment.' Phillip rolls his eyes. 'I'm just waiting to get my house back. The tenants are moving out soon.'

'Where's that? Your house.'

'Leyland Avenue.'

'Leyland Avenue?' Ken repeats, his voice a mixture of incredulity and annoyance. 'I live in Rokeby Avenue. We must be near neighbours.' He drops this on the table like a challenge. Every local knows that Leyland Avenue runs into Rokeby Avenue.

'What number?' Phillip scoops up the last of his second pasta portion.

'42.'

Phillip screws up his face in concentration. 'The brown house?'

'Yes.' Ken looks smug. I don't know this Ken either. Where is the lovely man who's let me weep on his shoulder so frequently?

'I'm just around the corner, number 18. Passed your house every day on my way to work.' He smiles. 'Small world.'

'Isn't it.'

'Anyone like a dessert? I have trifle. I didn't make it,' I babble. 'It's M&S, we have a food hall near us at work. Very handy.' I pick up our plates, stack them together and take them away before returning with the trifle and bowls. 'Help yourselves to trifle. Any more wine for anyone?'

Ken declines, citing driving again, but Phillip says he'll have half a glass. Half a glass? Would someone with a drink problem only have half a glass?

'You sure you wouldn't like more?' I'm testing him, aren't I?

'No. Thanks. I need take Betty out before the park closes. This trifle is really good, by the way.'

'Good old M&S.' I say, sounding both coquettish and childish. 'Haven't you already been to the park?' As in sitting there all day.

'No. I haven't had time today.' He smiles. He looks genuine. Innocent.

'What time does it close?' Ken asks, calculation in his voice. I know what he's thinking; the sooner Phillip goes the sooner he can move in for the kill with me.

Or maybe I'm deluding myself.

'Eight.' Phillip takes a swig of his wine. 'Nice wine that.'

'Thank you,' Ken says, too quickly and too smugly for my liking.

'Eight,' I say, 'Oh, I didn't realise it was so soon. I

211

haven't taken Shadow out yet. I've been at work all day. She's only been in the garden.'

'I can take her if you like, Betty would like that.'

Out of the corner of my eye I see Ken cast a snide look over at the dogs.

'Would it matter if Shadow didn't go out for a walk, just this once?' he asks.

At the mention of the *W* word Shadow jumps up immediately and comes to my side with Betty close behind. They both bark and wag their tales.

'I think that answers that question,' Phillip says, laughing. 'I'll take them together. No problem.' He finishes the last of his trifle, lays his spoon back carefully in the bowl and stands up. 'Where's her lead?'

'I'm so grateful,' I tell him, as we stand at the front door while he clips Betty's lead on. I've told him not to let Shadow off her lead in case she runs away. 'When you come back, come in and finish off that wine. I don't want to drink the rest alone and Ken won't have anymore.'

'No. I won't, thanks. I've got a busy day tomorrow. Want to have a clear head.'

'Oh?' I try to make my voice sound neutral but open to more information. None comes.

I watch him walk down my front drive and along the street a little, a dog lead in each hand. Whatever dark and heavy weight he carried on his shoulders seems to have lessened slightly; his walk seems confident, strong.

'Interesting friend,' Ken says when I go back to the kitchen, raising his eyebrows in such a way that I know if I say just one critical thing about Phillip, then Ken will add ten.

'He is.'

'I suppose he'll be back at eight.'

'I hope so, I don't want him running off with my dog.' It's a joke, but the minute I've said it I wish I hadn't. Is that possible? Don't be silly, I know where he lives.

'Interesting him having a house near me; he doesn't look the sort.'

'What sort is that?' I ask, somewhat irked.

'Well, he looks a bit…' Ken pretends to search for the right word, but I know what he's thinking. 'Scruffy. Unkempt.'

'Doesn't mean anything.' I start loading the dishwasher.

'No, but I can't see Reynolds… well, you know, they have… standards.'

'Don't we all?' I move onto wiping the worktops and the cooker top.

'Would you like more wine?' Ken says, picking my half full glass up from the table.

'No. Better not. Work tomorrow.'

He puts the glass down.

'I was wondering,' he starts, looking at me with his intense, dark eyes, 'If you'd like to go out again. Another meal. Your choice of restaurant this time.'

'Um,' I say, wondering exactly how to tactfully turn him down.

'We could split the bill if you prefer. Like we used to.' He's referring back to our many outings when I lived at Mum and Dad's, when Ken was a truly good friend.

'I don't know.' I look him straight in the eye. This requires honesty. And tact. 'I mean, I don't know what you're expecting of me.'

'What do you mean?'

'Well, you've been… are,' I correct myself, 'The

greatest friend a woman could want, especially one who's been through what I have with your brother, but…' I've run out of tact now.

'But?' He's not going to make this easy.

'But I'm not…' Stop. I was about to say I don't want a boyfriend but Ken has never said he wants to be my boyfriend. Maybe I'm getting a bit carried away, maybe I've listened to Cat too much. 'I love having you as a friend but, as I said, I don't know what you want.' Ball firmly back in your court.

'Friendship, of course.' He looks affronted. Ken does affronted very well, I've seen him do it before, with Leeward, with their mother, Jayne, with soon to be ex-girlfriends. So, I'm going to take him at his word.

'Excellent. Because that's what I want. Friendship. Pure and simple. Because, I am *sooo* not looking for a man.' I giggle, it sounds appallingly false.

Ken nods slowly and a little smile, which doesn't look heartfelt, plays on his lips.

'Coffee?' I ask, filling the kettle.

'Sure.'

A loud rap on the front door interrupts any more awkwardness, or so I think.

'Have you told your new friend that you're *sooo* not looking for a man too?' Ken imitates my comment.

'Who? Phillip. No, of course not. He's not interested in me. He has enough woes of his own.'

'Really? I did wonder. What…'

'I better get the door,' I cut in before Ken gets a chance to ask his question. I've already said too much and I don't even know what I'm talking about. I'm just glad I haven't mentioned Cat's suggestion that Phillip was on Spice, even though I did believe it myself for a while.

'You were quick,' I say as I open the door to Phillip.

'Yes, sorry.' We perform a little smiley grimace which manages to convey apology and question at the same time. 'There was an incident in the park.'

'Oh. What?' I immediately glance down at Shadow and Betty who are both sitting to attention by Phillip's feet. 'Come in, come in.'

'Yes, these two ganged up on another dog.'

'Oh no. I hope they didn't...' I start as we shuffle along the hallway and into the kitchen.

'No. Don't worry. I stopped their little antics. I've given them both a good telling off.'

Ken doesn't attempt to suppress his snort of derision. I throw him a stern look.

'What happened? Is the other dog all right?'

'Oh yes, I stopped it before it began really, but it could have been bad because the other dog was tiny.'

I have a horrible sinking feeling in my stomach. 'She wasn't with a big guy who looks like Thor, was she?'

I hear Ken snort again and when I glance over at him, he has his hand over his mouth hiding his smirk, though not very well. He knows exactly who I'm talking about.

'No. She was with a little guy with starey eyes.'

'Did you get the dog's name?' I ask, dreading the answer.

'Yes. Daenerys. And the guy's name is Lee. He was fine about it. No harm done.' He hands over Shadow's lead and after I've removed it, I point to her bed. She slinks off without any objections. She knows she's been naughty. Of all the dogs in the park why did they pick on Daenerys?

'That would be my brother, I think,' Ken says, his voice dripping like syrup. He is so enjoying this.

Phillip looks intently at Ken and then frowns. 'That little guy? Your brother? Really?'

'Well, he has a small dog called Daenerys and lives on the other side of your park, so it seems likely.'

'This was a tiny dog, not just small. A Chihuahua, I think.'

'Yes, that's Leeward,' I mutter. 'He's Ken's brother.'

'Well, small world.' Phillip smiles over at Ken. 'You're not at all alike.'

'No,' Ken says, his tone and face expressionless.

'Would you like a glass of that wine?' I ask Phillip, hoping to change the subject.

'Oh, no, thanks. I need to get off. Early start and so on.' He gives me a shrug and a nod as though I know what he's talking about then turns back up the hall towards the front door. I follow him.

'Thanks for taking Shadow out,' I say as I open the door and he steps out.

'No problem. Well, not one that I couldn't handle anyway.' He laughs.

'Yeah.'

'Hey, sorry if I've spoiled your evening with your boyfriend.'

'He's not my boyfriend,' I say quickly. 'Absolutely not.'

'Oh. Okay. Sorry, I got the wrong end of the stick.'

'No, he's just a friend.'

'Okay. Well, thanks for the meal.'

'You're welcome. We'll do it again.' Why am I saying that?

'Okay. Night.'

'Night.'

After he's gone, I lean against the front door and catch my breath. Ken slinks out of the kitchen and catches me.

'Everything all right with your friend?'

'Yes, fine.' I smile and start back to the kitchen. 'Shall we have that coffee?'

'I won't,' he says, pulling on his jacket. 'Work and all that.'

'Yeah, me too.' It feels doubly awkward now.

'Goodnight, Lauren,' he says as he opens the front door. 'Message me with your choice of restaurant and some dates you can do.' He leans over and kisses me, very pointedly, on the forehead. I feel immensely patronised.

'Will do,' I say, waving at him as he leaves, promising myself that I will not message him.

'He described Leeward's eyes as starey,' I tell Cat on the phone ten minutes later. It's not even 8.30 and my tea/dinner party seems hours ago.

'Yeah,' she says. 'They are.'

'Really? Have you always thought that or has it just occurred to you now?'

'Always,' she says, sounding bored. 'Bit creepy, you know.'

'Really? I've always thought of them as deep and soulful. Maybe they've changed.'

'Mmm, maybe. It sounds like an entertaining evening. That's what you get for inviting druggies into your home. What are you like? What are you playing at? He knows where you live now. And Ken sounds well, like Ken...'

'You don't like Ken either though, do you?'

'I'm not fussed on him. Just be careful. That's all.'

'I've told him straight; I'm not looking for a boyfriend.'

'And he took it well?' She half laughs.
'Yes. He understands. He does.'
'Then that's fine, isn't it?'

Fifteen

The next few days pass without incident, I don't bump into Phillip, or Leeward and Alfie in the park and no one dies at work.

Saturday morning looms and I allow myself the prospect of a lie in. Except Shadow has other ideas, which is why I find myself at the park gates just after eight, watching the council man jump out of his van, unlock the gates, jump back into his van and drive off, all without so much as a nod in my direction.

Happily, I don't see anyone for the first fifteen minutes, not even one other dog walker, which is good because I'm not looking my best. I haven't even had a shower this morning because of Shadow. I'm going to luxuriate in the bath when I get back and have a bit of pamper morning. We've been round the park twice and are heading for home when I hear the familiar boom of Thor's voice behind me. I quicken my pace, yank on Shadow's lead in an attempt to urge her on but the little traitor is deeply involved in a sniffathon with a tree stump and is lagging behind me. Normally she'd be racing ahead and pulling me along.

'Hey, Lauren,' Alfie calls. Of course he's spotted me,

he's Thor with his godlike instincts. Why does this always happen when I look like crap? Will I never learn to always be box-fresh even when I take my dog out for an early morning walk. And I desperately need the loo now.

'Hey,' I call back, barely turning to acknowledge him while urging Shadow forward. Out of the corner of my eye I can see he's not alone. Please don't let that be Leeward. Please no. I start to wind in Shadow's lead.

'Lauren,' a voice says, and it's horribly close.

I turn slowly, careful not to show too much of myself.

'Hi Ken,' I say slowly. What? There they are, the three of them; two brothers and one lover. Leeward offers a half smile.

'You're out early for a Saturday morning,' Ken says. He, of course, is looking super fresh and handsome.

'So are you,' I snap back, still trying to encourage my dog towards the exit.

'We're having a family day out, early start,' Alfie says, his voice bright and guileless. 'Ken's driving us but we had to walk Daenerys first.' He bends down and strokes his dog's ears.

'Cool,' I mutter into my chest. 'Though I don't know how'll you all fit in Ken's little car.' I laugh, though no one else does.

'I have more than one car,' Ken says, his voice so superior.

'Yeah, we're visiting the new baby; Lee's brother and his wife have a little girl. Then we're off to a big family lunch with the mother-in-law.'

I stop and turn properly to face them all. Alfie is beaming his delight; Ken is looking away and Lee is frowning his annoyance at Alfie for being so indiscreet.

Not that Alfie knows he's telling me things he shouldn't. And, it would appear, they've made it up with Jayne too.

'Oh, that sounds nice.' There's an edge to my voice which neither of the brothers misses. 'Mother-in-law? Are you and *Lee* married now?'

'Not quite,' Alfie says as Leeward shifts awkwardly and starts glancing around looking for an escape. 'But I was proposed to last night.' He beams and holds out his hand to show me his ring.

Oh God. I want the ground to open up and swallow me. Here, right now. Then I see Alfie's face; the pleasure, the sheer joy and happiness spreading across it. I step forward and take his hand. I pull the ring up to my eyes so I can get a better look. It's manly but beautiful, a diamond set in a thick, solid platinum band. I remember the credit card payment to Leeward's favourite jewellers for our wedding rings, I wonder if he took them back or had one resized to fit Alfie's immense hand.

'Stunning,' I say, smiling. 'Congratulations.' I turn to Leeward. 'To both of you.'

'Thank you,' Alfie says, his smile, already immense, actually increasing. 'I wasn't expecting it, not at all. But this one surprised me.' He grabs Leeward's hand, pulls it up to his mouth and kisses it. Leeward looks mortified, Ken attempts to look passive but doesn't quite pull it off. I wonder if he can feel my pain, and my anger.

'Well, have a lovely day,' I say and force the biggest smile onto my face. 'And wish Steve and Sian all the best from me, and congratulations to them too, of course.' I turn and walk away and as I do so I can feel Leeward's and Ken's eyes boring into my retreating back. I glance over my shoulder and toss them a look, a look that says far more than words ever could. Alfie, meanwhile is playing, innocently, with Daenerys.

He doesn't have a clue. I would enlighten him but it would serve no purpose other than spite on my part.

After lying in the bath and spending far too long faffing about with my hair and makeup, I find myself in the kitchen enjoying a lazy brunch. Shadow is asleep, the sun is shining, the garden looks green and lovely – maybe a bit too green, I'll have to think about trying out that mower Dad has left in the garage – and, if I'm honest, I'm a little bit bored. I might pop round and visit my parents, I can even take Shadow with me, they won't mind.

I'm just securing the car dog harness and clipping Shadow in when a message arrives from Ken. It's overlong, wordy and quite pathetic. He goes on about this morning's encounter as being awkward for him, and embarrassing all round, except for *poor* Alfie who's innocent in all this. He hopes I won't do anything to make the situation worse – by that I suppose he means tell Alfie the whole story – and says that he, Ken, is stuck between a rock and a hard place. I wonder who's the rock and who's the hard place?

I don't reply because my instinct is to tell him to fuck off.

As I drive round to Mum and Dad's I think about what Ken has said. It might have been better if he hadn't messaged me. It might have been better if I hadn't bumped into them in the park. And it definitely would have been better if Leeward hadn't just asked Alfie to marry him.

But, I remind myself; I'm done with Leeward. There

is no going back for us. It's well and truly over. As the song goes – I will survive. I am surviving, more than surviving; I am thriving.

It still hurts though.

When I get to Mum and Dad's, Dad is out and Cat is sitting at the island unit chatting to Mum who is already making rounds of sandwiches. Is it lunchtime already? Judging from Grimmy's eager face as she watches Mum, I think it must be.

'The prodigal returns,' Cat says, laughing. 'Have you run out of food?'

'No. Shut up.'

'You can get in line for a sandwich,' Grimmy croaks from her corner. 'I'm first.'

'I'm not hungry,' I say, letting Shadow out into Mum and Dad's garden.

'I see you've brought the Heinz with you,' Grimmy says.

I refuse to comment, but it brings to mind my first bumping into Leeward in the park when he asked what *that* was when referring to Shadow.

After everyone has stuffed their sandwiches, Grimmy nods off in her chair and Cat, Mum and I sit in the garden with a pot of tea and a piece of cake. I *have* managed to find my appetite for cake.

I tell them about my surprise park meeting this morning.

'What?' Cat says, inhaling cake crumbs and nearly choking. 'You've got to be joking. Engaged? Really? Hasn't he learnt his lesson?'

'What do you mean?'

'Well, you know…' Cat stumbles over her words. 'It's not even a year since your wedding…'

'Well he obviously loves Alfie more than he did me.'
I can feel my throat catching.

'More fool him, then,' Mum says.

'I thought I was over him. But this morning, I… I
just wanted to die, just for a moment.'

'You're better than that, better than anyone,' Cat
says, patting my shoulder.

'I know. I know. But, it's just that, you know, it's
bad enough being dumped for someone else, but when
that someone else is of the opposite sex, it, well… it
stings.'

'Stinks, more like,' Cat snaps. 'Anyway, he didn't
dump you, you dumped him and in spectacular fashion
too.'

'Yeah, but humiliating, for me as much as him.'

'And you really think that this Alfie has no idea
what's gone on?'

'None. He's so sweet and friendly towards me. He
thinks I'm just an old friend of Leeward's.'

'It's a shame they live so close to you, all this
bumping into them isn't helping anyone, is it. And he'll
find out eventually. He's bound to. Someone should tell
him, poor sod. I almost feel sorry for him.' Cat sits back
and folds her arms.

'Well, it's not going to be me.'

Neither Mum nor Cat reply to that and we sit in a
sad silence suddenly broken by a croaky voice.

'Am I getting any of that cake? Or is it just for you
young ones?'

'You fell asleep, Grimmy,' Cat says, jumping up. 'Let
me help you back to your seat and we'll sort out your
tea and cake.'

'Why, what are you talking about that you don't
want me to hear? I hope you're not thinking about

putting me in a home. I don't like the sound of that one you work in, Lauren.'

It's my turn to jump up. Grimmy looks worried, genuinely afraid. I suppose when you're her age being put in a home, against your will, is something you dread.

'No, Grimmy, we're not talking about you. We're talking about Leeward and his new lover.'

'Oh, that. Gollum.' Grimmy turns to go back to her chair while Cat and I shuffle along with her and Mum cuts her a piece of cake and pours out a cup of tea. Once in her chair, her grim smile returns now that her worst fears are not being realised. 'Is he getting married again?' she asks with horrible prescience.

'How did you know? Were you listening?' Not that it matters, why shouldn't she know? It really doesn't matter, does it?

'No. Never heard a word. Doesn't surprise me, that's what happens. They go off and marry quickly. Seen it so many times in the past. Thank you, Lisa,' she says as Mum puts her cake and tea on the little table in front of her.

'Yes but, Grimmy, Leeward's marrying a *man*,' Cat cannot resist saying. I thump her on the arm; there is no need for our nonagenarian great-grandmother to hear that.

'Doesn't surprise me,' Grimmy says as our mouths drop open in shock. 'He always seemed a bit bent, a bit queer to me. And he has very shifty eyes.' She takes a sip of her tea followed by a bite of cake.

'I used to adore those eyes,' I say, mostly to myself as I wander back out to the garden.

'Let me read that message again,' Cat says, sitting down next to me and reaching for my phone. 'That

Kenton is a duplicitous bastard too, isn't he?'

'What could he do? Cut himself off from his own brother? Would you do that to me?'

'No. I wouldn't. But I also wouldn't be sniffing around your ex either, would I? Get him out of your life. And soon. I told you no good would come of keeping in with Ken.'

'Actually, you told me to keep him sweet, which I did.'

'Yes, and I subsequently told you to ditch him, which you haven't. How are you going to reply to this message?'

'I don't know. Maybe I won't bother.'

'That's no good. He'll see that as an invitation to pop round and explain in person and you don't want that.' Cat's fingers fly over my phone. 'There,' she says, handing it back.

I read Cat's reply. *Fuck off, tosser.*

'Cat,' Mum says after reading the message over my shoulder. 'That's not very nice.'

'No, it's not, but it is appropriate.'

I don't know whether to laugh or cry.

'I'm not sure if the ring wasn't recycled,' I say quietly.

'One ring to rule them all,' Cat sniggers. Then Mum joins in, then so do I. We're soon cackling away like the witches from Macbeth.

'Jayne can recycle that outfit and her headdress,' Cat says, gasping for breath between her words.

'Maybe the venue will give them a discount for repeat business?' I add, sounding as catty and bitchy as I feel.

'You could lend them your bridesmaid dresses,' Mum joins in, then puts her hand over her mouth,

226

shocked at what's just come out of it.

'Muuuummm,' Cat and I chorus.

Laugh or cry? I'm choosing to laugh.

But I do feel sorry for Alfie, he's as much a victim in this as I was. And, I fear, he's going to find out the whole sorry story sometime, but definitely not from me.

Fortunately, Ken doesn't reply to Cat's message.

It's midweek at work when I pop in to see Archie, he's still got that cough.

'It's nothing,' he says. 'Really.'

'I'm going to get you more antibiotics, stronger ones.'

'There's no need. They did make my guts ache, that last lot.'

'I'll mention it to the doctor,' I say, knowing that stronger ones will probably make his guts ache more. To take his mind off his cough and the prospect of more drugs I change the subject. 'Hey, I met your grandson,' I say, realising then that I haven't seen Phillip since our meal at my place with Ken.

'Which one? I have so many.' He grins.

'Phillip. And his dog, Betty.'

'Ah, Phillip. Yes. How was he?' Archie's face drops and I begin to wish I hadn't mentioned him now.

'Yeah, good, I think.' Which isn't a complete lie, he was definitely better than he'd been on the previous occasions I've seen him.

'He's had a tough time.' Archie nods his head slowly. 'A very tough time.'

'Well, hopefully he'd over the worst of it now.' He certainly looked and sounded to me as though he had stopped taking whatever it was that had dragged him down, now I think about it, even his pallor had improved.

'Not the sort of thing you get over quickly,' Archie says, his voice soft. 'It's been hard for all of us. He loved that little girl. We all did.' He takes his large white handkerchief from his pocket and dabs his eyes before blowing his nose; he then has another coughing fit.

I really wish I hadn't brought it up. In trying to distract him from one nasty thing I've inflicted misery on him with another, and it's not helped his cough either.

'I'd better go and organise those antibiotics,' I say, edging out of the door.

'Thank you,' Archie says, though I don't think I deserve his thanks.

I hope Phillip is okay. I hope the fact I haven't seen him for over a week isn't a bad sign.

Or maybe he's got his house back and isn't using this park anymore. That'll be it. I hope.

Sixteen

Ken arrives two nights later with yet more flowers and wine just as I'm heading out of the door with Shadow for her evening walk. He looks sheepish.

'I'm surprised to see you,' I say, hovering on the doorstep while Shadow strains to get away.

'I thought I owed you an apology.'

'No need. Don't worry.' I step out of my front door and start to pull it closed behind me.

'Please, at least accept the flowers and wine.' He looks at me with pleading eyes.

I step aside and let the door swing open. He pops his apology gifts in the hall and steps back outside. I slam the door shut.

'Are you going for a walk?'

I don't even answer that, just raise my eyebrows at him. I'm afraid to say much in case I'm really rude, although Cat's message was really rude and that doesn't seem to have put him off.

'I understand why you were so angry with me on Saturday,' he says, keeping pace with me as I march towards the park. 'I know how it must have seemed to you.'

I don't answer, just keep walking with my dog.

'And I totally understand why you sent your reply.'

I don't correct him; I don't tell him I didn't send it.

'Even if it was rather crude and vulgar.'

The cheek of him.

'But I do understand how it must feel to be you.'

'Huh, I don't think so.'

We've reached the park and for some inexplicable reason and even though I've never done it before, I let Shadow off the lead and watch her run like hell.

What have I done?

'Shadow,' I shout as she bounds away.

She stops, turns, looks at me, then bounds further away. I start to go after her but Ken grabs my arm and despite my attempts to shrug him off, he stops me from chasing Shadow.

'I have to get my dog,' I snap.

'She'll be fine. She's a dog. They always come back.'

'She's never been off the lead before.' I turn back to where Shadow just was and can see no sign of her. 'Look what you've done. I've lost her now.' My breathing is increasing and I am starting to panic. I feel hot and sweaty and cold and clammy all at the same time. What if she's run out of the park and onto the road? What if she's been run over? 'I need to find her.' Ken lets go and I start to run to where I last saw her and Ken follows me.

'You're overreacting. She's a dog. She'll come back,' he says again. 'And if she doesn't you can just get another one.'

I stop. Even though I want to keep running, keep looking for Shadow, I'm so shocked, I stop.

'What? What?' I shriek.

'Well, they've got loads, haven't they, at the dogs'

home place.'

I'm not a violent person, apart from scraps with my siblings, especially my younger brother when we were kids, I've never hit anyone. But the resounding slap from my hand across Ken's face both horrifies and satisfies me.

And it's not just for Shadow, either.

'You mad bitch,' Ken says, rubbing his face.

'Fuck off, Ken.'

But Ken just stands there, his hand on his face and a kind of madness in his eyes.

'Lauren,' a voice calls from a short distance. 'Look who I've found.'

Phillip is walking towards us with Betty and Shadow trotting along together as though nothing in the world is wrong.

I rush towards them.

Betty's lead is threaded through Shadow's collar and the two dogs have their heads held high and are wagging their tails in unison.

'Did you let her off?' Phillip asks, smiling. 'Lauren, are you all right? You look red and…'

'Thank you,' I blubber and bend down to Shadow. 'You naughty dog,' I say, letting out little sobs of relief. 'I thought you'd got run over.'

'It is a worry when they run off, she's obviously not quite ready for freedom.' He takes my lead from me and clips it to Shadow's collar before unthreading Betty's lead. 'There you go,' he says.

'Thank you, thank you so much.' I'm starting to feel calmer now, my heart isn't racing anymore and the cold sweat is evaporating.

'No problem. Nice to see you, but I see your boyfriend is waiting for you.'

'What?' I snap, turning to see Ken still standing on the path where I left him. 'He's not my boyfriend,' I yell.

'Okay,' Phillip says, taking a backwards step. 'Nothing to do with me. I don't want to get involved.' He turns and walks away.

'Phillip, wait,' I call after him. He stops and glances back, a polite smile on his face. 'Thank you, again, and I'm sorry I snapped.'

'Okay, bye then.'

'I said she'd come back.' Ken is suddenly next to me.

'No thanks to you.'

'Come on, Lauren. Your dog is fine. Let's put all this behind us.' His voice is so liquid, so seductive it would be easy to agree with him.

'It's not just my dog, though, is it?' I sound like a petulant child.

Ken doesn't reply, doesn't even look at me.

I let a bit of Shadow's lead out and encourage her to walk on as I stomp along behind her. Ken, after waiting for a second or two, turns tail and leaves.

I can't pretend I'm not relieved.

I stomp around the park for at least an hour, my head spinning with everything that has gone on, as Shadow scampers about in and out of the trees and across the grass. I've let her lead out to maximum and hope I won't regret it. Nearly losing her earlier has made me realise that I need to train her properly. She needs to learn to come when called not run for the hills like a mad dog.

I finally turn to head for the park exit and home when I see Phillip sitting on the bench with Betty. I can't really slink past without him seeing me.

'Hey,' I say as I approach.

'Hi. Shadow behaving now?'

'Yeah.' I plonk myself down on the other end of the bench while Betty and Shadow snuggle together making their familiar furry yin-yang shape.

'Sorry if I was snappy earlier, it's been a bit of an evening.'

He offers me a cautious smile. It lights up his face. His eyes shine. If he put on a bit of weight, he'd probably be quite attractive, especially as he's now sporting a brand-new haircut. Then the smile fades and I remember what Archie had said about Phillip having a tough time and I want to ask him about it but I can't.

'Do you know of any dog training classes? I think Shadow needs some.'

'I don't,' he says.

'Oh, how did you get Betty to be so obedient?'

'I trained her when she was young. She's seven now, so knows how it works. How old is Shadow?'

'Three, I think. I don't know her full history.' I give a little shrug and look away. When I look back Phillip has his phone out and is flicking through it. It's a flash phone too. I know I shouldn't be surprised but I am. 'There's one at the church hall just down the road here on Wednesdays,' he says, passing the phone over to me.

'It looks perfect,' I say as I skim over the information. 'Just what you need,' I tell Shadow. I pass the phone back and fumble my own phone out of my pocket so I can look it up myself.

'Give me your number and I'll message you the link,' Phillip says.

'Okay. Thank you. That was quick,' I say as a message pops up immediately after I've told him my number.

'Not me, I'm not that quick. I haven't sent it yet.'

233

It's from Ken.

Please accept my apologies. I keep messing up with you. I know you're angry with the world but let's stay friends. We were such good friends.

I groan.

'Everything okay?'

'Not really.' I sigh. 'It's all such a mess.' I sigh again. 'I thought by getting my own place, by being on my own, you know, just me and my dog, a new start and all that, that life would be easier, better, but... I don't know...'

'Yeah, I know what you mean.' Phillip's voice sounds less whingey but more bitter than mine.

'I'd better go, you don't want to hear my whinging.' I stand up.

'I'm a good listener, if it helps.'

'You're all right, I've got my sister on speed dial to whinge to.'

'You're lucky.' He sounds wistful.

'Come on, Shadow.' I try to coax her away from her best friend.

'Well, the offer's there.'

It's very tempting. It might be good to get someone else's perspective on it, someone who doesn't know me or Leeward or Ken, or Alfie for that matter. But how can I add to Phillip's burden? Whatever it is, it sounds serious.

'Thanks,' I say, still trying to persuade Shadow to come.

'It might distract me from my own troubles.'

I look at him and, from the expression on his face, I'm not sure he meant to say that.

'Really?'

'Really,' he says, sounding emphatic.

I drop down onto the bench next to him and wonder where to start. Then it all comes out in a great big long moan fest, reminding me of my download to the solicitor, but that was many months ago and there's a whole new chapter to be told.

'That's where I recognise you from, as well as the home,' he says when I stop to draw breath. 'The video. I saw it. Very funny.' He laughs. 'Very funny.'

'Yeah, it went viral. I've never found out which bastard posted it either. I thought the song was brilliant at the time, until I saw it the next day on Facebook. In my head the words were perfect, they rhymed, they were clever, I was in tune. It sounded *so* good.'

He's pursing his lips to prevent himself from laughing.

'Then I fell off the stage and broke my wrist.'

'Oh, no.' He lets a little snort out and even I can see the irony and the funny side of it. Despite myself, I laugh along with him.

'All round, it was the worst day of my life and I thought I'd put it behind me until I moved here and bumped into them in *my* park. Repeatedly. And did I tell you they're getting married?' I follow this with another little laugh, a kind of manic one.

'Yes, several times.'

'And of course, Ken is a further complication in all this. I don't know what to do about him. I feel guilty, you see, because he's been such a good friend, but I don't know if I can trust him anymore. I think he wants something more than friendship. And he's wasting his time because no matter how good looking he is and all that, I am NOT looking for a man, least of all my ex's brother.'

'Are you sure he wants more?'

235

'Well *you* thought he was my boyfriend.'

'True. I did.'

'Why? What made you think that?'

'Just the way you are around each other, you know, easy, familiar.'

'Ah. Cat says he's just trying to get into my knickers.'

Phillip laughs again, it's really loud and I must admit it makes me laugh again myself.

'Sorry. I bet you wished you'd never asked.'

'No, it's good to know that…' He stops, clamps his lips together and looks away. He isn't laughing anymore.

'What?'

'Nothing. Really.'

And now it feels awkward.

'I'd better go.' I stand up and pull Shadow's lead. She disentangles herself from Betty and after several goodbyes we leave.

As I walk away, I cringe. Phillip now knows my whole tawdry story and the ongoing mess of it and God knows what he thinks of me. I was trying to present myself as this together, forward looking, independent woman and now I just look like a right mess.

I wish I'd never said anything.

As I round the corner at the top of my street, I can see Ken's car is still outside my house. Perhaps if I do several circuits around the block he'll give up and go home. I pull on Shadow's lead but her eyes are almost popping out of her head as she strains on the lead to go home; she's probably thirsty and so am I after all that talking.

Ken spots us and jumps out of his car. There's no escaping now.

'Did you get my message?'

'Yep,' I say, attempting to march past him.

'You didn't reply.'

'Nope.' I twist my shoulder so I can turn into my front drive.

'Can we discuss it?'

'I'd rather not.'

'Look, you have to understand that he's my brother and you're my friend.'

'Yep.' I manage to sneak around him and pull my keys from my jacket pocket.

'Please, can we just discuss it?'

I'm inside my house now and although Ken is close behind me, he hasn't stepped over the threshold; I could easily shut the door in his face.

His flowers and wine are still on the hall floor.

I turn back to him to say goodbye, to make it clear that this is the end.

'Look, Ken, I don't think this is a good idea.' I move to shut the door; he puts his foot in it, stopping me. 'Really?'

'Please can we just talk?' He sounds both pathetic and beguiling. It's quite a talent. I wonder if he uses this to get his own way all the time? He's the middle child, younger that Steve, older that Leeward, he's had a whole childhood to learn the art of manipulation.

'What's the point?' I lean on the door but he doesn't remove his foot.

'I'd just like you to see it from my perspective, to understand how I feel.' He blinks several times; his pleading is annoying me.

I shake my head.

'I just want you to understand. To forgive me. With all your brothers and sisters, your immense family, you must understand that I have to be loyal to my brother, he's my family. Anyway, I'd have to answer to our mother otherwise.' He smiles and takes a breath to start again.

'I only have one more sibling that you,' I cut in; irrationally, his referencing my family as immense annoys me.

At that moment my neighbour comes out, apparently to put a tiny bag of rubbish in her bin. Is she just nosy, or genuinely concerned for me?

'Then you understand how close we are,' Ken says and I can just see that he won't go away and he won't shut up. My neighbour is hovering in her garden. Do I want my dirty washing aired in public?

I step aside and let the door swing open and march towards the kitchen. Ken follows me in, closing the door behind him.

'Is it all right if I use your facilities?'

'You know where the loo is,' I say.

When he comes back he smiles his big, beautiful Ken smile. He certainly got the looks in their family. In my family we look similar, you can instantly tell we're related. I suppose that comes from having the same parents, both mother and father. But Ken and his brothers, there's basically no common feature they share, not height, not build, not hair and not skin colour. Jayne certainly put it about when she had her sons and, as she reminded me frequently, brought them up all by herself.

'Any chance of a coffee? I've been waiting for you for ages.'

'No. I don't do coffee this late in the evening, it stops me from sleeping. You can have a glass of water the same as me, if you like.'

'Oh. Okay. Thanks.'

I get two glasses and overfill them from the tap. Ken's is still dripping when I plonk it down on the worktop in front of him.

'Thanks,' he says after he's gulped half a glass back in one go as Shadow watches him nervously from her basket.

'Did you have a nice family lunch the other day?' I don't think in the whole ten years I was with Leeward that we ever did a family lunch, not with his side of the family.

'Yes. It was fine.' He reads my face and continues. 'It was Alfie's idea; he likes that sort of thing. He wanted to be friends with our mum.' Now he rolls his eyes.

'He knows nothing about me.'

'No.' Ken's voice goes up a notch in alarm. 'You're not going to tell him, are you?'

'No. I'm not. But someone should. He will find out eventually. Then how will he feel?'

'Not my problem.'

'No. Well, that's all right then. You can always step in to pick up the pieces like you did with me.' I cross my arms in front of my body as if to stop myself from exploding. Ken being here is making me feel particularly nasty and I just wish he'd driven off before I came back.

'Oh, Lauren,' he says with a sigh.

I keep my arms folded and I don't reply, just staring at him instead.

'I'm sorry, I'm piggy in the middle here but I can't just dump my brother, can I?' He looks at me for agreement. I give him none.

'You wouldn't,' he continues with another sigh. 'If it

was your sister. Anyway, you've always known that I was extremely fond of you, right from when you first met Leeward.'

I shrug.

'You can't pretend you didn't notice.' He waits for me to agree again. I don't.

'Oh, come on,' he says, sounding annoyed. 'Who was it who repeatedly told you, still tells you, how beautiful you look even when you patently don't? Who helped you through the fallout after your wedding went tits up? Who's been here for you? Me, that's who.'

'Yes, and I am grateful,' I say. 'You've been a good friend.'

'Friends. Of course. But I thought it was deeper than that. I thought you understood how I felt about you.'

'I've always thought of you as a brother.' I watch his face fall as I say these words, but they are true. Even though I might have been tempted, just a tiny little bit, the rational, sensible part of me always knew that it would never go any further than friendship. Not for me.

'Oh, come on, Lauren. Grow up.'

'What?'

'Did you think I've helped you all this time, had your snotty nose on my shoulder so you can cry about my loser brother, helped you get a fair pay off from him, just so we can be friends? Really? Did you?'

'So you did all that just so you could get in my knickers?'

'Don't be so crude. I've been the perfect gentleman, haven't I?' He waits for an answer and this time doesn't continue until I respond.

'I suppose so.'

'Well then. I have never done anything ungallant.'

It's hard not to laugh when he says that, only Ken could say *ungallant*.

'No, you haven't.' I bite back a smirk.

'Well… now it's time to…' he stalls, even Ken cannot continue.

'What? Pay my dues?'

'I wasn't going to put it like that, but…'

'Ken, no.' I hold my hand up. 'Stop. We've both been going along misunderstanding each other. I've always thought of you as my friend, as a brother as I've said before. I'm sorry if you thought otherwise. I really am. And, of course, I don't expect you to choose me over your brother, it's just that when I saw you all together, it brought back memories and it hurt. But no, I wouldn't choose you over Cat, so I do understand. But everything else… no. We are just friends. I'm not looking for another relationship. I'm done with men.'

He smiles. 'I'm sure I can change your mind.' He steps forward, I step back. Is he really going to attempt seduction when I've just told him clearly how I feel?

In her basket Shadow starts to growl and a look of irritation passes over Ken's face.

The doorbell rings.

Ken and I freeze. Shadow barks several times.

'Your nosy neighbour, no doubt.'

The doorbell rings again.

'I'd better get it.' I push past Ken on my way to the front door.

I pull the door open wide expecting to see my neighbour but it's Phillip's thin face that greets me.

'Hey, Lauren. You left your phone behind.' He passes my phone over the threshold.

'Oh, I hadn't even missed it. Come in. Come in. *Please* come in.'

241

Phillip frowns as he follows me to the kitchen where Betty skips around Ken and heads straight for Shadow's water bowl. The two dogs then yelp their excitement.

'Hi, err, Ken, isn't it?' Phillip says, and I don't know whether he genuinely has forgotten Ken's name or is just doing it for effect, for me, but I take a perverse pleasure in it.

'Yeah,' Ken says, his tone dismissive.

We stand in silence, Phillip and I, half smiling, Ken spoiling his beautiful face with a scowl.

'Am I interrupting something?' Phillip says, looking straight at me.

'No,' I say.

'Yes,' says Ken.

'No. Ken was just going, weren't you, Ken? I'll see you out.' I gesture towards the front door and Ken takes the hint.

'This isn't finished,' he says at the front door.

'It is, Ken. We want different things.'

'Right, so I've served my purpose then. Now you're ready to move on.' He glances back down towards the kitchen. 'With him? Really?'

'Not with anyone. I've said this once, I'll say it again: I'm not looking for a man.'

Ken leaves without another word. When he gets into his car he slams the door, starts the engine then revs hard up my tiny street.

I think he might be angry.

Seventeen

'Thank you for turning up like that. It was starting to get nasty.'

'Okay. I only brought your phone back.'

'I know.'

'Do you want to talk about it?'

'Huh. Do you really want to hear it? It's just a continuation of what I was whinging about in the park. I feel mean though, I feel as though I've used him. He probably thinks that too. He probably thinks I'm Super Bitch.'

'You? No. That title has already been awarded.' Phillip whistles for Betty after dropping this opener so I use his tactic.

'Do you want to talk about it?

'Ha, maybe some other time.' He follows this with a thin smile. I'm curious, or is it nosy? Either way I feel his pain and since he listened so patiently and without judgement to me, even made me laugh at myself, I feel I'd like to return the favour.

'Whenever you're ready.' I hope I don't sound too eager; I certainly don't want to pressure him.

'Yeah. But like you I suspect, I have work in the

morning.'

'Cool,' I mumble, because I don't know what else to say. It does explain the haircut.

'Yeah. Kind of. Phased return.' He stops, smiles then bends down to clip Betty's lead on. I follow him to the front door.

'Good luck with work,' I say as he steps out.

'Thanks.'

'Tomorrow your first day back?'

'Yeah. Three half days this week. Five next week. Then see how it goes.

'Cool.' Can I really not think of anything better to say?

'See you around, probably in the park.'

'Yeah. Bye.'

After he's gone I wish I'd invited him for tea again, but would it look like I'm just trying to find out what's gone on with him? Or would he think that having despatched Ken, I was now coming onto him?

No, because as even he knows, I am *not* looking for a man.

The rest of the week passes in peace, no dramas at work, no dramas at home. I hear no more from Ken and I hope that he understands and doesn't feel too bad about it all. I also don't see any more of Phillip in the park and I just hope that work isn't proving too difficult for him. Archie, his grandfather, seems finally to be responding to the latest antibiotics and his cough is definitely improving.

The weekend is soon upon us and, hurray, so is payday, it seems to have been a long time coming. I am going bed shopping. No more sleeping on the single blow up bed from my childhood. Although I do have quite a tight budget so I hope I'll be able to afford what I want, if not it will have to wait until next month.

I've had a good look on IKEA's website and seen something I like at a price I can afford. I was tempted to just order it, but Cat fancied a day out and has insisted that I view it in person. So that's my Saturday. Mum has even offered to look after Shadow after I said I was thinking of taking her with us, but as Mum pointed out she'd just be sitting in the car all day. I suppose I could leave her at home, but it feels mean when I do that every day when I am at work, even though it doesn't seem to bother her.

After dropping Shadow off I zoom round to pick up Cat and we're soon on our way. IKEA is only a twenty-minute drive up the bypass, so it's nice and easy.

'I think I might have the meatballs,' Cat says, leaning back in her seat.

'What?'

'For lunch. I love their meatballs. I know everyone says that, but they are great.'

I laugh. Honestly, if you could see my sister you would think she never actually ate food, just lived on supercharged air, she's so slim.

'I think it was about there,' I say, pointing ahead at a horribly familiar piece of grass verge.

'What was?'

'Where I stopped and read all of Leeward's and Alfie's porny messages. And pictures.'

'Oh. And that's where you also got grass stains all over the arse of your dress.' Cat seems to be fully embracing her new sweary self, and I think I have to take the credit, or blame, for that. I've never heard her swear so much as she has since my sorry wedding day.

'Yes.' I give a little ironic laugh. 'Just about sums up

that day really; grassy arse stains.'

'Never mind. You're past all that now. Onward and upward.' She pauses. 'Heard any more from Ken?'

'No. Thank God. I do feel bad about it though.'

'Don't. He's probably moved onto someone else by now.'

'Cat, that's a horrible thing to say. He's not like that.'

'He so is,' she says, laughing. 'I do wonder how you can be so naïve sometimes. I suppose it's all those years with Gollum.'

'Don't call him that.'

We pull up into the IKEA underground car park and head for the entrance.

'We should have lunch after we've done the furniture bit, then I want to go to the marketplace. I could do with some new glasses and I like the ones here because the kids don't seem to able to break them so easily. Or maybe we should start with a coffee and cake?' Cat has already mapped out our whole day.

'It's 10.30 and we've only just got here.' I roll my eyes.

'Okay. But lunch will need to be early. Probably better anyway, get in there before the hoards descend. At least it's not raining today so there won't be quite so many families just here for a day out and the lunch.'

'What are you talking about?'

'Well that's what we used to do when the kids were little. The lunch here is such good value. It's a cheap day out.'

'Are you insane? Nobody comes here unless they need to buy something.'

Now it's Cat's turn to roll her eyes. 'So naïve,' she mutters.

It doesn't take me long to find the bed I've chosen

online; it also doesn't take me long to discount it. It's just not right, but I do find another I like better, even if it is more expensive.

'Told you,' Cat says, her face so smug.

'All right, smart arse.' I pull my phone out and take a photo of it as well as the item number. 'I'll have to wait until next month.'

'Why?'

'I'm on a tight budget and this bed, no matter how lovely, is out of it. Come on, I can still afford my lunch.'

'How much out of your budget?'

'Too much.' I yank her arm to pull her away from the bed department. I can't pretend that I'm not disappointed but on the other hand, it won't kill me to wait. Another thirty nights on the blow-up bed isn't exactly perilous.

'I'll pay the difference.'

'No.'

'Yes. It will be your birthday present, so don't expect anything on the day.'

'I've just had my birthday, you bought me perfume and bed socks, remember?'

'Christmas then.' She laughs and picks up the order ticket, pops it in her pocket, links my arm and we head for the restaurant where Cat has meatballs and I don't.

'Right, ready for my favourite bit now,' Cat says as we leave the restaurant and she pulls me towards the escalator going to the marketplace where she grabs a trolley.

'A trolley? I thought you were just getting a few glasses.'

'I am. I can hardly put them in a yellow bag, can I? Anyway, I'm sure there are other things in here I might

247

have to have.' She winks at me and I shake my head. That's the trouble with IKEA, you can always find things that you must have that you didn't know you needed.

Twenty minutes later and we're still salivating over anything and everything when Cat spots something. She laughs then points it out to me.

'Isn't that can opener like yours.' She winks again; I'm beginning to think she has a twitch.

'Oh yeah,' I say, picking one up and examining it.

'You too?' says a deep voice from behind me.

I freeze. I cannot believe it. I just cannot believe it. Cat looks up at the speaker and her mouth drops open. Before I turn around, I use my finger to lift Cat's dropped jaw back up. Her eyes widen. She appears to be speechless, which is a first for her.

'Hi,' I say as I turn to face Alfie, who, mercifully seems to be on his own. 'Fancy seeing you here.'

'I know. What a small world. We'll have to stop meeting like this.' He laughs. Then he turns to Cat who is still staring at him. 'Hello. I don't think we've met.'

'Sorry,' I say. 'This is Cat, my sister, and this is Alfie, Leeward's fiancé? Is that the right word?'

'Certainly is,' Alfie says. 'And lovely to meet you Cat.' He offers his bear paw to shake.

'Hhhi,' Cat stutters. 'Did anyone ever tell you…'

'I look like Thor,' Alfie finishes for her. 'Yes, frequently, but as I told Lauren, I looked like this long before that actor.'

'What are these like?' Alfie picks up a can opener. 'We need one. We used to have one, I swear it was just like this, then it went missing. Lee says it went missing in the move, but I think it was before that.' He rolls his eyes in a theatrical way. 'We've been using the cheap one I already had ever since, but frankly, it's crap.'

'These are very good,' Cat says, now fully verbal. 'Lauren has one, it's brilliant, isn't it, Lauren?'

'Yeah.' I turn away from Alfie's innocent face. I could hit Cat right now.

'Lauren was just trying to convince me to buy one, weren't you?'

'Yes.' I edge closer to her and I think I might stamp on her foot if she opens her mouth again.

'I think I will,' she continues. 'I just can't decide which colour. Owww,' she yells as my heel makes contact with her toes.

'Sorry,' I say, narrowing my eyes at her.

'Yours looks like this but it isn't this make, is it, Lauren? Yours is a more expensive brand, isn't it?'

'Yes, I think the one we had was too, but it's gone.' Alfie picks up a can opener then, undecided, puts it back.

'Lauren, Lauren, is that you?'

Cat and I stare at each other. We both recognise that voice, last heard on my non-wedding day when the owner painted us up as drag queens.

'It is you. And Cat too.' Suzi jumps into our little group. 'Fancy seeing you here.'

'Hi Suzi,' Cat and I chorus.

'Wow, do you two know each other?' She points a finger at me, then Alfie, then swings it back and forth. 'Is it not a bit awks?' She grins.

'No,' Cat and I snap together.

'Anyway, what brings you here?' Cat is trying hard to keep Suzi from saying any more about Alfie, me, Leeward, the whole sorry mess.

'We just popped in on our way to lunch. Alfie was wittering on and on about a lost can opener and we were just approaching IKEA and I had a brainwave, didn't I Alfie? I said, let's pop into IKEA.'

'Yes,' he says, giving us all rather a quizzical look. 'I wasn't wittering though, was I? I mentioned it once.'

'Well, it looks like it's paid off, because here you are with the can openers. Haven't you chosen one yet?'

'About to.' Alfie's curt response suggests that he's not too fussed on Suzi.

'I think the whole world is here today, I've just seen someone from work. So funny. What are *you* buying?' Suzi now addresses her questions to us.

'Oh, just kitchen bits,' Cat says. 'I can't decide which colour can opener to get. What about you, Alfie. Red is nice. Lauren has a red one.' She hands Alfie a red can opener.

'Yes, I think I will.' He drops it into his yellow IKEA bag. 'I might get another one, a different colour, for Daenerys's tins.'

'Good, then we can be off.'

It's slowly dawning on me that Alfie and Suzi are going out to lunch together, but they can't be on their own, not judging from Alfie's face whenever Suzi speaks. Does this mean that Suzi and Ken are back together and they're all here? All four of them. How sweet.

'Ken, Ken, over here,' Suzi shouts.

Yep, they're back together.

Cat's eyes widen as a reluctant Ken saunters towards us, and an even more reluctant Leeward follows in his wake.

'Isn't this cosy?' Cat says and I can tell she's enjoying it. 'Hey are you two back together?'

'Yes,' Suzi says, her smile so broad it's almost breaking her face.

I clamp my lips together.

'Ahh, that's nice.' Cat's smile is as broad as Suzi's. 'You're having a family day out in IKEA. How sweet.'

Ken and Leeward roll their eyes simultaneously and I wonder if either is aware the other is doing it.

'Have you had lunch yet?' Cat is so enjoying this. 'The meatballs are delish.'

'No, not yet. We're on route to a pub like I was just saying,' Suzi corrects.

'Oh, sorry, I wasn't listening.'

I can't decide whether to stamp on Cat's foot again or kiss her.

'Well, if you change your mind, I can recommend the meatballs.'

'It's a bit mad in there, full of kids.' Suzi sneers, then linking arms with Ken, looks like the cat that has got the cream. I feel both happy and sorry for her.

We all stand and give each other embarrassed half-smiles. I look Ken full in the face but he just looks away. Leeward refuses to meet my gaze too.

'Oh, a decent colander,' Alfie says, spotting it across the aisle and striding off.

Suzi pulls at Ken's arm and Cat slinks away towards the glasses, which is the only reason we're even in this department. It's all her fault we've bumped into this lot.

Suddenly, it's just me and Leeward.

'Well,' I say. It's not a question, in fact I don't really know what it is or why I said it.

'Well what?'

'I don't know.' This is the first time we've been alone, in person, since the day we bumped into each other in the park – and the shock of that didn't allow me to speak my mind.

Leeward starts looking for an escape but Alfie has

moved further away and I can't see anyone else either. It feels as though it's just us in the entire store.

'Have you told Alfie about me?' I say, keeping my voice low. I know damn well he hasn't.

Leeward opens his mouth to speak, changes his mind then closes it.

'You need to.'

He raises his eyebrows at me, alarm, horror, it's hard to tell. 'Or what?'

'Oh, he won't find out from me. I like him. He's lovely. But he will find out, eventually. Someone will say something. You need to tell him. Suzi almost blurted it out just now. It's only a matter of time…'

Leeward purses his lips and looks away. He starts shuffling and I know he's just revving up to run off but somehow he's trapped himself between two display racks of pans. He would have to barge past and knock some over to escape.

'I'm just saying, that's all. Be honest with him. He'll forgive you.'

'I don't think this is the place to discuss this, Lauren. Anyway, it's not really any of your business.'

'No. It's not. But…'

'I need to go now.' He waits for me to step aside.

'You never even said you were sorry.'

'Oh, for fuck's sake, do we have to do this now? Here?'

'No, not here, not now.' I smile. 'But I do need closure.'

'You didn't say that,' Cat screeches when I tell her about it in the car on the way home. 'It sounds so…'

'What?'

'Psychobabbly, I suppose.'

'And…'

'Well, no, that's fine. But well, closure….' She laughs.

'I didn't even know I felt like that. I didn't even know I was going to say it until it came out of my mouth. Anyway, we've agreed to meet up; he's coming round to my house tomorrow morning when Alfie is at work.'

'No. No.'

'Yep. Then we'll see what he has to say for himself.' It was my idea and I'm already beginning to regret suggesting my house as the venue for our showdown. But, he's right, it does need to be private and I didn't want to go to his place, not that he invited me.

'You should get that can opener out, have it on display.'

'Stop it.'

'And what about that Ken? So brazen. Poor Suzi. I wonder if she knows she's sloppy seconds.'

'Stop it. You're becoming so crude lately. Anyway, I don't think that's the correct use of that phrase.'

'Whatever.' She sounds like one her children. 'You were right to tell him where to go. Told you so. He's a sneaky arse who just wanted to get inside your knickers. It certainly didn't take him long to move on, did it? Or is that a move back?'

'Stop it.'

I've walked Shadow, hoovered the house from top to bottom and polished every surface, I've even put toilet cleaner down the loos. Not that I'm going to show him around or anything like that, because I'm not seeking his approval, am I?

It's 10am and Leeward is late.

Bastard isn't coming.

I'll give him ten minutes then I'll start bombarding him with messages and calls. He's not getting away with it.

The longest ten minutes in the history of time pass and I pick up my phone just as there's a knock on the door.

'You're late,' I say as I open the door.

'Sorry. Not intentional, it was her. Alfie says she needs the exercise but she doesn't think so, sits down at every opportunity.'

I look down at their little scrap of dog who sits quivering on the doorstep.

'You could just have carried her; I think she's used to that. Pop her in your pocket, or something. Come in.'

Shadow is delighted to have a new playmate and Daenerys is soon lapping up water from Shadow's bowl. Funny how friendly they are given how recently Shadow and Betty ganged up on Daenerys. Dogs, eh, as fickle as humans.

'Would you like a drink too?'

'Only if you're having one.'

'Coffee then.' I pull two mugs from the cupboard.

Once done I take the coffee to the table and pull out a chair, gesturing for Leeward to do the same; he's been hovering like a dirty smell while I've been making our coffee.

He sits down opposite me and waits.

'Well?' I say.

'Well what? You wanted this meeting, not me. I haven't anything to say.'

'Really? Nothing? Really?' I'd forgotten how exasperating he can be.

He looks away.

'Okay, you can start with an apology, because you've never given me one for what you did.'

He harrumphs. 'Me apologise? You weren't exactly innocent in all this, were you?'

I'm left speechless, staring at him, my mouth opening and closing like a fish.

'Me? Me? What did I ever do? Except agree with you and go along with your plans for that grandiose wedding. Oh, and sell my car to pay for it.' My voice has gone up a notch in pitch and I am barely controlling my anger. I so didn't want it to descend to this level, and so soon.

'What about that bloody song and that fucking video posted all over Facebook.'

'Not by me.'

'*You* posted it on *my* timeline. Don't even attempt to deny it,' he says through gritted teeth. 'I had to close down my account because of that.'

'Yes, but that was after the event. I had been thoroughly humiliated by then, why should you get off with it?'

He looks away, he hasn't got an answer for that.

'Anyway, you're missing the point, Leeward. That song only happened because of what you had already done, it came after the main event, not before it.' There, take that. I fold my arms and purse my lips.

He looks at me, looks me up and down but still says nothing.

'I don't know why you came if you've got nothing to say.'

'Huh. Really?'

'Yes. Really.' I take a sip of my coffee and it tastes bitter, but I think it's the bile rising into my throat rather than anything wrong with my coffee.

'Because you will tell Alfie about us otherwise, you made that perfectly clear yesterday in IKEA.'

'I never said that. Definitely not.'

'You implied it.'

'No, I didn't. I said you should tell him before someone else does.'

'Exactly.' Now it's his turn to fold his arms, and he cocks his head in that slightly smug way he has. I see it now and wonder why I never did before.

'No, I didn't mean me. I wouldn't do that. I told you that yesterday. I said I wouldn't.'

'You said it in a way that suggested you would.' He looks at me with those eyes, those eyes that I used to find so deep and soulful; Cat's right, they are creepy.

'No, I didn't.'

'You fucking did.'

'Fucking didn't.' This is so pointless. 'Why don't you go? If you can't apologise or at least explain then there's no point.' I stand up.

'Explain?'

'Yes. Explain.' Was he always this dense? Perhaps he was and I just never noticed because I was so besotted with him.

'Explain what?'

'You're hard work.' I flop down into my chair again. 'Explain why you went off and had an affair in the run up to the wedding *you* wanted. Why you still wanted to marry me even though you and Alfie were exchanging so many *I love you* messages, and, while I think of it, when you became gay?'

'I'm not gay, I'm bi.'

'That's all right then.' I drop my head into my hands. This isn't going the way I wanted, the way I expected. I thought he'd just say sorry and we could forgive and forget. That's all I really wanted, or so I thought. 'Does Alfie know you're bi? Or are you lying to him too?'

'He knows.' His tone is flat.

'Have you always been bi? All the time you were with me?'

'Yes, obviously. I don't think it's something you develop as time goes on. I just never acted on it before Alfie.'

'Good for you.'

'I never went looking for love with a man. It just happened. I met him at the gym, he was my trainer.'

'But why have an affair with him when we were getting married?'

'I don't know. I sort of couldn't help myself. I just fell in love with him. You've seen him, you've met him. He's just the b…'

'Whoa.' I hold my hand up. 'Enough. That still doesn't explain why you were marrying me.'

He sighs. 'No. I haven't really got a proper answer. I have thought about it a lot, I suppose I thought if we got married my affair with Alfie would fizzle out. We'd been together a long time, you and me; we were moving onto the next step in life. I thought we'd be having children next. I didn't want to hurt you.'

'That worked out well, didn't it?' I shake my head in disbelief. I get up and take my cup to the sink. Leeward hasn't drunk his. Then I return and take his full cup to the sink too.

'Oh, but I,' he starts, then shuts up.

'And you took him on my honeymoon. New Zealand wasn't it? What was it like? Did you go to Hobbitland?'

He rolls his eyes when I say Hobbitland, which I

knew he would which is why I said it.

'That was a spur of the moment thing. I didn't plan it.'

'Ha, you must have spent all day Sunday rearranging the tickets.'

'Yeah. I did. I didn't want to waste the money.'

'We sold my car for all that.' I flop back down into my chair. 'And you bitched about giving me some money.'

'But it was my house.'

'Which I helped fund for almost ten years. Then I was homeless. You kicked me out without even telling me to my face. Then you went on my honeymoon with your lover…' I stop, we're going around and around in circles, I've started repeating myself.

We both sit and stare. The clock in the kitchen ticks away the seconds; I'd never even noticed how loud those ticks are until now. I lean over and look at our dogs, nestled together in Shadow's basket as friendly as Betty and Shadow are.

'And you never let *me* have a dog when we were together. And you wouldn't let me call you Lee.'

Leeward shakes his head and stands up. He fumbles in his pocket for Daenerys's lead. Shadow and Daenerys, who have been watching our exchange like spectators at a tennis match, both jump up and trot over to us. Leeward bends down and clips Daenerys's lead onto her collar.

'And you stole my wine, didn't you?'

'What wine?'

'The one I had from work, the one they gave me when I went on leave to marry you. Did you and Alfie enjoy it?'

He shakes his head and sighs, but he doesn't deny it.

I know he took it and never let on when I asked if he'd seen it.

He's silent and so am I as I see him to the door.

'Nice place. Very you,' he says, with a small smile.

'I don't need your stamp of approval,' I snap back.

'I know you don't. I was trying to be nice.'

'Don't bother.' This was so not a good idea. Why did I think it was? Stupid me.

I lean past him to open the door but he stops me, gripping my hand and it sends tingles down my arm. Oh God, it brings back so many memories, so many *good* memories. Treacherous body.

'I am sorry,' he says. 'Really, I am. I suppose I was so wrapped up in myself I didn't see how hurt you were. I was angry at the way you trashed our wedding; I was...'

'*You* trashed our wedding.'

'Yeah, well, we both did. Look, I'm trying to apologise. I really am. I'm trying to be honest here. I can see how, and why, it's all made you so bitter.'

'I'm not bitter.' I keep my voice as flat as I can. Am I bitter? Am I?

'Well, I'm still apologising, profusely. I was a selfish bastard. I'm sorry.'

'You're just saying that so I won't tell Alfie.'

The alarm registers in his eyes.

'I'm joking. I won't tell him. But someone will.' I shrug. 'Up to you. None of my business.' I lean over and open the door.

I stand back so that Leeward and Daenerys can shuffle out.

'Bye then,' he says.

'Yeah, bye. Oh, and in the interests of full disclosure, while we're being honest and all that, Ken came onto

259

me.'

'What? When? The fucker.'

'Recently, just before he got back with Suzi. Bye.'

I shut the door and lean against it, my heart beating in my chest.

Eighteen

'Did you feel better after delivering that?' Cat asks when I recount the details of the conversation to her on the phone. 'Especially the Ken exposé?'

'A bit.'

'It was spiteful, wasn't it?'

'Yep.'

'And bitchy.'

'Yep.

'Well done. They'll all shits. Even Suzi for making us look like pantomime dames on your wedding day.'

'Alfie isn't. I feel sorry for him.'

'Hey, I didn't want to say this yesterday but I can see what Leeward sees in him. I mean, my God, he's a god. Literally.'

'Don't.' I'm halfway between laughing and crying.

'Well, he is hunky if a bit camp.'

'Do you think? First time I met him, in the park, I didn't think he was camp at all.'

'No, you fancied him.'

'I, I didn't.' Did I?

'Well I did, yesterday, just for a millisecond.' Cat laughs. 'Anyway, did it work? Did you get closure? Is it finished now? Can you put it all behind you and move on? Can you get your priorities right now? Not waste any more time on him? On any of them?'

'I have moved on.' How can she not see that? I have my house, my dog, my car, my old job back, I most emphatically *have* moved on.

'Good. Got to go, stuff to do.' She does a little mock sigh which means the stuff isn't for her.

I have moved on. I have. Cat's comment about moving on has irked me. I keep thinking about it, even when I'm taking Shadow for her evening walk and I'm running to keep up with her, I can't stop thinking about it. Then, when I catch myself scanning the horizon on the lookout for Leeward and Alfie, I check myself, retract Shadow's lead and head for home.

I toss and turn in bed. I've spent the evening inwardly wittering to myself too, even watching reruns of *Poldark* hasn't distracted me. At 3am I get out of bed, go down to the kitchen and make myself a hot chocolate, that should help me nod off. Shadow, briefly woken from sleep in her basket, raises a lazy eyebrow at me but doesn't get up. Typical, even my dog can't be bothered to give me sympathy.

I take my drink back upstairs, sit up in bed and sip it slowly. Despite all the nasty stuff that's gone on between me and Leeward, prior to our wedding day I loved him more than I loved myself.

He broke my heart.

Then he ripped it from my chest and stamped all over it. With Thor's mighty boots and probably his hammer too.

Seeing him today brought back so many feelings, so many emotions. I remember the good times. I remember the fun. I still mourn the life we had together, I loved it.

I don't love him anymore, I hate him.

And that's the problem.

I have to get over that hate, I need to feel indifferent, neutral.

I finish my drink, turn off the lamp, lie down and drift into a deep sleep.

The sound of my phone pinging wakes me up. Did I set the alarm? I didn't think I had because, despite my lovely new curtains, the light still gets in and does a good job of waking me.

It's not the alarm. It's Leeward and Phillip. I read Phillip's first. There, that's getting my priorities right.

Wish me luck, first week of going to work every day, even though it's only mornings.

Bless him. I'm honoured that he's messaging me and so early too. It's only 7am.

Knock 'em dead, I write back and after I've pressed send, I wonder if that is the right thing to say. Too late now.

He sends a smiley face back, so maybe it's okay.

Leeward's message isn't so upbeat.

Told Alfie last night. He's not speaking to me now and has gone to work early and without a word. He's very upset. Hope you're satisfied.

I'm not satisfied, though I am sorry for Alfie. Why did I even get myself involved? Who am I to give relationship advice?

I don't reply because my gut response would be along the lines of *not as upset as me on our wedding day*. No, I resist the temptation and go and have a shower instead.

'Oh, Lauren, Mr Evans wants a word with you,' a new care assistant says to me as soon as I get to work. She's loitering in the office and I don't like being given instructions by anyone, especially when they know my name and I don't know theirs.

'Who?'

'Cruise passenger,' she says, without looking at me. 'He's in the day room.' She slopes off without another word. Who the hell is she to be giving me orders? And I don't like the way she's referring to one of our residents. I'd better go though, in case he's ill.

I find Mr Evans, as instructed, in the day room on the dementia floor.

'Ah, there you are. Thank you for seeing me.'

'My pleasure,' I say, giving him a quick look over. He looks well, actually better than he did when he first came in here. He's put on a little bit of weight and it shows in his face, a definite improvement. His clothes are still immaculate so his family must be keeping their word and laundering everything themselves, because one cycle through the laundry here and there would not be so much as a knife edge crease in sight because everything is tumble dried to oblivion. 'How are you settling in?'

'That's why I needed to see you.' He wipes an imaginary crumb from his shirt sleeve. I notice he's wearing cufflinks; gold cufflinks. 'I wonder if I could move deck? Is there another cabin I could have?'

'Um, I don't know.' He's on the dementia floor because it's secure, downstairs is not and residents can come and go as they please, although most of them aren't physically up to it and rely on their families to take them out.

'I'm sure you'll be able to sort something out for me, my dear, what with you being the chief steward.'

'Right.' He sounds so lucid, if only this *were* a ship. 'Why do you want to move? Is everything okay with your room?' If that's the problem I'm sure I can get it sorted out.

'My room is fine, better than fine, and my cabin steward is a darling. No, it's the other passengers.'

'Oh.'

'Yes, they're somewhat unsavoury.'

'Oh, really? In what way?' I'm dreading the answer.

'Terrible manners, especially when eating.' He glances around the day room, then leans in closer and lowers his voice. 'Some even wear bibs, like babies.'

'Ah.' There's no denying that, sadly.

'And some even wear…' he hesitates, takes another look around then whispers, 'Nappies. And they need them, believe me.'

'Right. Um…' I really don't know what to do about this. Sadly, some of our residents have dementia that is so far advanced that they have reverted to childhood and that includes incontinence. I hope this isn't a fate he's destined for, but think it likely as he's been diagnosed with dementia.

'Can I leave that with you?' He pats my hand and smiles. It's funny, he seems such a sweet old man, but if that action took place outside in the *real* world, someone would probably be screaming sexual harassment, even though it's really not.

'I'll see what I can do.' God knows what I can do. I say goodbye and hot foot it back to the office where I pull his file out.

When I've finished reading it, I ring up Clare, the home manager and ask to see her.

A day later and after a lengthy meeting with Clare, and several complex phones calls to each of his three daughters, we move Mr Evans to the floor below. We've agreed that he should be happier there for the time being, the front door is secure – though that's mostly to keep people out rather than in – so he should be safe. We all agree it's a temporary measure, but who knows how long that might be? And Mr Evans seems delighted with his new cabin on a lower deck. We all, except Mr Evans, know it's just temporary, but it might be years before he's so bad he needs to move upstairs. Alternatively, it might be months, it will be my responsibility to monitor him.

Later in the week I receive an email from Clare commending me on finding an excellent solution for Mr Evan's complaint. She's also wondering if I'd like to sign up for management training with a view to becoming her deputy and ultimately a nursing home manager myself. I have to admit, I've never even considered it before, but now I'm wondering if it's time to focus on myself, advance my career, look to the future. I might even start by having a discreet word with that rather rude and disrespectful care assistant. I'm feeling rather good about myself.

If only my private life was so rewarding.

I'm with Shadow and we're queueing up outside the church hall waiting for the dog training to commence. Shadow is behaving impeccably, sitting by my side and not reacting at all to any of the other dogs; it's almost as if she knows she's going to be tested.

We trot in and take our places, which in my case means shuffling along and fitting in with everyone else as the lessons started two weeks ago and they've squeezed me in. There are nine of us and the dogs vary greatly in breed and size.

'What breed is your dog?' asks a lady who looks and sounds like she's just popped down from the local stately home, she's even wearing tweeds, and a scarf around her head, reminiscent of The Queen.

'Mongrel,' I reply, because I'm not going to get into all that nonsense that I've heard being repeated around the room and in the queue about pedigree names and lineage. I really don't care. Shadow is a lovely dog and I don't care what *flavour* she is. And when she can learn to not run away in the park, she'll be even better.

'Mine too,' The Queen says, patting the head of a giant dog which I assumed was a Great Dane. 'They're far nicer natured.' She gives me a quick wink and I smirk back. I think I might have found an ally at doggie training already.

We start off with walking to heel and all the things that Shadow actually does quite well. I'm really quite enjoying myself and so is Shadow when the door is suddenly hurled open from the outside making it bang against the inside wall.

Everyone jumps and we all turn to look and in walks a tiny little dog, a Chihuahua.

My heart does a little lunge before it rattles against my chest, because I know what, or rather who, is coming next.

'Sorry everyone, I'm running late.' Alfie, channelling full Thor persona in a leather waistcoat and massive boots, strides in. He brushes his extravagant, dirty-blond hair away from his face.

The women in the hall swoon collectively.

He sees me and offers a half-smile.

Don't come and stand next to me, don't come and stand next to me, don't come and stand next to me.

Alfie takes three giant strides and positions himself between me and The Queen. Great. For fuck's sake.

We do a few doggy manoeuvres and, try as I might, I cannot get away from Alfie. If I move away, he just follows me. I know the hall is full of people and dogs, but really, can't he take a hint? Shadow's achievement of coming back to me from across the hall when she's off the lead is completely side-lined by Alfie's insistence in following me so closely.

Finally, the class is over and I plan a hasty retreat. But, it's not to be. The Queen comes over and asks if I'll be here next week then tells me her dog is called Muttley because he's third generation mutt, which is quite funny, and when I finally get to leave, Shadow has entangled herself in Daenerys's lead.

'Everyone's very friendly,' Alfie says as he creeps up behind me, quite a feat given the size of him.

'Yeah,' I say, not looking at him. I tug on Shadow's lead as though it will magically untangle.

'I'll just sort that.' Alfie bends down and pulls their leads apart.

'Thank you.' I start to march towards the door.

'Are you walking home?'

I want to say no, I'm flying. *Just go away Alfie. Why are you and Leeward and bloody Ken always butting into my life?*

'I'll walk with you,' he says, evidently not getting the message that I just want to escape. I'm obviously not emanating enough hostility via my body language.

There's no point in trying to outrun him either, is there? How could I move faster than Thor?

'How's your week been so far?' he asks.

Oh no. Enough of this. I stop, turn and face him. 'Alfie, I know you know who I am, Leeward has told me he told you. He also said you're upset about it and not speaking to him. I just want to say that I'm sorry and all that, but really, it's nothing to do with me, how you feel about it, I mean.'

Alfie stares at me as though I'm speaking another language which is probably how I sounded, and for a second or two I wonder if Leeward has lied to me and actually not told Alfie anything and I've just dropped Leeward in it.

'I know it's not your fault. Of course it's not. You're quite blameless.' Phew, he does know.

Is he being sarcastic? Did Leeward tell him I sort of forced his hand, made him tell Alfie. Is he going to have a go at me now? I glance up and down the street for somewhere to run and hide.

'It's me who should be sorry. I took him away from you.' He blinks several times; I hope he's not going to cry. It will look very strange, he's so Thor-like and everyone knows gods don't cry. 'When I met him I had no idea he was with you, with anyone actually.'

I shrug. What can I say to that?

'I'm so sorry, Lauren.' Then he steps forward and envelops me in his great bear arms and hugs me. I have to admit it's really rather nice and he does smell… well, godlike. 'You've had a terrible time and although I'm not to blame any more than you are, I know you must have suffered greatly. And, I'm really sorry about that.'

Okay, this is getting really embarrassing now. I can feel my throat constricting, all this sympathy is going to make me weep. Like a baby.

He keeps on hugging me and I keep on breathing through my nose to stop myself from crying. Of all the people to give me sympathy, I didn't expect it from Alfie.

'It's damn Lee I'm angry with,' he says, finally letting go of me. 'If he'd been honest from the beginning, I probably wouldn't have pursued him the way I did. I only found out he was bi after we'd been together a couple of months. I assumed he was out and proud, like me. He certainly gives off that vibe.'

I laugh. I can't help it. 'Does he?' Have I been missing something all these years?

'Err, yes,' Alfie says, a big smile on his face. 'And I'm not the only one who thinks so. Let's just say that Lee could have chosen from several suitors down the gym.' He gives me a gentle nudge.

'Is it a gay gym then?' Does such a thing exist? Have I said something insulting?

Alfie grins. 'Not officially. Come on, let's get home, it's getting late.'

He walks me to the end of the street and, just as he's turning to leave, I invite him in for a coffee. After I've said it, I immediately regret it, but he smiles and accepts.

An hour later and we're gassing away like old girlfriends. We've dissected Leeward's habits and giggled over his penchant for dark, minimalist décor and regimented wardrobes.

'I've told him I won't live like that,' Alfie giggles. 'I'm much more decadent when it comes to furnishings. You must come round and see.' He stops when he sees my face. 'Well, maybe not just yet,' he continues before getting up to leave.

At the door he gives me another hug.

'I do want us to be friends, Lauren. I really like you.'

'Yeah, me too.' I'm actually being genuine, I do want to be friends with him, just not too close.

'Cool. Come on, Daenerys, Daddy's waiting.' He

clips on his dog's lead. 'He's messaged me three times since I've been here.' He rolls his eyes and strides off. 'I expect he thinks I'm sulking.'

Later, I lie in bed and scan through the past and look for signs of Leeward's gaiety. Is that the right word? Probably not.

Nineteen

The following few months pass with surprising calmness. No more drama.

I go to doggie training every week and even though I see Alfie there and we exchange pleasant chit chat, I don't feel any pressure. Even when a torrential downpour means that Leeward comes to pick Alfie up afterwards and offers me a lift, which I have to accept or get soaked, the atmosphere in the car is pleasant. Leeward and I are never going to be best friends, but at least we can be polite and civil. I'm even starting to not hate him anymore. I go for days when I don't even think about him or the life we had and when I do it's to reminisce and look back with happiness rather than sorrow.

Lauren Nokes has moved on.

I say this to Cat one evening from the comfort of my fab IKEA bed – which only took me and Dad two hours to put together.

'Yes, I think you finally have,' she says before pausing.

'Hello?' The silence has gone on for so long I think the call has been cut, but according to my phone, it hasn't.

'Sorry,' she says. 'I was just thinking. Perhaps I was a bit harsh when I told you to move on. You know, tough love.'

'D'ya think?' I laugh.

'No, seriously. I've never been through what you have, it can't have been easy. I mean, finding out the man you've been with for ten years is gay. Then all that crap at your wedding.'

'Bi,' I correct with a giggle. 'And don't go on about it, you'll wind me up again.'

'No, what I'm trying to say is,' she pauses again, 'Well done, Lauren. You are your own woman now.'

'Maybe I am.' Now it's my turn to pause. And think. Cat's always saying things like that to me, but what about her?

'Lauren?'

'Cat, I was wondering…'

'Yes?'

'Are you your own woman?'

'God, no.' Her tone implies I've said something so incredibly stupid that I should be ashamed of myself. 'Another ten years before I can even start to reclaim myself. Once the last one flies the nest, then maybe. Anyway, got to go,' she adds before I question her further. 'I'll see you at the weekend. Looking forward to the 'middle of Lidl'.'

'Okay,' I laugh. 'Small things, eh?' I can't believe how excited she is that a Lidl store has opened in our town and we're making a trip there.

'I know. We know how to live. IKEA, Lidl.' She laughs as she ends the call.

I ponder on Cat's words about moving on as I snuggle down with a bit of bedtime reading – a management book which I've been told to read ahead of my three weeks of intensive, offsite training which starts next week.

Yes, Lauren Nokes has moved on. I am my own woman.

If I have one regret; it's Phillip.

I haven't seen him since he went back to work. We've exchanged lots of phone messages, even had a lengthy phone call after his first week full-time, he basically just needed a friendly ear to download to, and as he put it when he rang me, I owe him one for drowning him in the Leeward-Alfie-Ken saga. But other than that, I haven't seen him, not in person. We're obviously out of synch with the dog walking in the park regime, either that or he's moved back to his own house. Wouldn't he have told me? Maybe not, we're not *that* close.

On a whim and even though it's ten at night, I message him.

Hope all well with you? How's work going?

I don't expect a response immediately so I'm surprised when he messages me back straight away.

Funnily enough I was just thinking about you. Would you like to meet for a walk around the park with our little furry pests? Work is okay, well better than okay – I'm coping well and it's a good distraction.

I reply that I'd love to meet and ask when. He suggests Saturday morning at ten. I don't dare ask what work is a distraction from.

Just as I'm dropping off to sleep I suddenly jerk awake. Should I have asked him? Is that why he put that in his message? Oh damn, it's too late now. I'll have to wait until Saturday. All I know, which isn't much, is that it involved a little girl. Taking Archie's comments alone — *he loved that little girl, we all did —* implies she has died, but Phillip specifically stated that no one had died.

Saturday morning can't come soon enough now. I make an effort. Wash my hair, dress nicely, appropriate for dog walking in a soft top and long shorts, but nice, and, of course, matching shoes. The weather is warm, the sun is climbing in the sky, the birds are singing and my dog has now achieved the milestone of being capable of not running off when let off her lead.

If it wasn't for Shadow getting so excited when she sees Betty approaching us, I would walk past Phillip. He looks so different.

'Wow,' I say as we meet. We exchange awkward hugs. 'I didn't recognise you.'

'Really?' There's genuine puzzlement in his expression and his tone of voice.

'No. You look…' I stand back and survey him. 'So different.' He's put on weight and the faded jeans and white t-shirt he's wearing fit him well. His hair is still short, in fact it looks freshly cut and his face stubble is groomed and tidy.

'Yes,' I mutter, feeling embarrassed for commenting on it. 'Being back at work obviously suits you.' I look down so I don't have to look him in the eye.

'Well, it's a distraction.' He bends down and pats Shadow's head. 'How's she doing after the dog training classes?'

'Good. Look.' I unclip Shadow's lead and wait. Nothing happens, she doesn't run off but mainly because she's far too interested in saying hello to Betty.

Phillip unclips Betty's lead and suddenly the pair race off together, side-by-side, furry yin-yang.

'Will she come back?' he asks.

'I hope so. She usually does now.'

'Good. We can sit then.' He paces over to the bench where I first saw him, Spice man. Then waits for me to catch up before he sits down. We sit beside each other scanning the horizon and watching our dogs, who are having the best of fun darting left then right, chasing an imaginary rabbit, at least I hope it's imaginary.

'I'm knackered now,' he laughs. 'I've been round the park twice.'

'Oh, sorry, am I late? I thought we said ten.'

'No, not at all. No. I just needed to get out and about. The sooner I move out of that nut house the better. There was an almighty row going on in the shared kitchen this morning about fridge shelves and milk. It's worse than my student days, and these are supposed to be *professional* people.'

'Oh. Sounds grim.'

'It's not for much longer. I get my house back in two weeks and two days. Not that I'm counting.' He turns and smiles at me. His blue eyes twinkle in the sunlight. He's fit, actually now his cheeks are no longer sunken and his pallor is normal, he's really fit. I suddenly feel hot and uncomfortable. Subtly I move away, just a little, just to put some cool air between us and I return my gaze to my dog in the distance.

'That's good.'

'Yeah. Who knows what sort of state it will be in? The last lot redecorated in vibrating pink and lilac, I had it all painted out in magnolia before these ones moved in, but you never can tell with tenants.'

'Surely they're not allowed to do that.'

He gives an ironic laugh. 'No, not allowed but that doesn't seem to stop them. Just good that I put my furniture in storage and let the house empty.' He shakes his head. 'I'm relieved I never sold it. I must have known…'

I let his words hang in the air while I analyse them. Is this a lead for me to ask what he means? Why do I hesitate? I pluck up the courage.

'Known what?' I squeak.

'Oh, you don't want to hear it.'

'I do if you want me to. I'm a good listener. And I owe you one for the Leeward-Alfie-Ken story.'

'No, that's been paid back. I downloaded about work.' He smiles, more to himself than me.

'Well, I'm here if you need me. You've heard my nightmare so you know I can take it.' Oh God, that sounds so flippant. I didn't mean it to sound like that. I feel myself flushing; I'm quite literally hot under the collar. I pull at the neck of my top. There's a long silence, then he speaks.

'I know what happened to you was awful,' he says, also keeping his eyes focused on our dogs. 'But, believe me, it's not in the same league as my sorry tale.'

I stop myself from speaking before I put my foot in it again. Instead I reach over and squeeze his hand, just gently, then I let go. I'm curious, of course I'm curious, but if he wants to maintain his privacy, that's fair enough. When he starts speaking again, his voice is quiet, measured.

'I met Belinda, she prefers Bel, on a night out. It was a stag night. I hadn't gone on the long weekend to Spain, so this was the local one. You know the sort of thing. Too much drink, money being spent as though it has no value, everyone behaving like louts. Not me at all. I hadn't wanted to go but… well, there I was being almost as loutish as the rest of them.' He stops, waits.

'Mmm,' I say as though I do know. Of course I know what he means but it's a long time since I went on the female equivalent. Even my own hen party was a very sedate affair.

'She winked at me across the bar. I didn't think it was for me, I looked behind me but there wasn't anyone else there. I gave her a smile back then looked away but I kept glancing back. Couldn't help it. She was stunning. This glossy dark hair, poker straight and long, just falling down her shoulders. Big eyes, big smile. She was way out of my league.'

I already don't like the sound of Belinda, Bel.

'She sashayed around the bar and came towards me.'

'Sashayed,' I find myself repeating. Stop judging.

'Only way to describe it.' He gives off a bitter little laugh. 'To be fair she'd been drinking herself too, out with her friends, though not as loutish as us, they were loud.' He stops again, and I sneak a quick sideways glance at him; he's right back there, with Bel, The Stunner.

'Mmm,' I offer to encourage him.

'She did all the talking; said she'd been watching me for a while. Liked the look of me. I had no witty one-liners to offer back, not even any compliments because I couldn't trust myself not to say something dumb about how she looked. She flirted, I smiled. It was very one sided. I was flattered. She was stunning.'

I want to say that so was Leeward, that he knocked me off my feet the first time I met him, but that would be childish, wouldn't it?

'We were soon kissing and groping in the corner. Sounds seedy saying it now, but at the time... well, we exchanged phone numbers. I didn't message her the next day or the day after that, I thought once she'd sobered up and remembered me, she'd be regretting it. I didn't want to put her in that position. Or myself, if I'm honest, it's horrible being knocked back.'

I don't understand why Phillip is so lacking in confidence. He looks hot. Stop it. Maybe he looked more like Spice man back then.

'*She* rang *me*. Not messaged, rang. She suggested I buy her dinner. She was very forward.'

'Oh. Right.' Is that the best I can do?

'I liked it. I hadn't been in a relationship for over two years. I wasn't looking. But it felt good to be chased by such a stunning woman.'

If he says she's stunning again I might be sick.

'We went out for dinner and it went from there. Rapidly. Within weeks we were seeing each other four, five times a week. We went out, but mostly I went to her place, she had a son, he was three at the time, he only went to his father's every other weekend. I didn't meet her son, Edward – she called him Teddie – for six, maybe seven, weeks. She didn't want to confuse him, which I thought was fair enough. When I did meet him he was a cute little kid, dark hair and eyes just like hers.' He stops again and swallows hard.

'Yes,' I mutter, nodding.

'It wasn't serious between us. Just a bit of fun, she made that clear. And it was fun, immense fun. She was a…'

Please don't say *stunner* again.

'Good laugh,' he continues, mercifully without using the 's' word. 'Her husband – they were still married, just separated – had gone off with a colleague, a younger version of Bel. She was still smarting from the rejection. She just wanted a bit of fun. I was happy with that. I was more a revenge shag than a serious relationship.'

Well, so far this isn't a tragic story.

'Then she announced she was pregnant. Which surprised me, I thought we'd been careful, but evidently not careful enough. It was a shock. She said she understood if I didn't want to continue seeing her but she'd be keeping the baby no matter what I did. I could hardly walk away, could I? My own child. What sort of man does that?'

There are tears running down his face, he makes no attempt to wipe them away, but he also doesn't make a sound. I reach over and squeeze his hand again.

My mind is racing ahead, I know something happens with the little girl. Maybe she's ill, or injured, or something. I want to know but I don't want to know. I'm not sure I can bear it.

He sniffs then uses the back of his hand to wipe his face. I want to offer a tissue but I don't have my bag with me, just my keys and phone stuffed into my pockets.

'She was seven months pregnant when I moved in with her. I thought about selling my house but with her not being divorced it was complicated. Her husband still co-owned her home. I let mine out, the rent covered the mortgage, even after tax. Then I paid a substantial amount towards their mortgage every month, Bel's and her husband's. It seemed a fair arrangement. Josh, her husband, he liked it because it meant he could rent somewhere better for himself. It was all very amicable. Tidy. Bel didn't want to do anything permanent until her divorce was sorted out. Then, we could both sell our houses and buy somewhere together. Josh paid something towards Teddie so we managed fine.'

He pauses again, I look over at him and see his

Adam's apple going up and down as he swallows rapidly.

'Oh.' I jump as a large wet splat hits my arm, quickly followed by another one. For a stupid moment I imagine Phillip is crying again and these are his tears.

'Rain,' he says.

We both look up at the sky, no longer blue, it's covered by a dark cloud.

'I hadn't noticed it getting darker,' I say, jumping up. 'Shadow,' I call. 'Shall we go to my place, it's the nearest?' I am so presumptuous.

He hesitates for a second or two. 'Okay.' He whistles for his dog and they both come running.

'I've been practicing that,' I say, implying I'm as good at whistling as he is.

'Easier than shouting.'

By the time we reach the end of my street the rain is gathering pace, falling in fat drops that splat on the ground, on our faces, in my freshly washed hair. We scoot down the street, our heads down.

'There you are?' a familiar voice says.

'Cat?' I look up and see her standing under an umbrella next to her car.

'I've been banging on your door and ringing you.'

'Oh, um, right.'

'Lidl,' she says, prompting me. 'Middle of Lidl.'

'Yes, of course.'

'Oh, hello,' Cat says, turning her attention to Phillip, her eyes widening.

'Let's get inside.' I yank my keys out and we all dart for the door.

Once inside, Cat turns to Phillip. 'I'm Cat, Lauren's sister.'

'Phillip,' he says. 'Nice to meet you.'

'You too.' She gives him a megawatt smile before turning back to me. 'I've got Grimmy in the car.'

'Why?'

'Once she got wind of where we were going, she wanted to come. Seen the adverts, heard about it, needs to see for herself.' She rolls her eyes. 'Also, Mum and Dad needed to do some things. So I'll have to go back out in a min. You know what she's like.' She starts fumbling with her umbrella again as she opens the front door. 'Oh, it's stopped. Weird weather.'

'It has,' Phillip says, peering out. 'Look, I'll get off so you can go to Lidl with your sister.' Is he smirking?

'Oh but…' I start. 'I can…'

'Some other time.' He gives me a quick peck on the cheek – which is rather nice – pulls on Betty's lead and he's gone.

'Soon,' I call after him. 'Just got to use the loo and get my bag,' I yell to Cat who's now getting into her car.

'Did you forget about us?' Grimmy accuses when I get in the back seat.

'No, just lost track of the time, that's all. Anyway, I didn't know you were coming, Grimmy.'

'Well, I am,' she says.

'Cool. It'll be fun.'

In the back of the car I message Phillip and apologise. He replies with several laughing faces.

'You kept *him* quiet,' Cat whispers as we trundle across Lidl's car park in search of a trolley while Grimmy waits for us in the car. The car park is heaving because Lidl has only been open a few days and there's a multitude of opening offers on.

'No, I didn't. I've told you about him before.'

'No, you haven't.'

'I have.'

'Haven't.'

'This is juvenile.'

'No it isn't.'

'Stop it, Cat. It's not funny.'

'Well who is he?'

I wonder what I should say. Will I regret telling her? 'Spice man.'

'Nooo. Spice man? Really? I thought Spice man was all thin and scruffy and trampy and slept in the park.'

'Well he doesn't now.'

'No, he's rather dishy. I mean not quite Thor standard, but…'

'Shut up.' We trundle back to the car and wait for Grimmy who lowers her window.

'I think I might stay here now. I've seen enough. Too many people,' she says. 'You can bring me another day, Cat, in the week when it's empty.'

'Oh Grimmy,' Cat says, struggling to hide her annoyance. 'It'll be fine once we're inside.'

'No, you go and enjoy yourselves, girls, while I wait for you. Don't be too long.'

'Okay, Grimmy,' we chorus between gritted teeth.

'How does she manage to suck all the joy out of everything?' Cat says as we head towards the shop.

'She's old, she's had a tricky life in some parts…' I'm defending Grimmy when really I'm just as irritated as Cat. We'll have to be quick now because we're already fretting about leaving an old lady in the car on a very warm and muggy day. Even if she can open the window.

'I suppose.' Cat looks at me and smirks. 'Says the new tragedy queen of the family.'

'No I'm not. Shut up.'

'Oh, look at the bakery.'

I wouldn't really call it a bakery, but I have to admit that the cakes and pastries on display look amazing. So amazing that we choose a selection. Cat has some for her family, I have some to take home, we get something for now to eat in the car before we leave and some to take home for Mum and Dad. We're barely through the store door and we've spent a fortune on cakes.

'I'll have that one,' a croaky voice says from behind us.

'Grimmy. I thought you didn't want to come in.'

'You were taking too long, I thought I'd come and see what all the fuss was about. Don't worry, I've locked the car. A nice man helped me.'

'I'll just go and check,' Cat says, a look of alarm in her eyes.

I grab Grimmy's choice of cake and put it in a bag.

'And I'll have that one for later,' Grimmy says, pointing a crooked finger at a large, lemon doughnut. 'That'll be nice with a cup of tea. Cat can do that for me when we get home.'

'All right,' I say with a smile. Lucky Cat. 'Everything okay?' I ask when Cat quickly returns.

'Yes, amazingly,' she mutters under her breath.

'Told you I'd locked it.' Grimmy tuts. She really doesn't miss a thing.

We move on down the shop, Cat picks up some tomatoes, I get a hand of bananas, neither of us needs to do a *big* shop, but some things just look too nice to miss. Finally, we arrive at the middle where all the exciting, and in some cases, downright weird stuff, is displayed. Cat looks like a kid in a toy shop.

'In there a café in here where I can go and sit down? All this standing and waiting is giving me leg ache.'

'No, Grimmy, there isn't.'

'No? Oh. Well there is in Sainsburys, we should have gone to Sainsburys.'

'That's not the point, Grimmy,' Cat explains.

'What's not?'

'Well, this is a different kind of shop and we wanted to come *here.*'

'It certainly is if there's no café for weary shoppers to rest their legs.' Grimmy starts casting her eyes around looking for a chair. She's so dinky that she could almost fit in the kiddie seat in the trolley. Cat sees me looking between the seat and Grimmy.

'Don't tempt me,' she says.

'Tempt you? I'm not tempting you.' Grimmy scowls at Cat, and Cat scowls back.

'You're in a funny mood today, Cat,' I say before turning to Grimmy. 'Shall I take you back to the car?'

'Yes, I think so. I'll take my cake with me too. I can have that while you're in here. But don't be all day.'

I rummage around for Grimmy's cake and we head for the tills where the queues are long and winding and where everyone has trollies full of the weird stuff from the middle.

'Oh, Grimmy, shall I just get your cake later? We'll be ages waiting.'

'Old lady coming through. Very old lady coming through. I'm nearly a hundred,' Grimmy tells a man with a chainsaw and cake decorating set in his trolley.

Astonishingly people let us pass until we're pushing in at the front of the queue to pay for one cake. I fumble the cash out of my purse, which is all in 5ps and 2ps, because I don't have much actual cash on me since I always pay by card. This all seems to take ages and I can feel people's hostility bristling around me.

285

'Thank you all for your help,' Grimmy croaks, addressing our audience. 'I was in the Blitz, you know,' she adds. 'In London.'

'Let's go.' I link arms with her and attempt to hurry her away. Talk about cringeworthy.

And I have to go back in there in a minute.

'That was quick,' Cat says, when I return. She already has a trolley full of stuff, two pairs of rubber shoes, a sequin top, a kitchen bin. She catches me examining her shopping. 'Everything is so cheap,' she says defensively, 'And good quality. Grimmy okay?'

'Yes. For now. She was already moaning we'd been too long. Told me to hurry you up. I don't know why you brought her. You know what she's like.' I know I shouldn't complain about her, I should be – no I am – grateful that she's so sprightly, so with it at her age. When I compare her with some of the residents at the home, she's absolutely, bloody amazing, I know that. But she can try the patience of a saint. And I'm no saint.

'Had no choice. Mum wanted to marzipan Grimmy's cake and her new chair was being delivered today. It's going straight in the garage until the party, but you know what she's like, she wouldn't miss it and that would spoil the surprise.'

'Oh yeah.' I'd almost forgotten about Grimmy's birthday party. In four weeks' time she will be ninety-five. The party isn't exactly a surprise, she will expect something but it's usually just a family party. This time Mum and Dad have invited everyone who knows her. It's another five years until it's a big one again, *the* big one, who knows if she'll make it. So it makes sense to celebrate big when you know you can.

'I hope the weather's good that day then we can spill out into the garden. Hey, you can bring your b...' The b word hovers on her lips before she corrects herself. 'Friend,' she says, grinning at me.

Twenty

Back home, I unpack my shopping. I've spent more than I intended, including a new pale blue toaster with matching kettle that tones in with my kitchen décor and certainly looks better than Mum and Dad's castoffs.

I've also bought the ingredients to cook a lovely meal tonight, including wine.

For two.

I pick up my phone and stare at it for too long. Silly really. Then I ring Phillip. I'm almost relieved when it goes to voicemail, but then flustered about what to say.

Hi, Lauren here. Just wondered if you fancied a meal tonight. At mine. I'll cook. Bye.

Now I feel stupid.

Does it look as though all I want is to hear the rest of his story? Isn't there an element of truth in that? A big element. Is that so bad?

I unpack my kettle and toaster, arrange them on the worktop and stand back to admire.

'I don't know why you need a four-slice toaster,' Cat commented as she scrutinised the items in my trolley.

'That's the only size they do in that colour.'

She narrowed her eyes at me and grinned.

'Stop it.'

'What?'

'That. If I didn't know better, I'd think you'd been drinking. You're behaving weirdly.'

'Just enjoying myself.'

'At my expense.'

'No. No. Not really. Anyway, why was your friend sitting in the park all day doing Spice?'

'He wasn't doing Spice.'

'So?'

'He was ill and now he's not.'

'What was wrong with him?'

'I don't know. I haven't asked.' Which is true, I haven't. But whatever happened to him obviously knocked him for six. And when I do find out what it is, I won't be telling Cat.

'Well, he's looking good now, you could do a lot worse.'

'We're just friends. We sometimes walk our dogs together. Just stop it.'

'Much more *you* than Leeward.'

I nudged her hard in the ribs then and she performed a theatrical howl which made everyone in the middle of Lidl turn and look at us.

'You should definitely bring him to Grimmy's party,' she said, before dodging to escape a second elbow to her ribcage.

My phone pings.

I'm expecting Phillip, but it's Alfie.

Thought I saw you in Lidl today. What did you think? Did you grab any bargains? We got a toaster with matching kettle.

My heart sinks. Is nowhere safe? Now even the

middle of Lidl is tainted. I can't even imagine Leeward wandering around Lidl, he hated supermarket shopping when he was with me, even Waitrose wasn't good enough.

I leave it ten minutes before I reply. I have to reply because if I don't, he'll take offence and nothing of this situation is *his* fault, not really.

Me too. What colour did you get?

Red. Suzi egged me on. □*Lee hasn't seen it yet.*

How sweet, he's out shopping with Suzi. Again.

Lol, I reply then promise myself that's an end to the conversation and plonk my phone on the kitchen worktop.

But my phone pings again. I snatch it up. It's Phillip.

That'll be great. Glad to escape the nut house, more loud arguing going on about nothing. What time?

I message Phillip back and smile to myself. It'll be a treat to cook for him especially since it's just us and our dogs and Phillip won't be making a play for me the way Ken did. Not that Ken cares two hoots about me now he's back with Suzi. It didn't take him long to move on. I bet Jayne is pleased. The thought of Ken turning up with me in tow at a family get together and Jayne's face is enough to make me laugh out loud. Shadow, lapping up water from her bowl, stops mid-action and frowns at me, yes, definitely frowns.

'Don't worry,' I say, because of course my dog understands everything I say, 'Your friend Betty is coming this evening too.' I swear Shadow's tail wags at the mention of Betty's name before she trots off into the garden.

I make chicken stuffed with cream cheese and wrapped in bacon, with potatoes and green beans. I even go so far as to make a baked cheesecake for dessert. I'm excelling myself. I toyed with making pasta but since I don't need to prove a point to anybody, namely Ken, I've gone for something I think, hope, Phillip might like. Now I'm panicking in case he doesn't eat meat. Too late. I'm sure I've got some crisps in the cupboard somewhere.

He arrives at the time I've told him clutching a bottle of wine.

'White,' he says, 'I hope that's okay.'

'Any colour is good for me.' I laugh and sound stupid and awkward. I do hope tonight isn't going to be awkward. We are, after all, just friends sharing a meal together.

Betty bounds past me in the hall and gallops off to meet her friend.

'I hope you like chicken and I hope you're hungry,' I say as I put his wine in the fridge and pull out a bottle of my own. 'Wine now?'

'Yes, yes and yes.'

I pour us both a generous glass and as I hand his to him, I notice he's changed his clothes, darker jeans now and a shirt. He looks good, just as good as he did in the park. Too good. It makes me feel jittery and silly.

I really need to calm down. What the hell is the matter with me?

'How was Lidl?' Is he smirking? Yes, he definitely is.

'Not without its minor dramas,' I say before telling him about Grimmy and her queue jumping and the cakes we've stuffed ourselves with.

'Any left?' He glances around the kitchen.

'No, sorry. But I have made a cheesecake.'

'Sounds good.'

He sits at the table while I bring the food over. We

serve ourselves since this will allow him to eat as much as he likes without me constantly asking if he'd like more.

'Help yourself,' I say as I put the plates down.

We eat and drink in a kind of strained silence, or maybe it's just me. He eats quickly but maybe that's because he just wants to get it over with and leave. Shadow and Betty play in the garden; after this afternoon's downpour it turned back into a warm, bright day and now a lovely evening.

'That was great,' he says, after his second helping. 'So nice to eat in civilised surroundings.'

'What do you normally do?'

'Lately I've been eating lunch at work. So much better. We're in a shared building so we have a shared restaurant. It's good too. Prior to that, hit and run in the shared kitchen in the nut house.' He grimaces. 'Ready meals, mostly. There are three fridge freezers, and three microwaves but only one oven and hob, so I think the owner knew how it would be.'

'How many rooms are there?'

'Seven, I think. Might be six. Oh, and there's a dishwasher, but no one wants to load or unload it. I do it whenever I cannot stand the mess. It's ridiculous. Counting the days…'

'Until you get your house back,' I finish for him. 'Cheesecake? More wine?' We're about to start on his bottle now.

'Cheesecake yes, wine maybe later. I'd love a coffee with that cheesecake.'

'Me too. We could take our dessert out to the garden.' I have even acquired some second hand garden furniture, another castoff from Cat's mother-in-law.

We sit out here, side by side on my bench, and eat

our cheesecake – he has a second helping – and drink our coffee. It's nice. Watching our dogs makes it feel less awkward than staring at each other over the dining table. I open my mouth to speak then close it again. I'm deliberating with myself. If I bring up what he was telling me about this morning does it look as though I'm just being nosy? If I don't, does it look as though I don't care?

I get up and pick up our plates and cups.

'Wine?' I ask. 'We'll be starting on yours now.'

'Why not?' He smiles but he looks distant, distracted. Maybe he's wondering how soon he can leave without looking rude.

I bring the bottle and two glasses back.

'The bottle.' He raises his eyebrows, takes the bottle from me and opens it.

'I couldn't unscrew it,' I lie. 'Anyway, save getting up again. Just got to remember to put it in the shade between glasses.'

He pours me a glass and hands it to me before pouring his own. His actions are slow and deliberate. I think.

'Where was I?' he says, looking at me.

I shake my head slowly and do a little shrug pretending I don't know what he's talking about. Perhaps I don't. Perhaps he's talking about something else. Perhaps I'll never get to hear what took him so low.

'Ah yes, Bel and the baby. Huh, sounds like the title of a book, don't you think?'

I just smile, not too much, no teeth showing.

'Well, I was ecstatic when Lucia Victoria arrived. I held her first. She looked at me with eyes as dark as her mother's and blinked. She had a thatch of matted dark

293

hair, a cute little nose. I've never felt love like it. Never.' He stops and stares past our dogs, past my garden; he's somewhere else altogether.

I reach for the wine bottle but it's only me who needs a refill.

'7lbs 11oz of pure love.' His Adam's apple is working overtime now. He takes a breath. 'We went home and we were a family, albeit a fractured one where one little boy went off to his real father's every other weekend, but the rest of the time it was the four of us. Lucia was a cute baby, everyone said so. My parents came down from Scotland when she was three weeks old and fell in love with her. Mum said she reminded her of me as a baby, she had my chin, my face shape. Everyone else thought she was the double of her mother, and that became more apparent as time went on, but that was okay, because, as I've said, Bel is a stunner. In looks. Bel and I rubbed along fine. It wasn't a great love between us, but we did okay. We wanted the same things, which was mostly the best for our children. To be honest if it hadn't been for Lucia, I think the thing between Bel and me would have fizzled out. She was too high maintenance for me.' He stops, looks at me, expects me to say something.

'In what way?'

'Salons.' Air escapes through his nose quickly, almost like a snort. 'Hair every two weeks, it seemed that the lovely dark hair I'd so admired and that was supposedly from Bel's distant Italian heritage, hence calling our baby Lucia, needed dyeing frequently. Nails. Tans. Facials. Getting ready to go out, even to go to the supermarket took two hours. But I didn't care because Lucia was such a delight. Cute, funny, smiley. All the things a father could want. Oh she cried like a baby, of course, but…'

He's silent now and it goes on for a long time. I'm about to reach over and squeeze his hand when Betty comes pattering over and rests her head on his lap. Shadow follows and does the same, to him, not me.

'It's all right, girls,' he says, patting their heads. 'I'm okay. I'm fine.'

'More wine?' I ask, picking up the bottle.

He glances down at his glass under the bench, still full, and shakes his head. The dogs run off.

'Bel went back to work when Lucia was a year old, her idea, not mine, only part-time but it did help our finances, well, it paid for her salon sessions.' He laughs. 'God, she was high maintenance. And that was us, doing okay. Until the day before Lucia's third birthday.'

He takes a long swig from his wine glass, quickly followed by another then searches around for the wine bottle before refilling his glass and then mine. I'm starting to feel lightheaded with all the wine, I've certainly had more than him.

'Bel had been going out on work dos, you know, the usual thing, drinks after work, the odd evening, nothing extraordinary, nothing I even thought about. Then he turns up. Josh, her ex. One Saturday night when the kids were in bed and it wasn't his appointed weekend. We were watching a movie on Netflix, a romcom, with Jennifer Aniston. Bel's choice, not mine. He'd had a few drinks, he wasn't drunk, he was quite coherent, but I could smell it on his breath. I answered the door and he strode in, pushed past me, marched into the lounge, started shouting, asking Bel if she'd told me yet? I assumed he wanted more access to his son. Maybe Bel had refused but I didn't really see what it had to do with me. Or maybe it was to do with the divorce, they still weren't divorced. I edged out of the room. Bel always said there were things that were too difficult to sort out. I didn't force the issue because I didn't want to marry Bel, she didn't want to marry me. But we were content, you know, doing okay.'

I want to go to the loo now, all this wine and coffee has filled me up. But I can't just get up and go, not now that he's getting to the part where I suspect it all goes wrong. I fidget.

'Where's your toilet?' he says, standing. 'All this drink, eh.'

Grateful for the break, I direct him to the downstairs loo and run upstairs myself. He's hovering in the kitchen when I return, the dogs are in Shadow's basket and are settling down to sleep.

'Shall we go in the lounge?' I ask, leading the way.

We sit on opposite sofas, him staring into the distance, me trying not to look at his face too intensely.

'He, Josh, called me back in. Made me sit down. Told Bel to tell me, but she couldn't even look at me. I worked it out pretty quickly, they were having an affair. Or, not an affair since they were still married, so technically I was the affair. I saw it all play out, me having Lucia every other weekend, him back in the marital home when I'd been paying his mortgage for the past three years. I could hardly believe it, yet it had a certain symmetry, an inevitability.' He stops again, swallowing hard.

'I'm sorry. That must have been awful.'

'I could live without Bel. In fact, in the few seconds it took me to realise that I was the interloper now, not him, I felt almost relieved. As long as I was Lucia's father and saw her frequently, I was going to insist on *every* weekend, it would be okay. It had never been a great love affair between me and Bel. I'd survive. I had Lucia.'

He stops again and it seems as though he's gasping for air.

'By this time Bel was crying and begging Josh to stop but Josh was just shouting, *tell him, tell him.* I waited for her to tell me it was over between us, that our cosy domestic life was over, but frankly I didn't need her to do that, it was blatantly obvious. Then Josh said something about if she couldn't, he would, which made Bel cry even more. So I said it was okay, I knew it was over. I even pretended I'd seen it coming, though I hadn't. No idea. Bel by this point had almost collapsed on the sofa begging Josh to stop, but he just kept telling her to tell me or he would. I got up, started to walk away, to leave the room, but Josh grabbed me, hauled me back again.' There are tears rolling down his face now, he's sobbing in silence again just like he did in the park. He turns to look at me and I know, I know without even thinking about it.

'She wasn't yours.'

Phillip stands up and reaches for the tissues I keep on the window sill and blows his nose.

'Sorry,' he says, watching me watching him.

I shake my head. 'Don't be.'

He just stands there, staring out of the window into the fast approaching twilight.

I stand up too and wrap my arms around him. I've got nothing to say, nothing that will make it any better or not sound stupid or trite. No wonder he sat on the bench in the park looking so wretched.

'You guessed. I didn't. Josh told me, blunt and to the point, but to be fair not gloating or cruel. Not then. I didn't believe it. Wouldn't. Couldn't. Then it all turned to shit. I just walked out there and then, Bel still sobbing on the floor, Josh just looking at me, pity in his face. And all the time Jennifer Aniston's perky little face tweeted away in the background. I'll never watch another romcom again. I walked the streets, finally fell asleep on a bench just as dawn was breaking, not *our* bench,' he adds with a brief smile.

Our bench. I always think of it as *his* bench.

'I went back home later that Sunday morning, well, their home. I used my key to open the door only it didn't open, it was deadlocked from the inside. I banged on the door. Josh answered. No sign of Bel or the children. He wouldn't let me in, just handed me a bag of my stuff, work clothes, toothbrush, toiletries. And Betty, who looked like I felt. Poor Betty, it wasn't her fault. Then we got nasty with each other on the doorstep of the house that had been my home for the previous three years. I suppose that's how he must have felt when I moved into his home. I said I wanted proof. I wanted DNA. He said they'd done it already but I could do it too, it would only prove I wasn't Lucia's father. He was right, it did. He threatened to call the police if I didn't go away right then.'

'Oh God,' I mutter into his chest because we're still hugging.

'I left. Turned up at a mate's house late afternoon, having spent several hours in the pub. He let me sleep on the sofa, not that his wife was very happy about it, especially as she didn't like dogs and I had to leave Betty at theirs the next morning when I went to work. But work sent me home before lunch because I had a meltdown in front of a client. Apparently. I don't remember. My mate's wife wanted me out, said it wasn't good for their children, three little boys, to see the state of me every morning. The mate helped me find the place I've been in ever since. At least I could afford it, I had my phone, my wallet. I had to buy another phone charger though, she never put that in my bag. And once my phone was charged, I stopped all the direct debits that paid the bills, that ran their house.' Wow, that sounds familiar.

He lets go of me and I have to loosen my grip too. He sits back down on *his* sofa and I perch on the edge of mine.

'I did things I vaguely remember, things I'm not proud of. I went back to the house when I knew they'd be at work. The locks had been changed. Already. I went to Lucia's nursery, the staff called Bel. It didn't stop me. I went again, but Bel had instructed the nursery to call the police. Josh took out an injunction against me, I couldn't go within half a mile of them, of Lucia. I couldn't even get my belongings until they said so. I stopped asking, I didn't care. I started to slide down into an abyss of self-despair, self-pity.

'I went to the doctors, or rather my mate took me. I just sat there like a zombie. I got antidepressants. They made me worse. Then work stepped in and sent me for help, for counselling, for CBT. Thank God. It doesn't stop it hurting though. Then I found out about the birth certificate, because I hadn't been there, I wasn't on it, Bel had arranged a visit to the registrar without me. It didn't really change anything, just rubbed salt in a festering wound.'

I want to stop him and ask about the counselling, the cognitive behavioural therapy, but he's so in the moment, so determined to get everything out that I just nod and listen.

'Bel knew, deep down, subliminally. I think she'd

always suspected. I think she confided in Josh once they were having their affair, not that technically, legally, it was an affair. I was the affair.' He reminds me of myself, repeating things just like I do.

'And you've not seen Lucia since?'

'No. Just that once glimpse at nursery. She waved and her face lit up. I don't suppose she knows what's going on? They won't have told her, not everything, obviously. But she's three, she'll miss me, she'll ask questions. She'll ask where Daddy is.' Tears drip silently down his face. He cuffs them away.

'Yes,' I whisper.

'And the rest you know, because you've seen me in the park.' He gives me a sly look. 'Looking like a drug-crazed zombie.' He winks. Has he heard me describe him as Spice man? He can't have, surely.

'When did this all happen?'

'That night, the Jennifer Aniston night, 4th September. I'll never forget it. The day before Lucia's birthday. Huh. They went ahead with the party, too. Without me. I'm dreading the anniversary.'

I gasp, hold my hand over my mouth. I can feel my heart start to beat out an old, familiar pattern in my chest. Horror mixed with panic.

'Me too,' I say. 'That was my wedding day.'

It's also the date of Grimmy's birthday party.

Twenty-one

Grimmy is sitting in her new chair in her corner of the kitchen looking regal.

It's a lovely day and many of the guests have spilled out into the garden. I go over to give my great-grandmother a hug and kiss, even though she winces.

'Happy birthday, Grimmy.'

'You didn't say and many more.'

'I have in my card, it's on the table with all the rest.' You just cannot win with Grimmy.

'Who's this?'

Phillip stands behind me, he's watching Grimmy as well as looking around. Fortunately, although there are many people in the room, all of my family are in the garden. So the full inquisition won't start just yet.

'I've brought a friend. Grimmy, meet Phillip.' I wave my hand at Phillip, then at Grimmy. 'And this is my great-grandmother, Grimmy.'

'Grim by name and grim by nature,' she says, giving me a lop-sided wink.

'What?' I can't help it coming out of my mouth.

'I keep telling you I'm not deaf, Lauren. I'm not stupid, either.' She laughs, well cackles.

'It's lovely to meet you,' Phillip says while I stand there open-mouthed. 'I've heard a lot about you.'

'*I* haven't heard anything about *you*.' She looks him up and down, making no attempt to pretend she isn't appraising him. 'Why didn't you tell me about this one, Cat?' she calls over my shoulder.

Cat appears at my side, carrying a tray of drinks, a grin on her face.

'I didn't know anything about him, Grimmy.' Well, it's almost true. 'Got to go, I'm playing waitress at the moment.' She gives me a sly smirk.

'He's good looking, I'll give you that, Lauren,' Grimmy says without any shame.

I mouth a sorry to Phillip but he just smiles.

'It's a relief really,' she adds.

'What is?' I've no idea what she's on about now.

'That you've found a man, because now I can stop looking for one for you. I won't need to bother with that tinderbox thing now.' She turns to Phillip and addresses her next comment at him while I stand there, my mouth gaping like a goldfish and my face blushing horribly. 'I found a lovely gas man for her, but she turned her nose up. Wouldn't even meet him. Still, you look a lot better than Gollum. His eyes were too close together and scary. Yours look quite normal.'

'Phillip and I are just friends, Grimmy. I've told you enough times that I'm not looking for a man.'

'Have you told him that?' she says, nodding at Phillip who has turned away, hiding his face from us, his shoulders going up and down as he laughs to himself.

'Grimmy,' I mutter.

'Stand back,' she says, gripping the remote control and propelling herself to an upright position in just seconds. The new chair is certainly faster than the old one. 'Young man, if you're not with her you can escort me.' Cunning old great-grandmother, she doesn't need any help getting around, unless it suits her convenience.

Phillip turns and smiles, first at me, then at Grimmy. 'Love to.'

'I'm like a queen with my young prince,' she says to me, with another wink.

'I I..' I'm speechless.

Grimmy clutches onto Phillip's arm and off they go, parading out into the garden.

'Well, if you don't want him, she'll have him,' a sneaky Cat says from behind me. 'That's how she snared all the other husbands.'

'Stop it.'

'Who's a sly one then? Glad to see you brought him.'

'We're just friends.'

Cat narrows her eyes. 'Shall we?' She links arms with me and we follow Grimmy and Phillip.

'How's your management course going?'

'Finished. I really enjoyed it. Just got to put it into practice now, turbo charge my career.'

'Good. You're your own woman, Lauren Nokes.' She sniggers.

'Shut up. Did you know Grimmy knows why we call her Grimmy?' I watch Cat's face for a response.

'No, she doesn't.'

'She does, when I introduced her to Phillip she said "grim by name and grim by nature." She seemed to think it was funny. I think.'

'Ooops.' Cat giggles.

'Oh, Lauren,' Grimmy croaks from the other side of the garden, when she spots us. 'My old chair is in the garage, you can take that with you when you go, for your house.'

'Nooo,' I mumble into my chest.

'It'll fit a treat in your lounge. Just lovely.' Cat nudges me.

'What's got into you?' I unlink arms with my sister, she's starting to really annoy me now.

'I'm happy for you. I'm just pleased you've moved on.'

'Phillip and I are just friends. I brought him here as a friend. I'm beginning to wish I'd come alone,' I snap. And I'm not about to tell Cat that I brought him here so he wouldn't be alone on the anniversary of his own misery.

'Ahh, don't be like that. Will you be able to fit that chair into your car?'

'I haven't brought my car.'

'Never mind, Dad can drop it round tomorrow.' Cat is so full of mischief now.

'Shut up.'

'Okay?' Phillip asks five minutes later, after he's deposited Grimmy in her garden chair. 'Just been chatting to your brother Sam, he was asking about *us*.' He rolls his eyes then smiles.

'I'm sorry. I should have known better. I shouldn't have brought you. I just thought it would be a distraction, you know.'

'It's fun. Your family are great. Grimmy especially.'

'Oh God, I'm so sorry. She's just so rude.'

'No, really, she's a character. It's all quite amusing and it is a distraction. I'd almost forgotten the date.'

We exchange grimaces. It's not actually Grimmy's birthday for a few more days but we're having her party a little early to fall on the weekend. And we're lucky today, the weather is good, it's both sunny and warm.

'Let's get ourselves a drink.'

After I've told every member of my family that Phillip and I are just friends, I start to relax and enjoy myself. By the time everyone is assembled in the kitchen to sing happy birthday, I'm feeling quite calm and jolly. As Grimmy attempts, aided by several of her great-great-grandchildren to blow out the candles – Mum has chosen candles in the shape of a nine and a five rather than ninety-five actual candles – I've had enough drink to have not a care in the world.

Grimmy shuffles back to her new chair after the exertion of the candle blowing.

'Lauren, Lauren.' She waves a crooked finger at me.

'I'm being summoned,' I say, giggling to Phillip. 'Better go.'

I wander over to Grimmy and Phillip wanders along beside me.

'What were you doing this time last year?' Grimmy says, her dentures dropping slightly from her gums.

I feel my heart quicken pace; I also feel Phillip freeze beside me.

When I don't answer, Grimmy reminds me.

'You were singing that awful song, do you remember? It was very funny though, until you fell off the stage.' Grimmy starts to cackle.

I want to cry.

'Grammy,' says Dad coming up behind us, 'That was cruel, bringing that up.'

'Oh, was it? I didn't mean it to be. I was just pointing out how far Lauren has come in a year, that's all. Sorry, Lauren. I didn't mean to upset you.'

I blink back my tears. I think that's the first time that I've ever heard Grimmy apologise.

'I didn't mean any harm,' she reiterates.

'Not to worry, Grimmy,' Phillip says, 'Lauren's over

all that now, aren't you?' He turns to me and looks into my eyes. 'You're okay, aren't you?'

'I think I am. What about you?'

'Getting there,' he says. 'Getting there.' He links my arm and walks me out to the garden.

'Trust Grimmy,' I say. 'Honestly, she's just so tactless.'

'I'm grateful she doesn't know about me and my woes.' He half laughs. 'God knows what she'd make of that.'

'She might have a bit of sympathy for you. She's been through a lot of crap in her life too.'

'Not quite like mine though.'

'No, but she had her own daughter when she was very young, shotgun wedding and all that, though not actually with a shotgun, obviously. Then her daughter ran away when she was sixteen, came back pregnant at seventeen, father unknown. Then died when she gave birth to my dad. So Grimmy and her husband, who would have been my grandad except he died long before I was born, had to bring Dad up. She's lost two other husbands since then too. So it's not all been roses and lemonade for her.'

'Ah,' Phillip says, sounding pensive.

'Yeah, that's why she's so grim.' I grin and so does he, though our black humour is probably being augmented by all the Pimm's and homemade elderflower wine we've consumed.

We start to sway together as soft music plays around the garden. We're in our own little bubble. He moves in and places a brief and sweet kiss on my lips. I rather like it.

But this isn't right.

'Phillip, don't feel you have to do that because you

feel sorry for me.'

He laughs. Too long, too loud.

'Because I'm not looking for a man.'

'Good.' He smirks. 'And just so there's no misunderstandings in the future, neither am I.'

Postscript

Two years later...

This is sooo not how I expected life to pan out.

I was perfectly happy, thank you very much, in my little house with my little dog, Shadow. I definitely did not need a man to save me, because I wasn't in any danger. At all. Even if I had been, I'm more than capable of saving myself.

And, once I'd overcome the Leeward/Alfie/Kenton complication, life was just settling down and becoming nice and tidy. I even had a lovely new career on the horizon, well, not new as such, but improved.

Then what happened? Well, what do you know, but I fell down that rabbit hole called love. Again. You'd think, after all I'd been through, the over-the-top wedding I never wanted, Leeward's betrayal and all that followed, you'd think I'd have learned my lesson.

But no, oh no not I...

'Are you ready?' Phillip asks, standing in front of me and casting an eye over my outfit, it's tight to say the least.

'As I'll ever be.' I've examined myself enough times

in the mirror, even been through my wardrobe several times hoping something better will magic itself into existence, but no such luck.

'We don't have to…' he starts, but doesn't finish.

'We do.'

'People would understand, given the circumstances.'

'Grimmy wouldn't. I can assure you we will never hear the end of it.' There is no way we are going to miss Grimmy's birthday party. No way on earth.

'If you're sure?' There's still a question in his words.

'Absolutely. Dogs walked?'

'Absolutely. I'll just get Archie. You go on down.'

I stomp down the stairs of *our* house, we've only actually lived in it for thirteen months. A bit of advice for anyone who cares to take it: do not move house when you are eight months pregnant. That said, once the shock and horror of the move, the stress of selling two houses and packing everything up was over, it was sooo worth it. I love this house. I chose it, with Phillip. We chose together. Just as we chose the furniture, the decor and the carpets together.

And the name of our baby. Archie. Not that he's such a baby now. He's just had his first birthday. I cannot quite believe how quickly that time has flown by.

You see, despite my not looking for a man, and despite Phillip needing a bit of space too, we sort of fell in love when neither of us was looking. Funny how that happens. It started, as you might expect, at Grimmy's ninety-fifth birthday party. When we left, we left together and we went back to my house and we christened my bed. I use that word euphemistically because of course you don't actually christen a bed, but I'm sure you know what I mean. After that we hurtled along at such a speed that I don't think either of us stopped to draw breath. All the time we both agreed that *we* were just what *we* needed. That is, a nice, cosy affair, nothing complicated, because we'd both been bruised by love and neither of us wanted to experience *that* again.

But we saw each other every day. And I do mean every day. After work, then before work, and almost by accident we were living alternate days at my house or Phillip's. At the same time, I got a demanding new job as manager of a new nursing home, and Phillip got a promotion. I don't think either of us stopped to consider what was going on. It was exciting, exhilarating. Fast, fast, fast.

We were dashing around like mad things and loving every minute of it, and each other. Not that there were any mad declarations of love, or any assumptions. Neither of us was falling down that crevice again, thank you very much. It wasn't love at first sight for me like it had been with Leeward – and look where that had ended up. It wasn't lust at first sight like Phillip had felt for Bel, his love had all gone to the little girl he thought he'd fathered.

Then I realised I was pregnant. And it was decision time. I sat on that little nugget of information, that delicate little secret, for a few weeks. It might sound selfish, hell, I know it does, but I just didn't want anyone, not even Phillip, to influence my decision about the future. And, if I'm completely honest I was petrified about how he might react, given what had happened to him. For starters, would he even believe it was his? Although, realistically, we spent so much time together that it would have been virtually impossible for it to be anyone else's.

But still. It's a big responsibility. Isn't it? Creating a new person.

I was always going to keep the baby, even if Phillip decided he couldn't cope with all that again. When I told him, he cried. I thought, oh hell, what have I done? But they were tears of joy; he couldn't have been happier. I told him I quite understood if he wanted DNA tests as soon as the baby arrived, but when Archie did finally appear two weeks overdue, there was no doubting who his daddy was. No doubt at all, they were like peas in a pod.

So here we are, our little family of three and we're off to Grimmy's ninety-seventh birthday party and we can't miss it because, as she has reminded us, it might be her last. She says that every year. At some point she will be telling the truth, I suppose.

'You were a long time? Had he fallen asleep?' I smile as my husband – oh yes, we're married, a tiny ceremony last year – carries our son into the sitting room where I'm waiting.

'I had to change his nappy,' Phillip says, with a wry smile.

'Ah. Lucky you.' I grin, because I'm the one feeling lucky; I escaped that treat this time.

I clamber into the car while Phillip wrestles our toddler into his car seat, alternately cajoling and singing the song that means he must wear his seatbelt. Don't ask, I made it up and it's become a family staple, but frankly it's as bad as my rendition of *I Will Survive*, without any swear words, obviously, but just as tuneless.

'Lauren, Phillip and my little Archie,' Mum says as we burst into her kitchen and I flop into the nearest chair.

'Everyone's in the garden, it's such a lovely day.'

'Bit too hot for me, Mum,' I say as Archie scrambles to get down from his father's arms and run off to see his much older cousins. 'Where's Grimmy?'

'On her garden throne,' Mum says, laughing. 'She's holding court as only Grimmy can.'

'Yeah.' Mum and I exchange a look, a smirk, a slight eye roll. God only knows what we'll all do when she does eventually go, she may be irascible but she's the centre of our family.

'Hopefully she's good for a few years yet,' Mum says, reading my thoughts. 'Though we have had to get her one of those alarm things you suggested.'

'Good idea. How's she getting on with it?' I had suggested to my parents that an emergency alarm might be a good idea for Grimmy. She's old and lives alone, and even if she does spend most of the day in my parents' kitchen, she goes home every night and sleeps alone.

'Well, it's gone off four times in the last three weeks.'

'Oh no. What was wrong? Why didn't you tell me?' I know why, they think I have enough to cope with.

'Oh, nothing was wrong. She just keeps taking it off. Dad has told her and told her she has to keep it on, says that's the whole point of it. She says it's ugly. I've persuaded her to tuck it under her clothes so no one can see it, although *I* think it looks good enough to pass for chunky jewellery.'

'I'd better go out and see her,' I say. Hauling myself up I grab the card and present we've brought her – a bottle of Johnny Walker whisky, as per her express instructions – and head out to the garden.

I find Phillip and our son and we present ourselves

to Grimmy who is, indeed, holding court from the luxury of her garden chair complete with parasol and footstool.

'Hello, Grimmy,' I say. 'Happy birthday.' Probably because I spend all my time singing nursery rhymes to a toddler it comes out as though I'm singing and I watch Grimmy grimace.

'Lauren, please.' She holds her hand up. 'I don't need to remind you that you can't sing, do I?' Grim by name, grim by nature.

I just laugh it off and hand over her present which she looks at for several seconds before resting it on her lap.

'Get the girl a chair, Phillip,' she barks across the garden. 'Look at her. And put it in the shade, next to me.'

Phillip does as he's told and soon I'm resting out of the sun and sharing Grimmy's parasol. Cat spots me from the other side of the garden, and mimes drink, which I nod to and soon she's in front of us both with a tray. Phillip has gone off chasing after Archie and it's just me, Grimmy and Cat.

'Open your present, Grimmy,' Cat says, giving me a sly wink. I don't like the sight of that.

Slowly Grimmy removes the wrapping paper and folds it neatly on her lap. 'I'll use that again,' she says before holding the whisky bottle up to the light. 'What's this? Do you all think I'm an alky?'

'It's what you asked for,' I say, feeling defensive.

'Is it?' she says, her dentures dropping a little, whether in disgust or disbelief I don't know. 'Put it with the others, Cat.' Cat places it on the opposite side of Grimmy's chair, and as I lean over to see *the others*, I count at least ten bottles of Johnny Walker's. 'You can have it at my funeral,' Grimmy adds, more to herself than us.

'How does it feel to be ninety-seven?' I ask, in my best jolly voice.

'I don't know, I'm still ninety-six for a few more days.'

'Oh yeah. So you are.'

Cat catches my eye and we smile.

'You're amazing though, aren't you, Grimmy?' Cat says, patting our great grandmother's hand.

'Well I've outlived everyone else my age if that's what you mean,' Grimmy growls, then turns to me. 'Lauren, why didn't you just have twins if you were going to have babies so close together? It's not good for you all this pregnancy.' She eyes my very pregnant stomach with distain. She's serious too. And she's not asking this because she's old or confused, because she's neither.

'It doesn't really work like that, does it, Grimmy?' Cat says, suppressing a smile.

'Yes it does. All this modern medicine makes that sort of thing easy, doesn't it, Lauren? You're a nurse, you should have sorted yourself out properly, shouldn't she, Cat?'

'Yes, Grimmy,' Cat says.

I kick Cat foot's as hard as I can, which isn't very hard since lifting my foot up is such an effort at the moment, but Cat milks it for all its worth and yelps.

'You can go now, girls,' Grimmy says. 'Here's your father and I need to talk to him about this stupid alarm thing.' She waves her arms around as though she's shooing flies away.

As I stand up, an effort in itself since I am, yet again, nearly two weeks overdue, I feel a warm gush between my legs – I am so glad I am standing on grass and not on the shiny floor of our parents' kitchen.

'Uh oh,' I say to Cat as I grab her arm and we waddle away together.

Our baby girl arrives less than an hour later. Like her brother she's her daddy's double, not that her parentage was ever in doubt. We're naming her Lucy Catherine. Catherine after Cat, who almost delivered her in the car on the way here and who held my hand and allowed me to bite her – yes, I know, it's so awful, isn't it?

And Lucy? I know what you're thinking, but you're wrong. We are not naming her after Phillip's nearly daughter, Lucia, not at all. Lucy is Grimmy's name. We're naming our daughter after her great-great-grandmother, because, after all, we named our son after Phillip's grandfather, Archie.

And, of course, we all lived happily, or should that be nappily, ever after.

Other books by CJ Morrow

 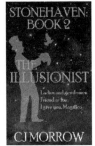 

One last thing...

Thank you so much for reading this book. I really do appreciate it. I am an Indie Author, part of a small imprint (Tamarillas Press) and not backed by a big publishing company, so every time a reader buys one of my books, I am genuinely thrilled. We've worked hard to eliminate any typos and errors, but if you spot any, please email:
TamarillasPress@Outlook.com

If you have enjoyed this book please leave a review on Amazon and/or Goodreads, and if you think your friends would enjoy reading it, please share it with them.

Many thanks
CJ

Email: cjmorrowauthor@gmail.com
Blog: cjmorrow13.wordpress.com
Twitter: @cjmorrowauthor
Instagram: instagram.com/cjmorrowauthor/
Facebook: facebook.com/cjmorrowauthor

Made in the USA
Middletown, DE
13 May 2020